SINFUL RUIN

USA TODAY & *WALL STREET JOURNAL* BESTSELLING AUTHOR

CHARITY FERRELL

SINFUL RUIN

USA TODAY & WALL STREET JOURNAL BESTSELLING AUTHOR

CHARITY FERRELL

1

———

Genesis

"I'm so sorry, Genesis." My father points a gun at me when I enter his office. "We were desperate, and they wanted you."

Classical music plays around us as he stares me down from behind his desk. His eyes are bloodshot, and sweat drenches his wrinkled forehead and shirt collar. A lit cigar in an ivory ashtray and a bottle of bourbon sit in front of him.

In panic, I slip my gaze from him to the gun. My heart beats so wildly that I feel it thrumming in my throat.

Carlisle Astor isn't a man of violence. He's a top donor to charities and politicians who vow to rid the New York streets of gun violence.

Before I can ask even one of the million questions floating in my mind, he straightens in his chair, struck by a sudden alarm.

"They're here." His finger toys with the gun trigger.

"Who?" I step out of his line of fire and follow his gaze to the shut door.

I stand there, waiting for intruders I'm unsure even exist.

Seconds pass as we wait.

Suddenly, a gunshot echoes through the office, and I jump.

One second. Two seconds. Three seconds pass.

The door remains closed.

My breathing shallows as I slowly turn to my father, and terror rises through me.

He's hunched over the desk, a gunshot wound marring his forehead. His arm hangs limply over the chair armrest, his lifeless hand still gripping the gun. Splatters of blood cover the wall, bookshelves, and the framed photo of us dressed as zombies for Halloween behind him.

"Dad!" I cry out, rushing to his side.

Blood seeps from his head, trickling down his neck, and covers my palm when I check his pulse.

Not even one weak beat.

I choke back a sob, telling myself to remain calm and not break down, as I frantically search for his phone to call for help since I'd forgotten mine in my car.

I find no luck on the desk or in the drawers.

My hunt stops when pounding comes from the other side of the door.

My father wasn't paranoid.

They are here.

Scanning the office, I search for an escape, but there's nowhere. My father put millions into this home. Why couldn't he have sprung a few more dollars for a hidden bookshelf leading into a secret room?

I duck behind the desk when someone kicks in the door. Peeking around the corner, I see three armed men enter the office. Their large frames darken the doorframe like the boogeymen in your nightmares.

My father's handgun has nothing on the automatic weapons slung over their shoulders.

"Come out, come out," the man in the middle taunts, his Russian accent thick. He whistles loudly while scanning the room. "I'm ready to meet my bride."

His bride?

I crouch lower, losing sight of them.

Screw the view.

I'm not about to become this psychopath's wife.

Had my father not just committed suicide or said, "They wanted you," I'd swear these men barged into the wrong home.

"You have three seconds before I blast that fucking desk with enough bullets to murder an entire fucking army," he warns, his patience thinning. "You don't want to piss me off, *nevesta*."

I don't move.

"*Seychas!*" the man screams.

Now.

I know my fair share of Russian.

Learning new languages was my father's form of bonding.

Reality sets in, and chills run down my spine.

I either have to give myself up or wait for this madman to *blast the fucking desk with bullets*. Standing, I raise my arms, and inch by inch, the men come more into my view.

I was right.

They are straight out of your nightmares.

And they've come to make mine a reality.

"There she is," the man in the middle, who appears to be in charge, says.

His cold eyes travel down my body. As they move back up, they reach mine, and his lips form a sinister smile.

A smile that promises destruction.

"My bride." He releases his hold on the gun to rub his palms together in satisfaction.

He's terrifying but—dare I say it—also attractive.

Tall, dark blond hair, a sharp nose, and a thick scar that runs along his jawline.

"The cunt is prettier in real life than her pictures," the burly man to his right comments, licking his thin lips.

The *cunt caller* isn't as attractive as his boss, and points are deleted for his comment and the way he's creepily staring at me.

If I wasn't terrified for my life, I'd give them all a lecture on how to speak to women.

"You're one lucky motherfucker, Dima," the creep adds. "I wish I were getting her. Maybe you'll share."

Dima's glare cuts to the guy. "You suggest that again, and I'll rip your fucking tongue out and feed it to my dog."

The man ducks his head. "Sorry, boss."

I use this opportunity to sweep my gaze over my father's desk, searching for a weapon. I tiptoe forward when my attention drops to the gun in his limp hand.

"Don't you even fucking think about it," Dima warns, creeping closer.

I glare at him, stumbling back and running into the bookcase.

Dima smirks, as if a terrified human is his favorite sight. "I can't wait to have my fun with you. You look like a fighter."

"You lay a hand on her, I'll fucking gut you and your men and feed you to your dog," a recognizable voice snarls behind them. "She's mine."

I slap my hand to my chest to tame my wild heart.

The three men separate, making room, as if they were the opening show and the main event has arrived.

Julian Bellini steps into my sight.

He looms over all three men, his presence heavier than the others combined.

While they're the boogeymen, he's the devil in the night.

The monster who controls them.

He wasn't trained to scare you.

He was trained to see you as prey.

To eat you alive.

To drag you into his hell.

Yet, with all that darkness, I've never seen a more beautiful man.

Julian towers over the other men, like a skyscraper taking over a village. His short black hair is brushed to the right, shaved shorter on the sides, with a slight part. Tattoos extend over nearly every inch of his exposed skin. His calculated cerulean-blue eyes stare me down.

Eyes that I've felt on me for years.

Eyes that I've *wanted* on me for years.

His face, lined with hatred yet sculpted like a god's, hardens when our eyes meet.

The music changes to a loud, thumping Beethoven.

Julian draws closer, his eyes anchored to mine, ready to crack open my soul.

He smirks widely. "Hello, Genesis. Looks like I arrived at the party just in time."

2

Julian

I PAID a pretty penny for Genesis.

Nah, I paid a pretty five hundred thousand dollars for her.

She'd better prove her worth.

Given my line of work, I'm not a man who makes lousy bets or poor financial decisions. I benefit from every investment, no matter fucking what.

Legit deals, illegal ventures with criminals—I'm always the winner.

The three Russians scowl as I walk past them, deeper into Carlisle's office.

Dima closes his hand around his AK-47's handle.

I smirk at him.

I fucking dare you.

"Read this." I smack a contract against Dima's chest. "I'm sure you know your father's signature."

Dima lowers the gun to stop the contract from falling to the floor.

Outbidding and outsmarting men is my favorite pastime.

That's exactly what I did tonight.

May this be a lesson learned for Dima.

As he reads the contract, I approach Carlisle's desk. This isn't the first time I've been in his office. Carlisle sold me and others who'd pay top dollar for insider trading.

Speaking of Carlisle …

He's seated in his chair, dead as a fucking doornail.

His soul delivered to hell.

I've staged enough murders into suicides that I know the wound was self-inflicted. I wish he'd waited until I arrived to pull the trigger. I'd have gladly done it for him.

My attention shifts from his dead body to Genesis.

She's far more entertaining as she grips the bookshelf as if preparing for an earthquake. I can't help but chuckle when I notice the family photo behind her.

All smiles from the parents who sold her out.

Nine times out of ten, greed prevails over bloodlines. Loyalty is the hardest heirloom to keep in this world.

Her eyes are wide, and the hand gripping the bookshelf shakes. She's in a room full of cold-blooded killers. With me at the front of the line.

Glancing over my shoulder, I see Dima's still reading the contract. Either he's illiterate or in shock that his father would make a deal that undermined him.

"He went behind my back," Dima hisses before shoving the contract into his blazer pocket and narrowing his eyes at me. "*You* went behind my back."

I scoff.

The idiot believes I owe him loyalty?

He could be in the direct line of a moving train, and I wouldn't offer him a helping hand. I'd push him further in front of it.

I click my tongue against the roof of my mouth. "Nah, I'm just a better businessman, Dima."

All eyes are on me when I grab Carlisle's lit cigar from the ashtray. I brush off the tip and offer it to Dima. He waves his hand through the air in disdain.

In his world, only one man can disrespect him. Yaroslav Morozova, his father, a notorious Bratva boss. Dima is next in line to take over the boss position.

I extend the cigar to the man on Dima's right. He shakes his head.

The other, who I know as Kuzma, bites.

Not that I blame the man who's merely a soldier.

It's a Cohiba Behike cigar.

Expensive and, since they're illegal in the States, extremely rare to find.

If Carlisle's slobbery, repulsive lips hadn't touched it, I'd keep it for myself.

The moment Kuzma accepts the cigar, Dima curses and snatches it from him. He flips Kuzma's palm to snuff the cigar into it. Kuzma howls in pain, attempting to tug away from him. Dima adds more pressure.

I roll my eyes in boredom.

Cigar burns are child's play.

Yaroslav should train his men to torture better. Dima should've at least gone for one of the eyes.

A burned retina is a great method to get your point across.

Smirking, I remember the last time I seared a man's retina. I didn't know if it would have blinded him since I put a bullet through his head three hours later.

"You don't take anything unless I tell you," Dima snarls at Kuzma.

Grinning, I divide my attention between their show and Genesis. She watches in horror as Dima instructs the other man to hold Kuzma down. Dima kneels beside him, opens his mouth, and shoves the cigar against his tongue.

I guess I underestimated the Russian son.

I offer him a mocking clap for his authority.

Forgetting about Dima's show of dominance, I notice Genesis tiptoeing toward the door and move in her direction. She stops when I nudge Carlisle's chair out of my way. His body slumps to the floor, and I step over it.

What a shame.

Carlisle had great potential had he not been such a selfish fuck.

"Genesis, get over here," I demand, snapping my fingers and pointing in front of me.

She crosses her arms and shakes her head.

I glare at her.

She needs to know I don't take kindly to disobedience.

Especially right now, when my annoyance level is at a maximum. I spent the past hour negotiating with Yaroslav. The Russians are a fucking headache to work deals with.

I shove my hand into my pocket and extract a switchblade. "For every second you make me count, I'll cut one of your pretty fingers off."

She doesn't move.

"One." I hold the switchblade out to inspect it. "We'll count that as your thumb."

She stubbornly shuffles my way, her deep chocolate-brown eyes meeting mine.

Genesis is drop-dead gorgeous.

She's also been off-limits to me for years.

But now? She's mine.

When she's within my reach, I snatch her wrist and tug her into my chest. For her earlier disobedience, I plunge my hand through her brown hair, tugging her head back. She hisses in pain.

"Fun is over," I announce to the room, motioning to the doorway and loosening my hold on Genesis's hair.

"Wait," she says. "We need to call for help."

"Help?" Dima scoffs. "For what?"

"My father," she hisses.

"He's already dead," I tell her. "Doubt he'll resurrect." What little slack I gave her hair, I take back. "Argue with me, and I'll test whether you resurrect after I kill you."

She slams her pretty mouth shut.

We follow the Russians from the office and through the foyer of Genesis's childhood home. We walk outside into the evening air, and she gasps when her eyes land on the two dead men on the entrance stairs.

Carlisle hired himself a few bodyguards.

Idiot found them on Yelp, as if searching for where to find the best chili dog. They might've had a five-star rating for protecting some mid-level politician, but their expertise could never match those of crazy Russians in need of a bride. Those men love contractual marriages and take them seriously.

"Sixty days," Dima says, referring to the contract as we walk toward our vehicles.

I open the passenger door of my black Escalade. "When it comes to money, I always hold my end of the deal."

He points at Genesis. "Not one fucking minute later, or she's mine."

Genesis whips her gaze to me in confusion.

"If that time comes and I don't have what I want, she's all yours to do with as you please," I reply before shoving Genesis into the passenger seat.

She stares at me in shock, and I can tell a million questions are floating in her head that she's too afraid to ask.

Good. I want her afraid.

"We'll be in touch," Dima says before sliding into his black Rolls-Royce, along with his men.

I nod, open the back door to grab a towel, and toss it at Genesis before slipping behind the steering wheel. "Wipe yourself off. I don't want a speck of blood on that seat."

"I need to get my phone from my car and call for help," she says, wiping the blood off her hands.

"You need to do what I tell you to do." I shut the door.

"Fine, can you *tell me* to get my phone out of my car to call for help then?"

"No." I shift the Escalade into drive and slam on the gas pedal.

"What the hell, Julian?" she asks as we surge forward. "Who were those men? Why were they there? Why were *you* there?"

I ignore her, driving through the iron gates of the property.

"Julian," she says, raising her voice, "answer me."

"Sit there and shut the fuck up. I'll explain later."

"Excuse me?" She smacks my arm with the towel. "Don't talk to me like that."

Now that the Russians aren't here, she's grown some balls, stupidly believing I won't hurt her.

"Don't test me, Genesis," I warn.

"Don't test me," she mocks my words, sounding too smug for my liking. "I'll test you until I get answers, Julian."

I swerve to the side of the road, put the Escalade in park, and snarl at her, "Genesis, you've seen the semi-nice side of me a few times—I'll give you that." I stretch across the console to get in her face. "You're also aware there's more evil inside me than nice. You keep running your mouth, and I'll prove it to you."

"I've never seen the nice side of you," she argues. "I only saw the nice side of your mother and *Mel*—"

Before she can finish her sentence, I clamp my hand over her mouth and get in her face more. She whips her head to the side, squirming to break free, and I creep closer to pin her to the door. I don't stop until my lips are inches from my hand on her mouth.

"You keep running that smart mouth, and you'll never see a side of me that isn't deranged again," I caution.

She narrows her eyes at me but stops resisting.

"Nod your head to confirm you'll shut the fuck up."

She slowly nods, and I feel her tongue graze my palm.

I pull back when my phone rings. As I dig it from my pocket, she runs a finger along her lips.

I relax in my seat as Derrick's name flashes on my phone screen.

Derrick is a Fed and also my informant, feeding me insider knowledge.

"Talk," I answer.

"Feds are headed to both places now," he informs. "Twenty minutes until they reach the Astor estate and thirty before they hit your girl's penthouse."

"Shit," I hiss, veering back onto the road.

The fucking Russians took too long making a deal with me.

I glance at Genesis while speeding down the road. "You're homeless now. If you want anything from your place that can be retrieved in five minutes and fit inside a single bag, you'd better rattle it off right now."

She blinks at me. "What are you talking about?"

"List your shit or get nothing."

She places her hand on the middle console. "I'm … confused."

"You get nothing then." I end the call.

3

Genesis

Or, in this case, a nightmare?

I'm stuck in a vehicle with Julian Bellini.

A cold-blooded killer in the Lombardi Mafia family.

His older brother, Damien, is the underboss of said family.

I also have history with this man.

For years, we've gone back and forth in a forbidden game.

He's like a nicotine habit I can't kick.

A drink I can't put down.

A craving that's sweet but deadly.

My heart thrashes against my chest, still recovering from him pinning me against the door. He told me to stop, but I kept talking shit. When I'm nervous, I run my mouth. My mother always said it was a habit that'd make it hard for me to find a husband. I, however, always found it to be more of an asset. *No, thank you* on a man who doesn't appreciate a little bit of attitude.

I peer over at Julian, taking in the way his jaw tics as he drives.

Deranged or not, he's the most gorgeous man I've ever laid eyes on.

I'll never forget the first time I saw him.

I was sixteen and in his parents' kitchen with his sister, Melissa. Marta, their mother, was showing us how to make the perfect cannoli. Even though my mother didn't like me at their house, claiming it was bad for our family's reputation, my father overruled her decision.

Julian stumbled into the kitchen, holding his side, while his father muttered Italian behind him. He was so calm at first, and I didn't notice the blood oozing from his side, soaking his white button-up until Marta scolded him for getting blood on the floor.

Melissa helped him into a chair while Marta scurried off, muttering, "Let me get my supplies."

Entranced, I observed him slowly take off his shirt and drop it on the floor. Melissa pressed a towel against his wound and didn't step away until Marta returned to help him.

In freak-out mode, I blurted that we needed to call the cops and take him to the hospital. Everyone stopped what they were doing and looked at me like I'd suddenly grown another head. You'd think I'd suggested we stab the other side of his torso so he could have twinsies wounds.

Julian took long swigs of vodka and watched me through a swollen eye as Marta stitched him up.

His wariness of me was apparent.

He didn't like me. That much was certain.

But me?

I was fascinated by him.

I stared, my eyes drifting from his face to his six-pack.

He was the most attractive man I'd ever seen.

I no longer cared about boys in my private school who wore designer sweater vests and loafers and bragged about which country clubs they belonged to.

I wanted my best friend's brother.

A man in the Mafia, who was dangerous and corrupt.

A man who didn't flinch at pain, who protected his family

and gave his mother a kiss on the forehead after she stitched up his wounds.

Deep down, I knew it'd never happen.

He was nothing but a crush to me.

And to him, I was nothing but a threat to his family, as if I'd been sent to destroy them.

I have so many questions for him.

Why did he show up at the office?

Why the actual fuck did that Russian psychopath think I was his bride?

Julian helped me, but I know he didn't do it out of the kindness of his heart.

"Where are we going?" I ask as he passes a car.

"My place." His phone rings, stopping our conversation, and he answers it. "I'll get there as soon as I can," he tells the person on the call before ending it.

As if he knows I'm about to play twenty questions, he turns up the music. When I reach forward to lower the volume, he snatches my wrist, slowly shaking his head.

Julian doesn't drive long, and we're still on the outskirts of New York City when he turns onto a private road and stops at a solid wood privacy gate, surrounded by a tall concrete wall.

He punches in a code, opening the gate, and drives forward.

I stare out the window, taking in the maple trees lining his driveway. He turns into an underground tunnel that leads straight into a garage.

As someone used to seeing sprawling estates designed to show wealth, I've never seen such a private setup before.

I unbuckle my seat belt as he parks. "Nice place. It gives very Batcave vibes. I'd ask if you're a superhero, but we both know you're the villain."

Not saying a word, he steps out of the Escalade.

I do the same, noticing two other parked cars—a black Mercedes and a Chevelle similar to the one his father had.

He punches in another door code, and I follow him inside.

The fresh scent of clean linen and lemon lingers in the air as he flips on the lights before dropping his keys on the kitchen island. I shut the door behind me and stand in the doorway, unsure of what to do.

The home is simple yet rich with plants, cream and dark-wood furniture, and sage-colored walls. Windows line the living room wall, revealing a patio, surrounded by more plants.

Since he's not giving me any direction, I head toward the living room.

"Keep your ass in here," he snaps, causing me to stop. "I don't want blood on my furniture."

I'm reminded I'm wearing my father's blood. I tried to wipe it off the best I could during the drive here, but there was no getting it out of my white cashmere sweater.

I cross my arms, turning to face him. "Who were those guys, Julian?"

He stares at his phone screen. "The Russian Bratva."

"Bratva?"

"Mafia, only the Russian version."

"Why did a man in the Russian Mafia—"

"Bratva," he corrects as if he doesn't want them affiliated in the same category as him.

I roll my eyes. "Okay, *Bratva*. Why did he refer to me as his wife?"

He finally lowers his phone and tosses it on the massive stone island. "Contractually, you were to wed him in"—he lifts his shoulder to raise his sleeve and checks his gold watch—"two days."

I roll my eyes again.

Asshole.

If he was looking for *days*, he needed to pull up a calendar, not look at his watch.

He clicks his tongue against the roof of his mouth. "But good news for you, I managed to save you from the Russians and cut you a better deal."

"A better deal?" I ask, raising my chin. "I'm not some Honda Civic, sitting in a used car lot."

"True. Your price was more along the lines of a Rolls-Royce, *shiny and new*."

"Why was a deal even made for me?"

"Your father owed the Russians a lot of money."

"Why would he owe anyone money? He's the richest man on Wall Street."

"That's what he led people to believe. Realistically, your father was the biggest fraud on Wall Street. He did things real rich men don't do to maintain their wealth."

"Things like what?"

"Insider trading, took on clientele not exactly the Wall Street type, and stole money from clients to maintain his lifestyle." He lifts his thick brow. "Now, he's dead, and you're fucked."

I swallow. "What does his debt have to do with me?" I swallow again. "Why am I *fucked*?"

"He borrowed money from the Russians and defaulted on his loan. He also poorly invested their money and eventually pocketed some of it. When the Russians came to his office for their money, Dima saw your photo and liked what he saw." His gaze drifts down my body, and he smirks. "Your father *and* mother signed a new contract. They had sixty days to pay the debt. If they failed, you'd marry Dima. That was sixty-one days ago."

"And now, I'm … free?" I ask, already dreading Julian's answer.

He runs his finger along his lower lip. "And now, *you're mine*."

I stumble back a step, nearly tripping on my feet. "Excuse me?"

His harshness turns into amusement as he approaches me,

unbuttoning his blazer in the process. "Genesis, I do nothing for free." He circles his arm around my hips, stopping me from backing away. "Every move I make ends in my favor. Bad deals are what put men, like your father, in caskets."

I gulp, and it takes me a moment to raise my gaze from the floor to him. Dread sits in the pit of my stomach.

"What's *your price*, Julian?"

He brushes a single callous finger along my jaw. "I need a favor from you."

I shiver, unsure if I want to smack his finger away or ask for more of his touch. "What favor could you possibly want from me?"

He's in the line of murder and gambling.

I'm not murdering anyone. That's for damn sure.

I doubt it's sex.

He's never had trouble getting women.

He's hot as fuck, he has money, and he's in the Mafia.

An instant turn-on for women.

Well, us insane women.

I also offered myself up to him before, and he declined.

Declined sex, but he had no problem touching me in the back of a nightclub.

"We'll discuss that when I return." He digs his finger into my lip before swiftly drawing back. Not another word leaves him as he returns to the kitchen, collects his keys, and walks toward the door.

I sprint across the room and block the door.

He raises his brow in humor.

"No, I want answers now," I demand.

He shoves me against the door, fastens his hands around my wrists, and slams them against the door over my head. I whimper when he presses his body against mine, lowering his mouth to my ear and sliding his tongue along the lobe.

"Which do you want more? Answers or protection from Dima?" he sneers.

I stare at him, lost for words, and bite my lip.

"Do you want to stay alive?"

"That's been my lifelong plan, yes."

"Then, you're going to have my baby." He pulls me away from the door, pushing me toward the kitchen. "And FYI, I have two men waiting outside who I've instructed to deliver you to Dima's doorstep if you try to leave. Or shall I have them drop you off at the altar?"

I rub my wrist and glare at him.

He cunningly smirks before leaving.

I flip him off as soon as the door shuts behind him.

4

Julian

"How's the Atlantic City location going?" Antonio asks.

"Growing," I reply, sitting across from him and Damien at the boardroom table at Lucky Kings Casino.

Antonio is the boss of the Lombardi Mafia family. For generations, my family has worked for them. My grandfather and father were both underbosses. Now, my brother, Damien, holds that position.

To cover their dirty-money trails and show legal wages on paper, the Lombardis started Lucky Kings. For the most part, it's run as a legit business, but we just also perform illegal dealings through it. Consider it a side gig.

After his father's death, Antonio gave Damien half the casino. Six months ago, I offered them a business proposal to open a second Lucky Kings location. I told them I'd fund the business and obviously provide them a cut. Being a competitor wasn't an option. Another business tried that, and people died on both sides.

We blew up all their construction locations.

They killed my family.

Damien and I became the only remaining Bellinis on our family tree.

We buried all the others.

We added one more recently—Damien's little girl, Alessia.

I can never leave the Mafia world, but I wanted something for myself, something that was mine. I'm not a man who enjoys working with others.

It was a no-brainer for Antonio and Damien, providing them further resources to funnel illegal money and another income source. They accepted the proposal, and I opened Lucky Kings in Atlantic City three weeks ago.

"Carlisle Astor is dead," I say with no emotion.

"Fuck," Damien hisses, leaning back in his chair. He scrubs a hand over his forehead.

"I figured his bullshit would catch up to him," Antonio adds dryly. "When I found out he was doing business with the Russians, I cut ties with him. I had enough problems on my hands."

I did the same. The man might've helped me make so much money that I could retire in the Caribbean, but I don't trust thieves. I believe if you steal from other people then you'll eventually steal from me.

Antonio rests his elbows on the table. "What happened?"

"He put a bullet through his own head." I crack my knuckles and slide an ashtray away from me. "A more peaceful death than what the Russians would've provided."

Though I'd have preferred he suffer their wrath. Instead, he left that nightmare to his daughter.

"Carlisle and his wife signed this before he blew his dumbass brain out." I open a manila folder and slide a contract to them.

Antonio reads it first. "Piece of shit," he hisses, passing the paper to Damien. "Men—*cowards*—like that disgust me."

Damien clenches his jaw as he reads. "I'll give him the

benefit of the doubt and hope he killed himself over the guilt of signing over his daughter."

"I'm not giving him the benefit of the doubt for shit," I snarl.

"If the Russians want her—which it seems they do since they traded her for a million dollars—she's theirs," Antonio states matter-of-factly.

Antonio doesn't know Genesis like Damien and I do.

I draw out the next contract from the folder and hand it to Antonio. "I fixed that."

He reads it and then peers up at me in curiosity. "You didn't pay the entire sum?"

"Why would I do that when I need leverage?" I ask.

"Leverage for what?" Damien takes the contract from Antonio.

"What I want from her," I say simply, motioning for him to read the contract.

Antonio glares at me. "If you default on the contract with Yaroslav, there'll be trouble for all of us."

"You know me well enough to know that won't happen," I reply.

Damien scratches his cheek. "Sorry to break it to you, brother, but you might be out half a million dollars. You know how stubborn Genesis is."

I shake my head. "Unless she wants to be a fucking Russian bride, she'll do whatever I say."

I FOUND out about Carlisle's deal with Yaroslav only two hours before Dima went to Carlisle's office to collect his bride. I immediately called Yaroslav, negotiated a new deal, and transferred the money into his bank account.

I smirk, loving that I stole Genesis from Dima.

While Yaroslav cares about his son's happiness, he loves money more. He also has the upper hand. If I don't pay the balance, he's half a million dollars richer, and Dima gets Genesis.

It's a win-win for him.

Though not for Dima, but he has to follow the chain of command.

Until Yaroslav dies or steps down, Dima must follow his orders. Money is a huge factor in keeping families thriving, and that's all Yaroslav cares about.

Dima will probably take his anger out on a poor soul tonight.

The need for violence when we're angry in our world is common.

It's also dangerous, and it has taken us to war multiple times.

Lately, it seems like war is all I know.

We went to war with the Marchetti family after Antonio kidnapped Cristian Marchetti's daughter. The Marchetti Mafia family is one of the most notorious and deadliest Italian Mafias in New York City. Antonio didn't only kidnap her, but he also forced her to marry him while we were in the middle of a war with Antonio's Uncle Sonny. Sonny wanted to take over, become boss of the Lombardi family, and Antonio had to kill him for it.

When that was over, we had to bail Damien out of a marriage contract with the Irish. And by bail, I mean murder the Irish boss and make it look like his underboss committed the murder.

Men start wars for several reasons—politics, religions, greed, *women*.

Women being in that category shows how powerful they are.

My phone rings, and I answer Warren's call.

"Did you draw it up?" I ask my attorney.

While I have the contract Genesis's parents signed and mine with Yaroslav, I don't have one with Genesis yet. No business is done without contracts, period.

"Yes," Warren answers.

"I'm on my way to your office now." I end the call.

Fifteen minutes later, I take the elevator to the fifth floor of his building and walk straight into his office. I pay a steep retainer to have round-the-clock access to Warren. The man loves money, which I have plenty of, and also fears me, which he should.

He clicks off CNBC when I enter his office and hands over the contract. "With any other client, I'd say this contract would be a hard sell, but what does this woman have to lose?"

"Everything," I state. "She has everything to lose." I read over the contract and then toss a banded ten grand on his desk. "Buy your wife something nice."

His lips form a smile. "She always says you're her favorite client of mine."

When I walk out of Warren's law firm, I spot an unmarked Tahoe and stroll toward it.

Derrick rolls down his window to hand me Genesis's phone. I instructed him to collect it from her car while the Feds raided Carlisle's home.

"If she wants anything, I can get her into her place later," he tells me. "I'll text you the details."

I salute him with one hand and shove the phone into my pocket with the other. He drives off, and I take it upon myself to look through Genesis's phone when I'm back in the Escalade.

Her password is her birthday—so fucking obvious.

"Hmm," I mutter, opening her messages. "Looks like I need to ruin some things for her."

5

———

Genesis

"You're going to have my baby."

Julian's words replay in my head like Beyoncé's "Single Ladies" did in 2008.

Talk about cliffhanger of the freaking century.

When he returns, I'm telling him he's batshit crazy and to take me home.

Is going home even safe?

I gulp.

Will the Russian war-fucking-lords come looking for me, thinking I'm Dima's wife to be, and Julian won't be there to protect me?

First things first.

I need to get out of these bloody clothes.

I kick off my chunky heels, undress to only my bra and panties, and walk upstairs in search of a closet. The only unlocked doors are bathrooms, and I find nothing. Defeated, I return downstairs and find the laundry room.

I open the dryer, and it's empty.

Just perfect.

As I make my way back to the kitchen, I spot a black blazer spread over the back of an island stool. I snatch it and put it on.

Unsure of what else to do, I snuggle on the couch and wait.

Wait and think.

Has my entire life been a lie?

My father was a well-respected Wall Street broker. He founded one of the largest investment firms in the country and managed billions of dollars for clients, ranging from tech CEOs to those on Forbes richest list and government officials in other countries.

No way he could have gone broke.

But why else would he have sold me and put a bullet in his own head?

Even if he did have a contract with the Russians, it's not like Dima could take me to court and force me to marry him, right?

I wish I had my phone so I could call 911. My father might've done a shitty thing, but he didn't deserve to be left dead in his office. I also need to get in contact with my mother to tell her everything and ask where she is. We haven't talked in days, but that's not unusual. Our relationship isn't the best.

I grab the remote and attempt to make myself comfortable.

My mind returns to Julian.

Why is he doing this?

I'm his sister's friend, yes.

But he made it clear he didn't like or trust me.

Why in the world would he want me to have his baby?

I saw my father shoot himself and haven't cried.

I'm numb, like it's hard to feel anything.

The loss and hurt are there, yes, but the tears aren't.

I don't know how much time passed before Julian returns, waking me.

He drops his gun, wallet, and a folder on the counter before walking toward me, slipping his hands into his pockets. He's no longer wearing his blazer from earlier. His black button-up sleeves are rolled to his elbows, and stress lines his face.

The blazer slips off my shoulder as I sit up, revealing my bra.

He halts in step, his gaze sweeping over me in slow motion. Blood rushes between my legs as his eyes travel over my chest.

He smirks. "This is a pleasant view to come home to."

I frown, hitching the blazer back up my shoulder. "Don't expect for it to happen again."

His smirk grows, a hum falling from his lips.

"It's time to tell me what's going on, Julian."

He cracks his neck. "Your father owes a lot of people a lot of money." He stops to correct himself. "Well, *owed*, given that he's now dead."

I wince at how cold he said *dead*.

"I'm sure you expected an inheritance upon his death, but all he left you was debt, possible criminal charges, and an obligation to marry into the Russian Bratva." His voice turns arrogant. "Or, if you behave correctly, I'll save your ass."

I cross my arms, goose bumps crawling up my skin. "I'll pay whatever he owes them." There's money in my bank account, and I'll sell everything I own if it means my freedom.

He strolls deeper into the living room. "The debt is a million dollars."

"I have that." My condo alone is worth two million.

"You have nothing, nor do you have access to any money. Your family's and your bank account were frozen hours ago. You also won't receive a penny from your inheritance or the sale of your condo."

"My father earned plenty of legitimate money. They can't take everything."

"They can. The Feds have been investigating your father for months and planned to arrest him tonight. When they arrived at his home after we left, they found his body and searched the home for additional evidence."

"How the hell do you know all this?"

"I know everything."

I snort. "Cocky much?"

"I did business with your father and have connections with a few Feds. He'd been on their radar, but I only learned about his deal with the Morozovas tonight."

"Morozovas are the crazy Russians?" I ask slowly.

He nods.

"You could've given me a heads-up about the whole Feds situation."

"You'd have done something stupid. The last thing I needed was them thinking you knew about or were involved in your father's crimes." He stalks to the wet bar, pouring two glasses of bourbon.

I don't take my eyes off him as he carries the glasses by the stems in one hand, and the bottle in the other while walking back toward me.

He holds out his hand carrying the glasses and offers me one. "I'm here to help you, Genesis."

I take the glass from him. "For a fee ... for a uterus."

"I don't do favors out of the kindness of my heart. If that's what you're seeking, good luck finding it in this city. Better yet, good luck finding it *anywhere*."

I glance down at my glass, wishing it had the answers I'm desperately seeking. "Melissa would've wanted you to help me. Helping her best friend would be the nice thing to do." I shut my eyes, the memory of Melissa always in my thoughts.

"I'd consider my offer very nice." He lowers the bottle to the wooden coffee table before taking a long swig of his drink. "In fact, I find it offensive that you see it otherwise."

"I find blackmail offensive. Do something for free for a change. Out of the kindness of your heart."

Who am I kidding?

He doesn't have a heart.

He peers up, as if deep in thought. "You want me to help you without reimbursement, *out of the kindness of my heart*?" When he lowers his attention back to me, he narrows his eyes. "I'll give you a hundred thousand dollars. Take it, build a new life, and try your best to hide from the Morozovas. But for a million-dollar price tag? I need more."

"I'll make payments." I slowly bring the glass to my lips, taking a sip to hide my anxiety.

"You want a loan? Go to the bank."

I glare at him.

He knocks back the rest of his drink and places his glass beside the bottle. "Now that you've learned your freedom lies in my hands, let's move on to the next order of business."

I chug my drink, refill my glass, and take a long draw of the alcohol before motioning for him to continue.

"I only paid half your debt." His eyes turn cold. "I'll pay the remainder when I get what I want."

"And what you want is a baby?" I swallow another swig. "You're nuts if you think that's happening. How about I clean your house for a year or babysit your plants?"

His face remains serious. "A million dollars in exchange for a child is a fair deal."

I shake my head. "My uterus is worth more than that."

"Genesis, your parents didn't even think your freedom was worth that." He straightens the collar of my—well, *his*—blazer and lowers his hand between the open gap. "You have two options, Genesis. Marry into the Russian Bratva or sign my contract."

I shiver when he caresses my skin with his thumb. He makes small strokes, as if torturing me.

Like I'm a victim in one of the sick games he plays with his prey.

I'm falling straight into his trap.

Straight down the hole.

Like Alice in Wonderland, but instead, he'll drag me straight to hell.

I shut my eyes, relishing his touch, and lose a breath when he abruptly pulls away.

"Now, drink up," he says, his deep voice breaking me out of my thoughts. He snatches the glass and places it against my lips. "If everything ends in my favor, you won't be able to consume alcohol for a good nine months."

I turn my head, refusing the drink.

He shrugs, pulling back, and I expect him to return it to the table. His eyes are on mine as he tips the glass down and splashes me in the face with the drink. I rear back in shock, wiping the droplets from my cheek, and glare at him.

"There are better places I can pour this. I suggest you don't test me."

I snatch the glass from him and chug it.

The more alcohol I have for this conversation, the better anyway.

"I want a contract." I'm shocked those words leave my mouth.

Am I really considering this?

Julian smiles smugly, stands, and returns to the kitchen. I watch his every move as he grabs the folder, stalks back to me, and tosses it in my lap.

"Your contract."

Well, damn.

I didn't expect him to have it on demand.

I steadily open the folder and flip through the pages of the contract.

His face is unreadable.

"Did you give me a drink before this to alter my comprehension while reading this contract?" I ask.

"Of course not." He rests his hand over his heart. "A man of my integrity would never."

I roll my eyes at his lie. "Why do you want *me* to have your baby? You could easily have some random woman do it without having to pay a million dollars."

"That's none of your concern." He bites into his lip, reaching down to skim his finger along my collarbone. "I will admit, though, coming home and seeing you like this, waiting for me, tells me I'm making the right decision."

I smack his hand away.

He moves it to my shoulder, running it down my arm.

The asshole is fucking with me, turning me on to turn off my brain.

I squeeze my thighs together.

Bad move since it draws his attention to my bare legs.

Fuck.

His eyes immediately dart to my thighs. Desire flashes across his face. I'm surprised he didn't pay more attention to my lack of pants before.

"You're asking for a lot here, Julian. It is my concern," I say.

"You'll be well taken care of and want for nothing."

"Well taken care of?" It takes me a moment to get the next words out. "Like marriage?"

That last word snaps his attention back to my face. "Marriage isn't necessary."

I raise a brow. "So, after we baby it up, I can marry another man?"

"Absolutely fucking not." He rips the contract from my hand, withdraws a pen from his pocket, sticks the cap in his mouth, and writes something on the second page.

He shoves it back into my hand, and I reread the page he wrote on.

No goddamn husband, is written in the footnotes.

I scoff. "I'm not spending my life alone."

He tears the contract from my hand, scribbles on it again, and hands it back.

I wait as he removes the cap from his mouth.

"I hope it doesn't come to that, and you change your mind," he says. "If you do insist, I won't expect us to have a traditional marriage."

"Hard pass on marrying a man who doesn't love me."

"Maybe you can convince Dima to love you." He caps the pen. "I'll send you a great wedding gift."

I glare at him.

"You'll have your own home, which I'll provide, and live a happy life with our child. We'll share custody. I get Christmas. You get Thanksgiving." He says everything so smugly, as if he knows I'll cave.

"I want Christmas."

"See, we're already off to a great co-parenting start. Arguing over custody."

I relax when he sits down. "Let's assume I *do* agree to this. How do I get pregnant?"

He cocks his head. "You do know how babies are made, correct?"

I so badly want to say *storks*, but this isn't the time for a jokey-joke. "Yes, but I mean, how will *we* …" I pause, my words dropping in the tense air.

"I'd prefer to fuck you. The fewer people involved, the better."

Every single nerve in my body lights on fire with the way he said *fuck.*

It's like he wanted to get me pregnant with that word alone, along with how he's looking at me.

"But if you feel more comfortable going another route, we

can." His lips twitch into a devilish smirk. "Though it's already been proven you enjoy me touching your pussy."

My cheeks burn hot as I remember that night, and I narrow my eyes at him. "Don't act like you weren't into it either. I saw your face when I orgasmed."

"Good news then. It appears we're compatible, and we can make our baby the natural way." He pours another round of drinks and raises his glass again, as if closing a business deal. "I'll make sure you come every time. It's a win-win for you, Gen."

"Not really. You never finished the job," I say with a smirk.

He works his jaw. "Genesis, had we not been in public, I'd have had you on your knees, choking on my cock."

He points at me with his glass, and I take a nervous drink.

Then, I choke.

On my drink, not his cock.

Though it's terrible timing.

"If you're trying to sound romantic, that won't work," I say when I gain control of my voice.

"I'm not trying to romance you. This is strictly business." He inches back, as if proving his point.

The man might fuck me, but he'll never love me.

What a dream man.

"It seems my only options are either you or Dima."

"Or death," he hums, taking a sip of his bourbon.

I sigh, my head spinning. "I need time to process and reread this."

He draws back some. "You don't trust me?"

"You're blackmailing me into having your baby."

He takes another drink, not bothering to reply.

I raise my chin, attempting to show some strength. "While I do that, you need to get my phone from my car."

Leaning back, he pulls my phone from his pocket. The furry pink case looks almost comical in his hand.

"Since you have my phone, I hope it means you have my car as well?" My tone is stupidly hopeful.

"You have your phone," he says, but it fully answers my question.

"Why not my car?"

"Your car has GPS on it. I don't want it tracked to my house."

"I need a car, Julian."

He hands me my phone, done with the car conversation. I immediately unlock it and go straight to my Contacts.

Only to find half of them gone.

"What the hell?" I show him the screen. "Did you go through my phone, you lunatic?"

He runs his hand over his jaw stubble. "I did."

"That's an invasion of privacy."

"I don't give a fuck."

"Why would you do that?" I scroll through the Contacts he kept.

There aren't many, but he did conveniently keep my OB-GYN in there.

"I needed to know what you were doing. Keep an eye on my purchase."

I decide to ignore the whole *purchase* comment and focus more on him going through my phone like some jealous boyfriend. "You can't just delete my Contacts."

He scoots in closer, his face and voice hardening. "I deleted the *men* in your Contacts. Men you should have no interest in communicating with." He holds a finger to my lips when I attempt to talk. "And since I prefer not to have this tedious conversation again, every man you met on that dating app of yours now knows you're pregnant with my baby and to never contact you again. I do business with the CEO of that app. You're banned from ever opening another account."

"What gives you the right?" I hiss through my teeth, using all my restraint not to throw my phone at him.

"Everything gives me the right. *A million* dollars gives me the right."

"I haven't signed anything." I'm so ready to rip that stupid contract to shreds. "You don't—*and won't*—control my life."

As if he can read my mind, he grabs the contract and moves it out of my reach. "Don't like my term? You're free to leave," he says nonchalantly, as if he can take it or leave it.

I mean, he really can.

He's not the one who'll be stuck marrying Dima.

He scrubs his hands together, ready to drive his argument in my face more. "As of right now, I'm only out half a million dollars, and I'll easily still sleep at night. As will you—next to Dima, of course." He lowers his hand to my thigh. "Consider what you're doing a surrogacy, if that makes you feel better. But let me make it clear— you won't find another man willing to give up that amount of money in exchange for pussy, no matter how sweet or wet it might be."

I cringe at his crassness. "Don't say it like that. You're asking for my uterus, not my pussy."

Saying it that way doesn't make me feel as cheap. I'm sure they sell uteri on the market for a pretty penny.

Big chance of them *not* being in someone's body though.

"Semantics," he argues.

Agreeing to his terms would seal my fate.

It'd be sacrificing my future and any hopes of being a traditional wife.

I'd be married to a man in the Mafia.

A dangerous criminal.

Endless thoughts consume my mind.

To somewhat put myself at ease, I stare down at his hand on my thigh. I inhale a deep breath, relaxing at the smell of his rich and smoky cologne.

I bite into my cheek, still tasting the liquor. "What would I tell my friends?"

"We fucked, and you got pregnant," he says simply.

I drop my phone to my side. "If I sign your contract, you can't continue to hang this debt over my head."

"Oh, Gen, I'll hold it over your head forever." He slides closer, getting in my face, and slips his hand between my legs.

I tremble, knowing I should pull away.

My heartbeat quickens.

My throat turns dry.

"Be prepared to hear it like a broken record." He dips a single finger beneath my panties, smirking at how wet I am. He removes his finger, rubbing his digits together to play with my juices. "The Russians are a fucking headache to deal with, and I did it for you."

"You expect me to lie down and spread my legs for a man who speaks to me like that?"

I'm surprised I'm able to argue with him with how turned on I am.

But arguing is one of my best hobbies.

I can do it in my sleep, turned on, turned off, drunk, on melatonin.

I hate how my body is falling for him.

I'm a fucking feminist.

I have an RBG bumper sticker on my car, for Christ's sake.

Well, my old car.

"What happens if I say no?" I ask.

"I'll offer it to someone else then."

"Was that your plan all along?"

"With how busy my life is, yes. I don't do relationships."

"What do you *do* then?"

He smirks, and I harden my glare at him.

His ringing phone interrupts our conversation, and I'm relieved at the break.

He takes the call, not leaving the room for privacy. Nodding, he listens to whatever is said on the other line before saying, "Yeah, okay."

After he ends the call, he looks straight at me. "I can take you to your condo in an hour. Make a mental checklist of what you want from it." He stands and starts loosening his sleeves around his elbow. "I'm going upstairs to shower. We'll leave when I'm done."

I gesture to myself. "Um, I need something to wear."

"Come on." He stops at the landing, waiting for me to stand.

I follow him upstairs to one of the doors with a code lock on it. He keys in the code, hiding it from me. We enter a bedroom that smells like his cologne and fresh laundry.

The walls are taupe, and I recognize his bed from the latest Restoration Hardware catalog. The room is clean, almost not lived in, and the brown bedding is perfectly made.

He guides me through a primary bathroom to an impressive closet—and this is coming from a woman with a closet larger than most New York apartments.

I huff when he shoves black sweats into my hands. He stares me down, not offering privacy like a gentleman would, as I slide the blazer off my shoulders. I use it to cover myself while awkwardly tugging the sweats up my legs. They hang loose on my waist.

"Tie the drawstring as tight as you can," he instructs. "Grab a hoodie."

I hold up the blazer. "What if I like this better?"

"I killed a man in that jacket a day ago. It's all yours, if you want."

I toss it on the floor as if it just caught fire, and he starts unbuttoning his shirt.

My jaw drops when he removes his shirt, revealing his tatted chest and six-pack. Snapping myself back into reality, I hurriedly turn around, yank a hoodie from the hanger, and flee the room, going into the hallway.

When I hear the shower start, I lean against the stair railing and call my father's attorney.

Henry will know what to do.

He's solved my family's problems for years.

Julian at least left his number in there.

Henry answers on the second ring. "Hello, Genesis. I've been expecting your call."

"Is it true?" I ask. "About my father?"

"Yes, and if you didn't know, they found his dead body earlier this evening."

I cover my mouth, hiding a gasp. Hearing him confirm it is a sucker punch to the gut. I'm also worried the cops or public may believe I'm involved in his death. If they watch the cameras, they'll see me fleeing the scene with a group of men carrying guns.

Will people think I did it for money?

For my inheritance?

Though now, it's nonexistent, apparently.

"Did he set up anything for me?" My voice shakes as the words leave my mouth.

"No."

My heart skips a beat.

"There's no money for you, but I can help set up an arrangement."

"What kind of arrangement?"

"I'll get you a home and give you money, and we can vacation together. You treat me well, and I'll take care of you. I'll also cover all your legal bills."

Wait ... is he ...

I clench my fist around the phone, wishing I were in front of him right now.

I'd throw something at his head and take all my frustrations out on him.

What a freaking creep bag.

"You're married," I snarl. "I went to school with your daughter."

The fucking nerve.

"And?" he huffs out. "This is a good offer."

Jesus.

It seems the only way women can get help around here is with sex.

Men will find any way to manipulate us if we're down on our luck.

"Are you asking me to be your mistress?" I snap, making sure I'm hearing him correctly. Or possibly giving him a chance to correct himself.

"Genesis, that's not what I meant."

"Then please explain what you meant because it sounds like that's your proposition."

He clears his throat. "You do for me. I do for you."

I grip the phone tighter. "I'm not that desperate."

I hang up on him.

It's just me, myself, and I.

Or me, Julian, and possibly a baby.

"Let's go."

I whip around at Julian's voice to find him standing in the doorway, buttoning a clean shirt with his pants still on. "I thought you were showering."

"Change of plans," he says, his strong jaw clenching. "We're leaving now."

I follow him down the stairs, nearly falling on my face since he's walking so fast.

When we're in the Escalade, I hold up my phone. "I need to call my mother."

Calling her should've been my first priority when I got my phone.

But deep down, I know she knew about the contract with the Russians.

After my father's first affair, she watched him like a hawk. She tracked his locations, checked his text logs, and made him spend nearly every hour with her when he wasn't at the office.

"Put it on speaker," Julian demands.

"What if I want some privacy?" I buckle my seat belt.

"What if I throw your phone out the goddamn window?"

I side-eye him but unlock my phone. "It seems you at least left her number."

"For you, though she doesn't deserve it."

"Don't insult my mother."

"She deserves more than insults after what she did. She signed the contract to sell you off, along with your father. She knew what would happen, which is why she fled the country." He points at my phone. "Call her. Put it on speaker. Let's hear her bullshit excuse or if she'll even own up to it."

My chest tightens at the ugly truth, and I want to vomit. "Wait, she left the country?"

He nods, disgust on his face. "She flew out on a private jet early this morning. Just like your father, she knew what was coming today."

A tear slips down my face, and I hurriedly swipe it off my cheek.

I hit her name, and she doesn't answer my first call.

Or my second or my third.

It takes four tries before she does.

"Mom, where are you?" I rush out, hearing reggae music in the background.

"Oh, hi, honey," she sings out. "I'm just in Tahiti."

Yes, she fucking sings it.

"Why are you in Tahiti?" I bite back the urge to scream that at her. I want to hear her sorry excuse for ditching my ass first.

"Mama needed a little vacation." She sounds as interested in this conversation as I was in Henry's offer.

"Bullshit," I hiss, losing that restraint. "You fled."

She's quiet.

"Dad is dead."

"What?" She at least shows emotion when hearing this news. Not a lot, but some.

"Dad. Is. Dead," I stress.

"How?" Her voice breaks just a twinge.

"He shot himself in the head in front of me."

Technically, it was behind me, but semantics.

I wince at how cold my voice sounds. It's as if Julian's attitude toward death has suddenly rubbed off on me.

"Honey," she says, her voice as smooth as, well, honey, "I'm so sorry."

"What are you sorry for?" I ask. "For his death? For taking the private jet without me? You left me here to deal with the consequences of your actions, yet you made sure you were safe from them."

"I didn't have time to call you. You know how bad traffic is in the city. I had to get out of there. I'll try to find funds to get you here soon. Just hang tight—"

"Have the jet come back and get me right now. If it was that easy for you, then it should be for me."

"The jet is parked. If we move it, the Feds will take it. Flying to the States isn't an option right now. We have to wait until all this clears up."

"Did you know about the contract?" I snarl. "The one that sold me off to a Russian psychopath?"

Her silence confirms she did.

"Did you know?" I grit out, needing to hear her admit it.

"I'm so sorry. We had no other choice." Her voice perks up, further increasing my annoyance. "Consider it a compliment. That a man of his wealth and status found you worthy of a million dollars."

Julian curses in the background.

Although he is one of those men.

I'm pretty sure I also hear him call my mother a cunt.

"How could you?" I say, fighting to control my emotions. I refuse to let her hear me break down. "As a parent, you're supposed to protect me."

A chuckle leaves her.

Yes, a fucking chuckle.

"Now, how was I supposed to do that, Genesis? I'm far too old for him, and you're *soo* much prettier."

"And you're dead to me." I end the call.

All I've gotten today is betrayal.

Tears build in my eyes.

My mother has always been selfish, but I looked past her faults.

My grandparents are dead.

My parents deserted me.

No siblings.

All I have are friends.

And Julian, it seems.

"Wait," I say when Julian cuts a right, driving in the opposite direction of my apartment. "This isn't the right way."

"We need to make one quick stop," he says, making another wrong turn.

I RECOGNIZE THE BUILDING.

I've been here with my father.

I grab Julian's arm when he puts the Escalade in park. "What are you doing?"

"No need to worry," he says, opening the glove compartment and pulling out a gun with a silencer at the end. "I have to make a quick errand, and then we'll go to your place. Start a list of what you need." He tugs away from my hold and opens the door. "Stay in here."

Before he gets the chance to lock me in the Escalade, I jump out. "I'm coming with you."

"Don't say a motherfucking word," he warns, snatching my hand, his grip so tight that I can't pull away. "Don't say I didn't warn you that this wasn't a good idea."

I, of course, say words.

I plead with him to stop as he drags me toward Henry's law firm.

I know Julian enough to know he's not here for a simple chat or for legal advice. His gun and the anger burning off him confirm it further.

He shoves the gun into his waistband and swings open the door. It's late, and most of the offices are closed. Only a few people are in the entrance lobby. I struggle to keep up with him as he leads me straight to the elevators. A couple attempt to join us, but he closes the doors in their faces.

"Rude," I snarl at him.

The elevator chimes, and my hands sweat when the doors open. The bright lights of the firm's lobby nearly blind me.

"Sir," the young secretary says when she sees us charging toward Henry's office, "you can't—"

He points the gun at her. "Sit your ass down. If you call for help, I'll push you out the fucking window."

She drops back into her chair, and I whisper, "Sorry, but listen to him," as I'm pulled toward Henry's office.

Julian kicks the door open even though there's literally a door handle, and I doubt it was locked. Startled, Henry jumps to his feet. His face pales as his gaze bounces from Julian to me.

"Julian …" His words trail off as his eyes find mine. "Genesis?" His voice trembles with fear.

"Sit down, Henry," Julian demands.

Just like the secretary, Henry collapses in his chair.

Julian releases my hand, and I don't move.

Stupid Henry suddenly reaches for his phone. Julian advances toward him and sweeps his arm along the desk. Henry's computer, phone, and papers fall to the Berber carpet.

Julian aims the gun at a quivering Henry.

Henry's back straightens, and he holds up his arms.

"Now, Henry," Julian taunts, standing directly in front of him, "you told Genesis you'd help her, correct?"

Shit.

He must've listened to our phone conversation.

"Yes," Henry stutters, his entire body shaking.

Julian walks behind Henry's desk, stopping behind him. "And what was your offer of *helping*?"

Henry violently shakes his head, not answering.

Julian grabs what little hair Henry has and forces his head back until he's looking him in the eye. "What was your offer, you fucking maggot?"

"I … I only said we'd vacation together, become friends— that's all."

Julian's hand leaves Henry's hair to wheel out his chair. "Get on your knees."

Henry stands and tries to make a run for it. He's too slow, and Julian catches him from around the neck and shoves him to his knees. Henry stares at me in horror as Julian tucks the gun back into his waistband, grips his head with both hands, and plunges his thumbs into Henry's eyes. He wails in pain, thrashing his body to the side to break loose.

I gasp, covering my mouth.

While I've always known Julian was a violent man, I never witnessed the full extent until tonight.

"Now, apologize to her," Julian says, removing his thumbs and forcing Henry to look at me.

"What?" Henry cries out, his eyes starting to swell.

"Apologize to her for being a scumbag," Julian demands.

"I'm … so sorry, Genesis," Henry screeches, his eyes pleading with me to control Julian.

Even if I tried, Julian wouldn't listen.

He'd probably make Henry's punishment worse.

Julian clicks his tongue along the roof of his mouth and pulls his gun back out, thrusting it against the back of his head. "That's not good enough."

"Julian, this really isn't necessary. I told him no," I finally say, stepping closer.

Julian slowly shakes his head at me. "It's completely necessary." He pushes the gun against Henry's head. "Now, say it again—and like you mean it. I want to hear the regret in your voice. I want to hear what a disgrace you are as a man. You're trash, a fucking predator, who doesn't deserve to enjoy another day in his life."

"Genesis, I'm so sorry." Henry presses his palms together in a praying gesture. "I shouldn't have done that. I'll give you legal services, free of charge. Whatever you want."

"She doesn't need your fucking services." Julian squeezes the trigger.

Blood splatters everywhere—the walls, the floor, the desk, on a family photo, on Julian, on *my cheek*. It reminds me of what happened in my father's office, and I swallow down the vomit rising up my throat.

Death seems to be the theme of the day. Henry's scrawny body sinks to the ground, blood gushing from his head, just like how my father's did.

I hear a gasp and turn around to find the secretary standing in the doorway.

"Try to run, and I'll shoot you next," Julian warns, aiming the gun in her direction again.

"Don't you dare," I say to Julian.

No way in hell am I okay with him murdering this poor woman.

With the gun still on the woman, he walks around Henry's body, dodging the blood, and stops in front of me.

He lowers the gun to smear the blood across my cheek. "Red looks good on you, baby."

I'VE SEEN two dead bodies and cleaned their blood off me in less than twelve hours.

Two men who'd been role models my entire life are now dead.

Two men I thought I could trust.

Moral of the story: Don't trust men, especially ones who love power.

Though does that mean I can't trust Julian?

After Julian killed Henry, he sat the secretary down, handed her a stack of cash, and told her if she kept her mouth shut, he'd send her more every month. He also offered her a better job with higher pay at Lucky Kings. It didn't even take her a minute to accept his offer.

She told Julian where the cameras were, and he erased all the data from the office and lobby. It's like I'm living in the *Veronica Mars* movie, only with way more violence. He told the secretary to tell the cops a man dressed in a suit came in, angry that Henry had lost his case and cost him money, and shot him.

The fact that it doesn't take Julian hours to do this is scary.

It's like he has it down to a science.

We leave, and Julian drives straight to my building in the city. He parks in the back, and we enter through the employee door. I frown, hating that I don't get the chance to tell my doorman or neighbors goodbye. Though it may be a good thing. I'm sure they have tons of questions if the Feds did go through my apartment or they saw the news.

Julian holds my hand tight, leading me down a hall and up a flight of stairs. I've never been in this way before.

My parents bought me the condo for my twenty-first birthday. I spent six months working with an interior designer, decorating it with bright colors and lush furniture. I also had a delivery of fresh peonies every morning.

It was supposed to be my forever home—or at least until I married and started a family. Now, that future is gone.

My cheeks flush from embarrassment.

I'm twenty-five, and my parents still funded my life.

It's not as if I spent all my life lounging at home and vacationing. I treated my volunteer work as a full-time job. It'd been my life for so long, and my parents had no issue financing my philanthropy work.

My father had me on payroll, but technically, I did *some* work for the company. I attended dinners when he asked and talked to people at events, convincing them to become clients and hand over their finances to his company.

On our drive here, I googled my father's name. Breaking news article after article popped up. The police raided our family home and found his body. The stories continued with the crimes they accused him of committing. I made Julian pull over and puked up what little was in my stomach.

I finally cried.

The shock wore off as reality set in.

The life as I had known it was gone.

We take the elevator to my floor, which opens directly into my kitchen. It's messy, not the way I left it, making it obvious that someone—or *someones*—was rummaging through my things.

A tall man, at least six-seven, wearing a black coat with an FBI badge, stands in my living room. A black cap is on his head, chestnut-brown hair sticking out from the sides. He pretty much solidifies that my father was in deep trouble.

"Julian," he says, jerking his chin toward him before offering me the same gesture.

I hold my hand up in a slight wave.

"Get your things," Julian tells me as the man walks in our direction.

Julian slips him money when he reaches us, and they move away from me, toward a corner.

I kick off my shoes out of habit and head toward my bedroom, moving slowly in an attempt to hear their conversation.

"They want to speak with her," the guy tells Julian. "Does she have an attorney?"

"No," Julian replies so easily, as if he didn't just kill mine—aka Henry—in cold blood. "But I'll get Warren to represent her." He turns, as if he knew I was listening, and motions toward the man. "Don't say a word to this guy. Get your shit and let's go."

The man laughs, jerking his head toward me the same way he did moments ago. "I'm Derrick."

"He's irrelevant." Julian glares at Derrick. "Don't talk to him without me."

Derrick chuckles. "I'm not irrelevant. I'm one of the men in charge of your father's case."

Does he even have a case?

I mean, it's not like they can charge and jail his corpse.

Or will that fall on me as well, like the whole Russian-bride situation?

"You're irrelevant to her because she had nothing to do with his crimes," he tells Derrick sternly before whipping his attention back to me. "Now, go get your shit."

I scurry away from them, run into my closet, and grab the largest suitcase I own. I throw some belongings inside—jewelry, handbags, shoes, and photo albums. I dump my bra and panties drawer into a tote bag—because *ew,* I don't want the *Feds* going through those.

"One minute," Julian yells.

I leave some of my expensive handbags. If what Julian said is true about my father stealing his clients' money, they'll sell them to pay the innocent families my father stole from. They'll need that money more than I will. I'll only take the items that mean the most to me.

I leave my bedroom with a bag draped over my shoulder and a Celine tote hanging off my elbow and wheel my suitcase behind me.

"In situations like this, do people not get *any* of their belongings?" I ask, my focus on Derrick since he seems to be the one in charge of seizing my shit.

He adjusts his hat, staring at me. "I'd guess they'll give you five, maybe six months before freezing the remainder of your assets and liquidating your belongings to pay your father's victims. You can keep some, what you have there, and you should be fine." He gives me a sincere look. "Sorry, and I'll also apologize in advance for when we have to interview you."

"You pull the *good cop, bad cop* shit on her, I'm killing you," Julian warns him.

Derrick laughs, as if Julian's threats are nothing new.

"Can I stay here tonight?" I ask as the realization that I'll be homeless soon dawns on me. "Until they kick me out, the place is mine, right?"

Julian takes two large strides in my direction, stopping in

front of me, keeping his back to Derrick. "Dima knows where you live," he says in a low tone.

I grip my suitcase handle. "Dima read the contract. He knows I'm not his, so I doubt he'll mess with me. Plus, it's not exactly easy to get into my building."

Well, not easy to get in through the front.

It seemed the employee entrance wasn't a problem.

"You're not staying here," Julian snaps. "Conversation over."

At this point, I don't want to stay here alone anyway.

I'll find somewhere to sleep that isn't Julian's.

It's after two in the morning when Julian helps me load my bags into the Escalade.

This has been the longest night of my life.

Yawning, I shut the door and pull my phone from my purse.

"Who are you texting?" Julian asks, not knowing the concept of privacy as I hit Favorites in my Contacts.

"Darcy," I answer. "I'll crash with her tonight."

"You're not staying with Darcy."

"Yes, I am."

"No, *you're not*."

"Why?"

"Her brother is a fucking creep. I don't like him."

"You don't like him because he asked me out."

Julian only knows this because he overheard me telling Melissa in their living room. He'd left his father's office, and apparently, he had ears like a hawk. He made a pit stop, told me to stay away from the guy, and left the room.

"That's one of the reasons," Julian says. "He's also a coke-addicted trust-fund kid who's been arrested twice."

I lean toward him in my seat and waggle my finger. "Now, if we're going to talk about criminals, I don't think you're on the nice list there either, Mr. Bellini."

"I'd think you'd be more careful with your words after all you'd witnessed tonight." He starts the Escalade and drives off.

"Did you know he felt me up once?" I say this to rile Julian up because I don't like him telling me where I can stay.

"Did you know I kill men who do things I don't like?"

I snap my mouth shut.

He plucks my phone from my hand and slips it into his pocket. "You can have this back when we're home."

I shake my head and mock his tone and words.

He turns to me, and even though I can't see his face in the dark, I know he's glaring at me.

"You'll stay here tonight," he says when we reach his home. "We'll discuss our plans tomorrow."

I have no other options.

Darcy is in Paris with her parents, so I'd still have to find a ride to her place. She'd also ask a million questions about *why* I needed somewhere to crash, and right now, my head is pounding too hard for me to even answer one.

"I'm not sleeping in your bedroom," I say as he pulls into the garage.

"Did I invite you into my bedroom?" He opens the door. "There's a guest room for you. Read the contract tonight and sign it."

6

———

Julian

"I'LL HAVE YOUR BABY," Genesis says, walking downstairs the following morning.

Her silky cherry-red pajamas display every single one of her curves, which she has plenty of. Her hair is pulled up in a ponytail, loose strands hanging in front of her eyes. Her large breasts bounce with each step she takes, and I lick my lips.

Dirty thoughts consume my mind as I watch her.

My cock twitches.

I chose Genesis for several reasons.

One, she's downright fucking gorgeous.

Perfection in my eyes.

The other?

She's my best option.

My parents loved her for a reason. They didn't allow many people into our lives, let alone my sister's. She spent more time at my parents' home than she did her own.

She's also always looked at me in a way no one else did. It was like she wanted me to open every door into my world for her and invite her in.

"Smart girl," I comment, breaking myself from my thoughts when she reaches me.

She plops down on the island stool and blows out a breath. "But I have a few conditions."

I chug my protein drink and set it to the side. "Hit me."

"You purchase a home for me *in my name* and *only* my name." Her voice is all business, and it's fucking hot. "I refuse to be stuck in the same situation that my father just left me in. I want what's mine to be mine."

I backtrack a few steps to lean against the cabinets, crossing my arms. "Someone sure has turned demanding, given her situation." I start counting on my fingers. "Homeless. Carless. Penniless."

She levels her palms on the island. "I'm not *penniless*, asshole."

"You're right. I'm sure you have some change in your wallet."

"*Moving on.*" She scowls at me. "I want a job to earn a paycheck."

"A job where?" I ask this more mockingly than I should.

"The casino, unless you know of anyone else hiring."

"I'll pay you for your services." I smirk, making a show of traveling my eyes down her face to her neck and stopping at her breasts.

Glaring, she pulls her pajama top up to nearly her chin. "I can deal cards—"

"Fuck no. No way am I having you on the casino floor." I scrub a hand over my face. "How about this? I'll give you a weekly paycheck while we sort this contract out. Then, we'll find you a position at the casino."

It's all a lie.

She'll never work at the casino, period.

She leans back on her stool. "You also can't stop me from volunteering."

I knew this would be a problem. "The shelter isn't safe for you."

"I've worked and been safe there for over a decade."

"Before, you didn't have a Russian who wanted to marry you or a pregnancy agreement with me. All of that makes you less safe, so someone needs to watch you. I can't have my men folding blankets and serving food when I need them elsewhere."

She groans, throwing her head back. "Please tell me you're not going to bodyguard me up like your brother did with Pippa."

Pippa is Damien's wife, and she's not allowed to go anywhere alone. She and Genesis became friends after Damien asked Genesis to take Pippa out for a spa day before their first date.

Someone is always watching Pippa. For a while, it was my job, which I fucking hated. That ended when I opened the casino.

I hadn't been made to play bodyguard to a woman I wasn't fucking.

I had been made to run an empire, to make money, and to get rid of those who got in my way.

I just need one more thing—a child to leave everything to.

"You want to volunteer, I'm bodyguarding you up," I say, hoping that'll change her mind.

Genesis is used to doing whatever she wants.

She needs to know that when she signs my contract, her life will change.

As will mine.

7

Genesis

How STUPID WAS I not to stash money aside in case my life fell apart?

I have a master's degree.

I should've gotten a job, but I saw my path in life as helping others.

That's why it's important I keep working at the shelter. They depend on me.

Julian showed me to the guest room last night and handed me the contract. I took a bath, reread the contract, and couldn't help but roll my eyes at the handwritten additions he'd added to it.

Can I really give up hope of finding true love and sign my life away to him?

One thing I do know is that I'm never trusting a man again.

Not with my finances, my heart, or any-goddamn-thing.

I wouldn't even trust one with my coffee order at this point.

Maybe a contracted marriage with no expectations—other than a baby and not marrying someone else—is the answer for me. I have no interest in a relationship that's doomed to fall apart, and if there's anything I know about Julian, it's that he's straight-up, no bullshit. So, I have my stipulations to add, and I'll sign.

"How long will it take me to get my own place?" I ask, changing the subject from volunteer talk. "Since you won't let me stay in the condo that's still legally mine."

He furrows his brow in frustration. "I thought I'd made it clear that you're staying here until we come up with a better arrangement. Finding you that arrangement is at the bottom of my priority list."

"What's at the top?"

"You meeting with my attorney since the Feds want to interview you."

I draw in a deep breath.

Never in my life did I think *talk to the Feds* would be on my agenda.

"You let my attorney do all the speaking," Julian continues with a stony stare. "Don't say a fucking word unless they ask you a specific question and my attorney okays it."

I make a zip motion across my lips.

I wouldn't know what to say to them anyway.

"Don't worry about it, okay?" he adds. "I'll keep you protected, Genesis."

IT'S NOT every day you have to select an outfit to wear to an interview with the Feds who might think you were involved in fraud. My options are also limited since I don't have a full closet any longer.

I went with a tan plaid pleated skirt, a collared white button-up, and flats.

Simple and not too flashy.

I stare at the New York skyscraper, where Julian's attorney's office is located.

Warren Gettinburg. I've heard of him.

He's expensive as hell but notorious for winning high-profile cases. If you're being charged with murder, he's on the list of attorneys to hire. Prosecutors have publicly said they fear when he takes cases because it makes their job ten times harder.

I unbuckle my seat belt and peer at Julian. "Will having an attorney make me look guilty?"

"No," he replies. "Even if it did, who cares what the Feds or the public has to say? Caring about people's opinions won't make you richer or happier. It'll only make you miserable."

I play with my purse strap. "That's easy for you to say. Everyone fears you."

He offers me a satisfied smile. "And that's my goal. I don't care if they like me."

Julian has done well at staying out of the public eye. He's not flashy with his money, nor does he care about the notoriety. Though, in his line of work, people know who he is and fear his name, but it's not as extreme as the attention Antonio gets. Most eyes are on the bosses of Mafia families.

Four Mafia families run New York—the Marchettis, Lombardis, Cavallaros, and O'Connors.

Lately, the Marchettis have started building relationships with the other families. They arranged a marriage with Benny Marchetti, the son of Cristian Marchetti, who's the boss of the Marchetti family, and Neomi Cavallaro, the daughter of Severino, who's the boss of the Cavallaro family.

Most recently—and shockingly—Cristian's daughter married Antonio.

That was a shit show and as arranged as I am a ferret. Everyone thought Cristian would murder Antonio at the altar. I attended the wedding, and Julian was there as well. I made sure to flirt with Cristian's nephew, Luca, to make him jealous. It worked.

"All right, Gen," Julian says, "you ready?"

He gives me a moment to take deep breaths.

I nod and grip the door handle. "Not really, but let's do this, I guess."

Emilio—another man who works for the Lombardis—is already at my door waiting for me to step out.

"We'll meet with Warren first," Julian explains when we're in the elevator.

My nerves are on fire, and I'm thankful he's with me.

And even though I'm throwing out attitude, I'm also grateful he rescued me from my father's office last night.

"Hi, Julian," the secretary greets, her tone too flirty for my liking, when we exit the elevator and enter the lobby.

Oh my God, am I already getting jealous?

I smile at her, telling myself to be nice.

Julian ignores her and takes my hand, and we speed-walk toward an office with glass doors.

Warren stands when we walk in, clad in an expensive suit. He smiles, his teeth pearly white, and shakes Julian's hand first.

When he takes mine, it's warm, and his grip is tight. "Hello, Genesis. It's nice to meet you."

He gestures for us to sit and takes his chair behind his desk.

I make myself comfortable on the leather chair while Julian stands behind me, like a guard protecting me from harm.

Warren doesn't seem surprised at Julian's lack of sitting and goes straight into questioning me. I answer as honestly as I can.

I had no idea what my father was doing and still don't understand why he did any of it. Reputation meant everything to him. I guess he preferred to die rather than hear how people are talking about him now.

My mother was also worried about her status and image. I'm

sure she's reading and watching everything the media says about her.

Good. She deserves their harsh words after what she did.

She knew what he was doing and helped him.

People have left comments about her fleeing the country, claiming it makes her look guilty.

They can't say the same about me.

I'm here, dealing with their consequences.

I deleted all pictures on my socials and disabled my accounts. I also removed all my connections to the shelter I volunteered at, worried the chaos would follow me there.

"Genesis," Julian says, snapping my attention back to the conversation.

I wrinkle my nose. "Does pleading the Fifth make me look guilty?"

"No, it makes you look smart," Julian fires back.

I glare up at him.

"They'll have no problem twisting your words," he says. "Inform them you had no idea of your father's crimes and you're learning the details at the same time as the media. Let Warren work his magic, and we'll get you out of this mess. Only answer a question when he nods toward you."

Julian's all business right now.

I need to be the same.

My freedom is on the line.

People could try to pin my father's crimes on me.

Just like with the Russians, I could be the one to face the consequences.

I offer Julian and then Warren a simple smile and nod. "Sit there and say nothing unless you nod an okay to me. Got it."

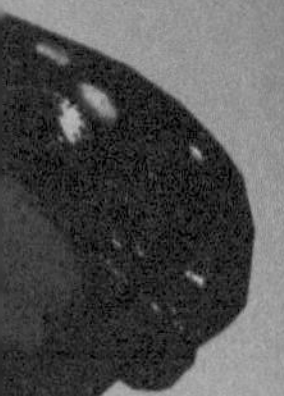

8

Julian

GENESIS IS a bucket of nerves when we sit for the interview.

Derrick's partner tried to stop me from being in the room with them but immediately shut his mouth when I told him, Fed or not, I'd have no problem slitting his sagging fucking throat.

My statement was before they turned on the camera, obviously.

I never leave traces of my threats.

Had he continued to give me trouble, I'd have waited until he left the building, followed him home, and slit his throat there.

During the interview, I scoot Genesis's chair closer to mine, and her body un-tenses an inch. I rest my hand on her bouncing leg, and it stops.

They ask her the same questions Warren said they would, and she replies as he directed her.

I'm fucking proud of the way she's carrying herself. She might not think it right now, but Genesis is fucking strong.

This interview had better get the Feds off her back. I'm worried they'll keep messing with her, needing to make an example out of *anyone* they can to scare others from pulling the same shit Carlisle did.

When finished, we return to Warren's office to discuss the marriage contract.

"Tell him the changes you want," I direct Genesis.

She recites what she said in the kitchen while also adding a few things.

"An allowance of twenty grand a month," is her first addition.

"Done," I reply with no hesitation.

"A monthly donation of five thousand to the shelter."

"Done."

"Agreement that I'll work at the shelter four days a week."

"Fuck no." That's one I'll put a stop to.

"Three days."

"One."

"Two."

"Fine." I motion toward Warren to add that pain-in-my-ass clause.

I'll figure out a way to get her out of volunteering even if I have to pay someone else to take her shifts there.

Maybe I should've chosen an easier baby mother. Antonio could've arranged a marriage for me that'd give us real estate, power, or money. Possibly all three.

Men in this world have no problem exchanging their daughters for deals.

Just like Genesis's father did.

A sour taste fills my mouth at the reminder.

I wish I could slit that fucker's throat. I'd have watched him bleed out with relish.

I never planned to take the *arranged marriage* route.

Forcing a woman to marry me always felt too Draconian.

My father wasn't a fan of them either. He made it clear to the Lombardis that Melissa was never up for sale.

I gave Genesis the choice.

She could've said no and walked away.

She didn't.

Fifteen minutes later, we both sign the contract that'll change our lives.

"I'm starving," Genesis says when we leave Warren's office. "After an anxiety-filled day, I either want to eat nothing or everything. It seems today, it's everything."

"I can stop and get you takeout," I reply. "You can also order something at home, and Emilio will pick it up for you."

Even though he tried to fight it, Emilio will be on Genesis-watching duty until I find another man I can trust.

"Home," she says around a sigh. "I don't have a home anymore."

"My home is your home."

"No, it's *your* home. I'm getting my own, remember?"

"You're getting *yours* after you have our baby. In the meantime, you live with me. So, get comfortable there." I brake at a red light and turn to look at her, my face serious. "Though, after I fuck you, you won't want to leave my bed."

She holds out her hand toward me. "Don't get your hopes up, buddy. Men who gloat about their sexual abilities usually lack in them. Most probably don't even know a clit exists."

"Are you forgetting I've made you come with only my fingers?" I hold up my hand and wiggle two fingers. "You don't think I can do that with my cock?"

Her mouth falls open, and I smirk.

I keep my gaze on her, even when the light turns green. "We can test it now, if you'd like?"

The car behind us honks, and I flip it off.

She shakes her head repeatedly. "I need to process all"—she

gestures back and forth between us—"*this* and figure out which route I want to go, getting pregnant."

I hit the gas in frustration.

"Want my advice?" I ask.

"Not really, but go ahead."

"It's much easier for us both for me to just come in your pussy."

"Oh, so romantic. We should write that on a Hallmark card." She sighs. "We also need to discuss what we'll do if we have sex and I don't get pregnant."

"That's when we'll try another approach. Might as well try the natural method first. Haven't you always said you like natural foods? Organic?"

"Oh my God, please never refer to your cock as a *natural* food again. I won't be able to even force my legs open to give you a chance to get me pregnant."

She's right.

The comment was weird as fuck.

Genesis brings something out in me.

A playfulness.

A man who attempts to joke.

I've always felt more comfortable with her than others.

She makes me feel two emotions—comfort or frustration with the need to strangle her when she tests my patience. And as a man who's *not at ease* ninety-eight percent of the time, that's saying something.

"Back to food," I say. "We can pick something up. I need to take you home and get going."

"Get going where?"

"Work."

"What kind of work? Casino or Mafia?"

"That's none of your concern."

"If we're having a baby, I think it's important for me to know your whereabouts." She slumps her shoulders. "I should've put that in the contract, damn it."

I grin that she didn't.

She can't make a fuss about it if it's not in the contract.

That's why I love contracts so damn much.

She perks up in her seat. "If that's the case, then you don't need to know my whereabouts." The delight of her comeback is clear in her voice.

"I'll always know every move you make, Genesis," I grit out. "You are mine now."

"Does that mean you're mine?"

"If you want to treat me like your husband, then I won't touch another woman. If you want to make your pussy mine, then I'll make my cock exclusively yours. The ball is in your court, baby."

She bites into her lip, and I love the way her cheeks blush. "I, uh …"

I also love that she's at a loss for words.

That doesn't happen often.

Normally, if Genesis can't find words that make sense, she'll just say random shit until she finds them.

"I want to go to the casino with you," she says. "I'll eat there."

"Absolutely not."

"Why not?" she whines. "It'll give me something to do. Otherwise, I might find trouble, and we both know my trouble is bad trouble."

So, it fucking seems.

I decide to go with a different angle. "You've had a lot going on. How about I treat you to a spa day with your friends?"

"How about *no*?"

"You love spa days." I know this because I've had to take her and Pippa before.

"I did, but there's this weird sense of guilt now."

"For what?"

"For spending money after what my father did."

"Don't feel that guilt, and you'll be spending *my* money."

"For a while, I'd like to be a normal girl."

"Fine," I say, giving in because I don't have time to argue. This situation has already caused me to lose enough work hours. "But you're keeping your ass in my office."

Genesis

My current to-do list:

1. Find a job.
2. Make sure Julian doesn't try to stop me from volunteering.

He agreed to two days, but I saw his face when he agreed to it. It was very much an *I'll agree to get this fucking over with* expression.

"Can I have a tour?" I ask Julian when we're in his office at the casino.

The room is tastefully designed with oak wood–paneled walls and hardwood that's slightly darker, giving it a beautiful contrast. A desk large enough for three people sits in the middle of the room. The wet bar in the corner, a stone fireplace, and tufted cognac-brown leather furniture add to the elegance.

There are two doors, but not a single window.

We came in through a door from the outside. I can only assume the other one leads into the casino.

"No," he says in irritation, walking behind the desk and punching a code into a drawer.

Him and his codes.

I hope he owns stock in whatever company he buys them from.

He's probably their biggest customer.

The drawer unlocks, and he takes out two menus.

"We have a few restaurants in the casino," he says, holding them out to me. "Pick what you want, and I'll have it delivered to you here."

I snag the menus on my walk to the couch and plop down. "I want you to eat lunch with me."

"Gen, I don't *lunch*. Save that for you and your girlfriends."

"As your future baby mama, I demand you have lunch with me. No lunch, no uterus rental." I shrug. "I didn't make the rules. I just follow them."

"Unfortunately for you, I don't give a fuck about rules." He withdraws a phone from the drawer before relocking it.

"Fine. I'll go downstairs and eat alone then."

"No, you won't." His tone is expressionless, bored almost, as if he knows he'll win this argument. He always does with people.

Too bad I'm not just *people*.

I'm a pain in the ass.

"Then, tell whoever my bodyguard is to come here and eat with me," I argue. "If you don't want to share a meal with me, find me another man who will."

His deep eyes narrow at me. "No one else is coming to my office."

I shrug, pretending to read the menu.

"My day is full of meetings," he adds.

"When's the first one?"

He checks his watch. "Forty-five minutes, but I need to go over paperwork and reports. I didn't want you to come here in the first place, so don't expect me to entertain you."

I frown. "I always hoped the man who knocked me up would be at least *a little* entertaining."

He drops the phone on the desk, and his jaw tics as he stalks in my direction.

I tighten my hold on the menus as he drops to his knees in front of me.

Reaching out, he grips my face in his strong hand. "You want me to fuck you on my desk as *entertainment*? Done. Lunching? No. The only time I entertain a meal is when it's closing a million-dollar deal or if that meal is pussy." He presses his knuckle under my chin to raise it. "We've already closed our business deal, and I didn't even have to wine or dine you. It seems tasting your pussy is the only other option you have to keep me in here."

I smack his hand away from my face with a huff. He draws back, a devious smirk on his lips.

"If you *ever* want the *privilege* of tasting or fucking me, you'll find a meal on one of these menus and eat *food* with me." I shove the menus in his face at the same time my stomach growls.

He ignores the menus and stands. "Fine, we'll fucking lunch. But we're eating in here. No arguments."

"Next time, we'll—"

"There will be no next time." He massages his temples. "I'm debating this entire agreement between us. My life would be much easier if I let Dima have you. I'm sure he'd have no problem lunching with you or killing you to eat your organs for lunch."

"Too late. The contract is signed. You're stuck with me."

"I can easily rip it up and pretend it never happened." His gaze is angry, as if he wants to rip me apart, along with the contract. "Consider it null and void."

I release a shallow breath. "That's illegal."

He stalks closer to me again but doesn't kneel this time.

Instead, he towers over me, threatening and irritated. "Oh, Gen, do you think I ever consider if an action is legal before I make it? Legalities mean nothing to me."

I cross my arms, hating that I'm losing this argument—something that usually doesn't happen with men.

We're arguing over lunch.

It's so damn elementary school.

Does he think he'll lose his perfect gunshot aim if he eats a damn sandwich?

"Fine," I say in annoyance. "Just feed me."

10

Julian

"Why aren't you touching your food?" Genesis asks, smearing a fry with ketchup.

She's seated on the floor, eating a steakburger and fries, and pops the fry into her mouth. While still waiting on my response, she takes a bite of the burger, moaning while swallowing her bite.

I don't blame her. I'm sure the burger is fucking delicious. The chef in the casino restaurant is one of the best in the state.

My untouched lunch is across from her. She laid it out, placing the silverware and condiments to the side, as if setting the table.

"I told you I don't lunch." I set the report I was reading aside and stand. "I ordered it so you'd shut up."

She frowns. "That's wasteful."

"Blame that on yourself." I stroll toward the bar and pluck a bottle of bourbon from the shelf of options. I might not lunch, but I have no issue day drinking.

"The burger I ordered is healthier than that," she comments, watching me pour a glass.

I chug the liquor in one gulp. "I drink when I get headaches. So, again, blame yourself for that." I pour another glass.

"That's rude." She takes a sip of her water. "You know what's also rude?"

"Don't know. Don't care." I guzzle my drink. "Now, be a good girl, eat your food, and entertain yourself." I set the glass down and head toward the door.

"Will you be late?" she calls out to my back.

"I'm always late." I leave the office without giving her the chance to reply.

It'll be a long night for her, but she asked for it.

11

Genesis

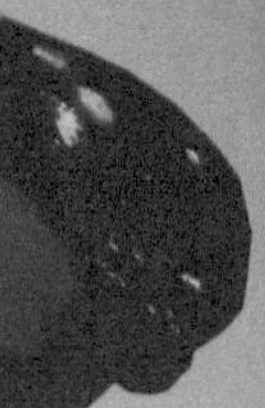

Did Julian forget what day and age we're in?

What am I supposed to do? Count my fingers and toes?

Sing the damn national anthem?

Us humans don't entertain ourselves anymore.

We let social media do that trick.

Unfortunately for me, I don't have that option. The moment I saw people commenting on my latest vacation photos, asking if it was funded by the money my father stole, I knew I needed a break.

After eating, I dump my food into the trash, then clean up Julian's, muttering, "Wasteful prick."

When I look around his office, my eyes land on the bar.

If you can't fight boredom with brain rot, might as well make yourself a drink.

I grab Julian's glass and sweep my gaze over the options.

There are no chasers. Just straight alcohol.

I eeny, meeny, miny, moe until my finger stops on an expensive tequila. We kept the brand regularly stocked in my college sorority house.

I fill my glass, grab the bottle, and take them with me to the couch.

I cringe at the first sip.

Straight tequila is not for the weak.

And I, admittingly, am the weak.

I make myself comfortable before opening Netflix on my phone. Julian gave it back to me earlier. As I drink and try to find a show, my gaze keeps traveling to the door Julian left through.

My curiosity is getting the better of me.

"Don't do it," I mutter. "Don't do it, Genesis."

To get my mind off possibly making a bad decision, I call Darcy.

Darcy and I have been best friends since middle school. We met in our private-school restroom when she asked me for a tampon. She, Melissa, and I became inseparable until Melissa's death. I'm grateful I had Darcy with me during that time. We were each other's grieving partner.

"Why haven't you answered my calls and texts?" Darcy asks as soon as she answers. "I've been worried about you!"

"Sorry." I frown and finish off my drink. "My life has been absolute madness the past twenty-four hours."

"Is it true? All the stuff they're saying about your dad? Is he…" She searches for the right word. "Dead?"

I nod, the alcohol threatening to make its way back up my throat. "Yes." The word hurts as it leaves my mouth.

"Are you okay?" she asks, sadness in her voice. "I wish I could come give you a hug. I'll book a flight home."

"Do *not* book a flight home. Stay there."

"Are you sure?"

"I need a second to … process everything." I can't hold back a sniffle.

Call me heartless, but it's hard for me to grieve a man who sold me like an expensive piece of art. He knew Dima was dangerous and would hurt me but didn't care.

"How's your mom?"

"Terrific." I roll my eyes. "She's lying out in the Tahiti sun, living her best life and hopefully getting a sunburn from hell."

"She really fled the country? I figured it was the internet just talking shit."

"She sure did."

"Damn, I'm so sorry, Gen. Is there anything I can do?"

I sigh. "Right now, just be the good friend you've always been."

Her voice softens. "Always."

I sniffle as a tear runs down my cheek.

I've never felt so lost in my life.

AFTER SPENDING an hour on the phone with Darcy, I peer back at the door.

I don't know why my brain is so curious about what's behind it.

Maybe because I want to walk into Julian's world.

To see more of it.

I wander over to Julian's desk and attempt to open a drawer.

Locked.

I try the others.

Same.

No shocker there.

I'm going to start calling him the Lock King.

Or maybe King of Locks.

Hey, that'd make a good book title.

Or a villain in a movie.

A blazer is hung over the back of his chair. I peer from side to side, as if checking for a spy, and shove my hand inside the blazer pocket.

Jackpot.

I smile, pulling out a wad of cash and counting it.

Two grand.

Look at me, living up to my family name now.

A little thief.

In my defense, if I push the marriage issue and Julian becomes my husband, what's his is mine, right? Plus, I doubt he'll mind missing a few thousand dollars. If he does, I'll pay him back. Maybe it'll convince him to give me a job to earn money.

I stop in my tracks when a thought hits me.

Is there a safe in here?

Maybe I won't have to gamble this money.

I can steal the cash and pay off the Russians.

Pfft, yeah right.

The man has a lock on a drawer, which probably consists of only pens and condoms. He's not leaving a safe open for easy access. I wouldn't be surprised if he had a passcode on his cock.

I return to the couch and shove the cash into my purse, a giddy smile on my face. That smile builds when I slowly open the door, finding it unlocked, and leave his office.

12

Genesis

I TIPTOE from Julian's office as if I were the Hamburglar, about to rob the casino for Big Macs, and land in a quiet hallway.

Every door is closed, and I hear voices behind one.

I turn on my heel and move in the opposite direction, toward the chaotic noise. I know I'm close to my destination when I hear loud music and the sound of slot machines ringing. When I hit the casino floor, I stand there in awe, taking in the scene.

I've been to the New York Lucky Kings, but not this location. Atlantic City puts the New York location to shame. When Pippa told me about Julian opening a casino on his own, I was excited for him. He'd always preferred doing stuff solo.

New York's aesthetic borderlines what you'd find in Vegas.

Bright lights, neon decor, and gold ceilings.

Julian's is ritzy and screams old money, reminding me of *The Great Gatsby*.

Like his office, it's sophisticated.

It's where you'd picture men in the Roaring Twenties illegally gambling in private rooms, smoking cigars, and making high-stake bets. Even the slot machines, while electronic, still appear like the classic ones. Crystal chandeliers hang from the ceiling, their lights reflecting off the machine screens.

I head straight to the blackjack table.

My late nanny, Sonya—*may she rest in peace*—taught me to play when I was seven. Playing cards was a regular pastime for us. When I couldn't sleep, she'd make me a cup of hot cocoa, and we'd play until I started yawning.

Three men are seated at the table, and they watch me in curiosity as I sit.

One smirks, as if he can't wait to take my money.

The other winks at me, perking up in his chair.

I force an innocent smile, excited to take *their money*.

The dealer furrows his brow, as if my sitting down annoys him. He cocks his head to the side, suddenly intrigued, when I pull out the cash from my purse.

I count out five crisp hundreds and slide the bills to the dealer. He exchanges them for chips, and my pulse speeds.

Here we go.

It's been a while since I played, but with all my troubles, it's like this is what I needed tonight.

A comfort, like all those cups of hot cocoa.

The dealer wins the first round, just as I planned.

The man at the far end wins the second.

I win the third, fourth, and fifth.

"Hello, Genesis."

I freeze, panic charging through me. Chills sweep up my spine at the voice that's haunted me for the past two days.

I struggle to keep my composure as Dima sits beside me—so close that he's nearly on my stool. His wide shoulder bumps into mine, and he steals a stack of my chips. The dealer's attention whips to me, and I slowly nod, not wanting to make a scene.

Dima's cologne is strong, almost suffocating. He's dressed in a black suit with a black button-up. A snake ring, nearly as large as his hand, is on his pointer finger. It matches the snake tattoo that runs from his hand up his wrist.

I don't say a word to him, only tell the dealer my calls, and win the round.

Dima grunts in disapproval, glares at the dealer, and steals more of my chips.

I win another round.

"Son of a bitch," he hisses, slamming his hand on the table.

I don't know why he's so mad. It's not *his* money he's losing. I'm just taking *mine* back.

Staring straight ahead, I lower my voice so only he can hear me. "What are you doing here?" I'm shocked at how assertive I sound.

"Watching you, *nevesta*." He edges so close that I feel his breath hit my cheek. "Keeping an eye on what's mine."

My stomach drops as I fight for words.

The reality is that there's a possibility that I will be his.

"Please go away." I ask, every muscle in my body tense. "I'm trying to gamble here."

"Ahh." His gaze latches on me, his lips forming a cunning smirk. "If your plan is to win money to pay off your father's debt with me, that'll never happen, *nevesta*."

He runs his hand down my thigh, and I shove it off.

"I have my eye on you, Genesis." He stands, towering over me, and lowers his mouth to my ear. "Soon, you'll be mine."

"Too late," I murmur, wishing I hadn't said a word and just let him walk away, but I keep talking. "Julian already signed a contract with your father."

He stands tall, straightening his sleeves. "A contract has never stopped me from getting what I want." Reaching out, he grabs a strand of my hair and twirls it around his finger. "I can't wait to tug on this when I force you on your knees to suck my cock."

I stare at him, speechless.

"No need to say anything," he says. "I prefer my women stay silent."

13

Julian

"I WANT them separated into three accounts." I stare at Caesar, the man I pay to run my shell company. "Better yet, add another for extra precaution. If even one account leads back to me, they'll never find your body in the ocean."

Caesar nods, scribbling down notes.

The average person wouldn't understand his notes.

They're coded.

Doing business with me is like getting in bed with the devil.

No changing your mind or going back.

No way in hell will I part ways with a man who knows where I hide my money. You end business with me, you cease business with everyone. I kill you, and your poor family spends the next week planning your funeral.

The casket will be empty, of course.

No body, no crime.

I grab my phone when it rings, answering a call. "Yeah?"

"Boss, we have a problem," Franko, the head of casino security, tells me. "We have ourselves a card counter."

Fuck.

Since Genesis is here, I hoped I wouldn't have to get my hands dirty tonight.

Stupid of me to think that.

There hasn't been a night in over a year that I haven't gotten my hands dirty. Whether it's violence or corruption, I always have blood on my hands.

I never take it easy on card counters. Who do motherfuckers think they are, coming into my casino and stealing from me? I'm the one who does the stealing.

I'll cut off every one of their fingers and shove them down their fucking throat. Then, so they can't count another card again, I'll plunge out their dirty-ass eyes.

Though that tactic is growing old.

I like to keep my punishments creative.

It helps me from growing bored.

"Be right there." I end the call and point at Caesar. "I want this done by morning."

Caesar shoves his papers inside his briefcase. "Can you give me until tomorrow night? It's my daughter's high school graduation tonight." Pride flickers on his face, alongside optimism.

I'm usually not one to give extensions. Normally, I'd tell someone it could be their birth of their daughter and I wouldn't give a shit.

Though, tonight, I'm feeling somewhat generous. Blame it on Genesis.

"Julian," Caesar says slowly, noticing my irritation, "you know I'm never behind. I'm telling you this: I can't make it happen. I won't let my daughter down."

He waits for my reaction, anticipating violence.

"I want it done by tomorrow evening, eight at the latest," I demand.

"Thank you." He buckles and locks his briefcase.

I show him out, then head straight to the security room.

For a moment, I consider stopping by my office to check on Genesis.

I'll do it after.

Card counters usually don't stay in casinos long. They get as much cash as they can and haul ass.

Franko is drinking an energy drink when I enter the security room. He wheels closer to the screen in his chair and hits the rewind button on the keyboard.

"Table ten," he says. "Woman. White shirt." He whistles. "Gotta say, she's the hottest card counter I've seen."

I step closer, shoving his chair to the side, and he gulps down his drink.

"Son of a bitch," I snarl, staring at the screen.

Franko picks up his two-way radio. "I'll tell Mossimo to bring her to us." Mossimo is one of our security men.

I shake my head. "No, I'll go down and get her myself."

I backtrack a step to leave but freeze when I notice a man take the stool next to her.

I slam my finger against the computer screen. "This man, find him."

"Okay, b—"

I storm out so fast that I don't hear the rest of Franko's sentence.

I grit my teeth so hard that my jaw burns as I charge straight to the casino floor.

I'm going to fucking kill her.

I'm going to fucking kill him.

Genesis is still at the table, and the dealer deals another round.

Dima is gone.

The closer I get to her, the more my anger skyrockets.

She turns, as if sensing me, seconds before I reach the table.

Snatching her by the elbow, I pull her off the stool.

The dealer abruptly stops, and the other men at the table gape at me.

I thrust my finger toward the dealer's face. "Don't you ever fucking deal her a card again."

The dealer's Adam's apple bobs. "Yes … yes, sir."

Genesis attempts to jerk out of my hold, but I only tighten my grip. She's lucky I'm not throwing her out of here and making her walk home.

Or better yet, chasing down Dima and handing her ass over to him.

No one fucks with my money.

It seems Genesis is doing that in every damn way.

I grab the chips she's won, shove them into my pocket, and don't say a word while dragging her off the casino floor.

Luckily, for once, she's smart enough to keep her mouth shut.

As soon as we reach my office, I open the door and shove her inside. I smile when she trips on her feet and nearly face-plants on my desk.

Serves her fucking right.

"What the hell?" she yells, gaining her balance and swatting loose strands of hair from her face.

I advance toward her, anger pouring from my body. "Where the fuck is he?"

I didn't watch the footage for long, but I saw him touch her.

Saw his slimy-ass hand brush her thigh and hair.

The fucker had the audacity to touch what's mine.

As soon as I'm done with Genesis, I'll pull up the audio and listen to every word of their conversation.

She squints, backing up against the desk. "Dima?"

"No, fucking Barney. Of course, Dima."

"He left."

"You didn't think to tell me he was here?" I snarl. "Matter of fact, why did you leave this office? I was very clear when I told you not to."

"I got bored."

"Maybe I should get bored with you and give you to the Russians."

"Maybe I should go to the Russians because I'm sick and tired of hearing you threaten me with it."

"You want him to kill you?" I ask, advancing toward her. "You want him to beat and rape you? Is that what you want? Because trust me, Genesis, he won't give a shit about a contract, or clauses you want, or taking care of you. He will fuck you, over and over and over, when he wants and how he wants. Is being a pain in my ass worth that?"

I'm toe to toe with her, pressing her body against the desk so tight that she can't move. Forcing her legs open, I stand between them.

"I was in a private place," she breathes out. "In *your* business. I'm safe here."

Raising my hand, I cup her face. "You're not safe anywhere." I squeeze her cheek. "What'd the fucker say to you?"

She tries to look away, but I don't allow it.

"He said soon, I'll be his."

I get in her face, my nose against hers. "Those words led you to believe you were safe?"

It seems Dima isn't giving up on his plan to wed Genesis.

He's about to become a goddamn problem.

I make a mental note to call Yaroslav and ask what the fuck. This isn't how deals are done. This is how men die over deals.

First, though, I need to handle Genesis.

I drop my hand to her throat to press her flat against the desk. Her pleated skirt rises, showing off her toned thighs and black panties. I lick my lips, hovering over her body, and smile at the feel of her pulse in her neck against my thumb.

Using my free hand, I push her skirt up farther and slip my hand beneath her panties. She's soaked for me.

"I don't tolerate disobedience." I spread her pussy lips, tilt her ass up, and shove two fingers inside her.

She gasps, her hips jerking backward.

I smile again and slowly drag them out of her. She fights for breaths as I backtrack a step and yank her upright.

Her lust-filled eyes clash with mine.

I smell the alcohol on her lips.

Crowding her again, I lower my head to run my tongue along her lips, tasting the liquor. "Tequila."

"Does it taste good?" she whispers.

Her pussy would taste better.

I ease my hand between her legs again but refuse to give her what she desperately wants.

"Please," she whimpers.

"I only reward good girls." I rip her panties, shove them in my pocket, and step away.

Thank fuck I'm a mentally strong man.

Any other human with a beating pulse would cave to Genesis's sweet pussy.

"That sure isn't a way to get me pregnant," she huffs, glaring at me. "Do I need to go into teacher mode and teach you sex ed? In case you didn't know, fingers don't jizz, meaning they won't get me pregnant."

The fuck is wrong with this woman?

Where does she even come up with the words that leave her mouth?

"The first time I fuck you, it won't be in my office." I harden my eyes on her in impatience. "And right now, I'm so fucking pissed that I'd fuck you so viciously that you wouldn't be able to walk for a week. Do you want me to fuck you like I want to kill you?"

Interest lights up on her face.

Fuck, she might actually.

Oh, I'm going to have some fun fucking her when the day comes.

But like I said, I don't reward disobedience.

I obviously can't gouge her eyes out, but I can withhold an orgasm.

That'll be her torture for her card counting and defiance.

She's lucky I'm not in the mood, or I'd force her to her knees and make her suck my cock.

"Is that what you want, Genesis?" My voice grows hoarse. When she doesn't answer, I stress the words. "Is it?"

She bites her lower lip. "I'm debating."

I start to loosen my tie, feeling the need to wrap it around her mouth so she doesn't say anything else to tempt me, but stop at a knock on the door.

"Boss," Franko says on the other side.

"Keep your fucking ass in this room," I snarl at her through gritted teeth. "Do you goddamn hear me? I'll have a man standing guard. If the door so much as opens, he'll kill you."

I don't wait for her response before charging out of the room. I lock the door and walk alongside Franko to the security room.

"He's gone," Franko tells me. "I have the tape ready for you."

"You'd better fucking have audio."

"I do."

Sitting in the security room, I listen to their conversation five times. I watch the video from four different camera spans and follow Dima's every move in my casino.

He knew where Genesis was and waited to get her alone.

I ball my hands into fists, pissed at my incompetence.

People don't usually trip me up.

I want to hunt him down and kill that motherfucker.

Genesis is only one day into our contract and already becoming a major pain in my ass.

Maybe I should let the Russians have her.
I don't need this goddamn headache.

14

Genesis

J ULIAN DOESN'T SPEAK a word to me on the drive back to the city.

And it's a *loooong* drive.

He does, however, take phone calls.

The asshole also keeps turning my music down each time I up the volume. He wants me to suffer in silence.

When he parks in the garage, he leaves the Escalade and slams the door shut.

So dramatic over a girl simply sneaking out and gambling.

It's not like I robbed the casino.

I thought red-flag men were supposed to love danger.

I pat my pocket, remembering the cash I have left from my thievery in his office. I'll be requesting the payout from the chips he took from me.

I won them.

Sure, maybe not fair and square, but I still won.

Julian keeps his butt-hurt attitude while inputting the code and opening the house door.

I sit there, play with my hands in my lap, unsure what to do.

"Get your fucking ass in here," he yells from the doorway.

"You have three seconds, and trust me, it'd be in your best interest not to test any more of my limits tonight."

"All right then," I say under my breath while getting out of the Escalade.

When I'm halfway toward the doorway, he turns and walks inside.

I keep my pace slow, giving him time to cool off.

When I follow him, he's in the living room, pouring himself a glass of bourbon from the same bottle we drank from last night. He chugs the liquor, slams the glass against the bar so hard that it shatters, and wipes the edge of his mouth.

He definitely wants to be nominated for Most Dramatic of the Night.

His eyes train on me as he snatches a glass shard, playing with it in his hand, not caring if it cuts him.

"Don't you dare pull that shit again." He points the shard at me. "Do you understand?"

I shift from one foot to the other.

No smart-ass comment will leave my mouth.

Julian is *mad*, mad and holding something he could easily slit my throat with.

"Is that understood?" Julian roars.

I cross my arms. "Don't talk to me like you're my father."

So much for keeping my mouth shut.

"Trust me, I'm far from him." He tosses the shard on the ground. His feet crunch against the glass as he steps toward me. "Unlike that bastard, I saved your ass. A little appreciation would be nice."

"Here we go with that bullshit." I spin on my heel and speed toward the front door. "You know what? I don't want you *saving my ass* again. Let me leave, and I'll take care of my-damn-self."

"Where'd you learn to count cards?" he calls to my back.

I stop, peering over my shoulder. "What?"

"Where'd you learn to count cards? A privileged woman like you doesn't run in circles that card count and steal."

I pinch my lips together.

There's no point in denying it.

He saw me on camera.

Julian snaps his fingers.

"My nanny," I murmur, turning to get a better look at him.

He strolls toward the kitchen and circles the island.

Opening a drawer, he pulls out a deck of cards and motions toward a stool.

"You're not going anywhere," he says. "Sit your ass down."

"A *please* would be nice." I glare at him, crossing my arms again.

He gives me a stern look.

"Ugh, fine." I dramatically sigh, throw my arms out to my sides, and stomp toward him.

He keeps his gaze pinned on me while I collapse on the stool and wait for his next move.

His wicked eyes stay on me as he stands tall and deals the cards. "I want you to play how you did at the casino."

Counting cards with only two players is difficult. I have a ninety-ten ratio of winning with at least four people. With two, it lowers to around fifty-fifty.

When I played with Sonya, she'd set up places for imaginary players and call out their plays. Or sometimes, her nephews would join us.

My parents were gone most of the time when I was growing up and trusted her with me.

She could've had me trafficking drugs or stripping, and they'd never have known.

Not that Sonya would've ever done that.

We played cards for fun.

I shut my eyes when sadness hits me.

I miss her. I miss her so damn much.

Unlike my parents, she wouldn't have turned her back on me. She'd be here, protecting me by any means necessary. *I hate you, cancer.*

Like Sonya did, Julian deals for two imaginary people.

Biting my lip, I debate whether to play dumb.

He decides our imaginary players' calls.

He barely blinks while I say mine.

Hit me.

Hold.

I win the first round.

I lose the second purposely, and from the smirk on his face, he knows it.

I win the third.

"I'm impressed." He collects my cards and shuffles them back into the deck.

"Did you ever think I *wasn't* impressive?" I lean in closer, a flirty smile on my lips.

Flirting with Julian isn't new.

Neither is attempting to seduce him.

Whenever I knew I'd be around him, I always dressed my best. I wanted him to *want me*—not see me as only his younger sister's rich, spoiled friend, who he didn't trust.

There's been a shift now though.

A somewhat scary one.

Back then, I knew the chance of us ever being *anything* would never happen.

Now, there's this uncertainty.

We'll have sex until he knocks me up, but then what happens?

I gulp down air, my stomach tightening.

What if I fall in love with him?

I raise my gaze to the ceiling.

Dear God, do not let me fall in love with this man. I'll never ask for anything ever again.

I've lusted over Julian for years, but I'll never make the mistake of trusting him with my heart. I know he'll break it with his unrighteous hands.

Julian snapping his fingers in my face breaks my silent prayer.

He holds up the cards. "You are aware card counting is illegal?"

I roll my eyes. "You, of all people, shouldn't lecture anyone on legalities. I think my crime is lower on the severity scale than yours." I use my hand to make a fake gun and pretend to shoot at the cabinet behind him. Then, for more artistry, I blow off the muzzle of my imaginary gun.

His never-ending stern stare remains. "This isn't a game, Genesis."

I lower my hand. "Trust me, I'm well aware. That's why I wanted to win some money—to get myself on my feet so you wouldn't have to pay as much." I was also bored out of my mind.

"You not only stole from the casino, but you also stole money from my office. *From me.*"

I pretend to study my French manicure. "I don't know what you're talking about."

"I checked my pocket before I put my blazer back on." He slams the deck on the island. "My cash was gone."

"All right, all right," I groan. "It's not like I broke into your safe. I just needed a little spending—*er, gambling* money."

His expression doesn't lighten up.

"I promise, I'm usually not a thief. Can we look on the bright side? I was just investing it back into your business."

His phone rings, interrupting us.

The man has the most active phone I've seen in my life.

"Yeah?" This seems to be his usual phone greeting.

No *hello, how are you* from him.

Just *yeah.*

If we have a child, I'll be the one in charge of teaching phone etiquette.

"I'll head that way in ten minutes," he tells whoever's on the other line before ending the call to make another. "How far are you away from my place?"

I grab the deck of cards as he nods and ends that call.

"Does *head that way in ten minutes* mean you're leaving?" I shuffle the cards.

He nods, slipping the phone in his pocket. "And your sneaking-out, stealing ass stays here."

"Rude." I hold up the cards. "I thought we were having a game night."

He shoots me a *not funny* stare.

"Is someone driving you there?" I ask, already feeling like I'm talking to a crappy boyfriend who lies.

"No."

"Are you ride-sharing?"

"No."

"Who was that on the phone?"

"Your babysitter."

"Hard pass. Pippa has told me too many bodyguard stories for me to agree to that."

"You don't have a choice."

I drop the cards on the island. "Where are you going?"

"Casino."

"I'm coming."

He shakes his head. "You ruined any chance of that happening again."

"Oh my God," I groan. "Are you going to hold that over my head forever now too?"

He snatches the top card from the deck, leans forward, and without saying a word, rips the first few buttons of my shirt until my bra shows. I gape at him as he slips the card beneath it.

His gaze deepens as he stares at my chest. "Gen, baby, as I

said before, I'm holding *everything* over your head." Grabbing another card, he flicks it at my face.

I shove his hand away, but he doesn't move back.

"Speaking of *head*, don't expect to ever receive it from me with that attitude."

He smirks before speed-walking around the island, as if I challenged him. I immediately start to stand, but he reaches me too fast. He grips my shoulders and slams me back onto the stool.

My throat turns dry when he spins me around to face him.

He presses his hands into my shoulders and dips his head to my level.

I swallow, the hair on my nape standing tall when his nose brushes against mine.

His lips are so close that I feel his smirk against my mouth. "If I didn't have to leave *right fucking now*, I'd spend the rest of my night proving your statement wrong."

I hiss when he bites my lip, holding the pressure there for a second after saying his words. He doesn't pull back until someone knocks on the door.

"Yeah," he calls out.

Fucking yeah.

The door opens, and Emilio walks in.

Oh, Emilio.

The man I've hardly spoken to but has seen me orgasm.

Not by him.

By the demon glaring at me.

Emilio is dark-haired, tall, all muscle, and handsome.

Call me biased, but I still don't find him as hot as Julian. But then again, I don't find anyone as attractive as Julian.

When I have a type, I have a type.

It seems crazy, off-limits psychopath killer is it.

Emilio also has the broody thing going on. He doesn't crack

jokes or get in playful moods. It seems to be a trend with these men. The Mafia molds them into emotionless assholes.

"Emilio will watch you," Julian tells me.

I spin in my chair to get a better look at Emilio and lift my hand in a teasing way.

Emilio jerks his head in my direction, completely impassive.

Julian lowers his chin to my shoulder to hiss, "He won't touch you," in my ear. "But don't make me shoot him in the goddamn arm for you attempting to charm him." He delves his fingers into my hair, jerking my head back. "Now, be a good girl and go to bed. I don't want any more trouble from you." He steps away and walks toward the door. "Behave, if you know what's good for you."

He pats Emilio on the chest and doesn't say another word as he leaves.

I've never been alone with Emilio.

He seems as disinterested in me as my first boyfriend finding my clit when fingering me for the first time.

"Do you just let him boss you around like that?" I slide off the stool and let out a huff when my feet hit the floor. "Would he really shoot you in the arm? That doesn't seem very friend-like."

Emilio stalks toward the living room. "Most likely. And FYI, if that were to happen, I'd shoot you in the arm next for giving me such an inconvenience. Bullet wounds are a pain in the ass."

Emilio isn't fun either.

Got it.

Since I'm exhausted anyway, I shrug and walk toward the stairs. "I'm off to bed. Make yourself at home, I guess."

He doesn't bother telling me good night as I stomp up the stairs. I pass the bedroom I slept in last night and keep going until I reach Julian's.

The door is locked, so I drop my bag on the floor and kneel to find my phone. I hit Julian's name and stand as the phone rings.

"Yeah," he answers—because of course.

"That's such a romantic way to answer your phone," I mutter.

He doesn't say a word back.

My shoulders slump. "What's your bedroom code?"

"Why would I tell you that?"

"If you want me in your bed tonight, you will."

There's a short moment of silence until he finally says, "Eleven twenty."

My chest hitches.

Melissa's birthday.

"Now that I've shared that with you—something I've never told anyone else—I expect your ass in my bed tonight," he says, his voice sounding almost bitter, not fitting his words.

He ends the call.

I input the code, hear the switch move, and walk inside.

I inhale a deep breath and flip on the light. As I move farther into the room, I run my fingers along the made bed. I strip out of my clothes on my walk to his closet and steal one of his sweatshirts.

Much better.

I don't bother grabbing sweats, staying in my panties, and tread into the bathroom. I open his drawers until I find a spare toothbrush. I'm too lazy to go to my room to grab my electric toothbrush and skin care. I'll have to sacrifice my thirty-minute-before-bedtime beauty regimen tonight.

Julian's drawers are clean and organized.

They're all filled with bathroom essentials, nothing unusual. I expected to find a knife or an Uzi.

After brushing my teeth and using his face wash, I climb into his bed, unsure which side he sleeps on. I send him a quick text, asking him to turn up the heat, but he doesn't reply.

The sheets smell like him—a comfort.

The room feels like him—another comfort.
Maybe I'm already feeling like this is home.

15

___

Julian

The Past

My soul has never felt more dead.

Sharp rain pours down on me, soaking my suit, as I stand outside the cathedral.

"You fucking did this," I mutter to myself. "You're the reason they're all dead."

I'll blame myself until the day I die.

Every action has a reaction.

The darker the action, the viler the reaction.

My family is dead.

Their home bombed.

All because of greedy men.

Greedy men feed off power. Always have and always will.

The overhead light shines above me as I stare into the black night. The funeral ended five hours ago, and I'm the only griever left.

I dig my Zippo lighter from my pocket, open it, and watch a hint of a flame flicker. The rain kills it seconds later, and I repeat the action, watching the same result.

I snap the Zippo shut at the sound of a car door slamming. Genesis, still dressed in her black funeral dress, circles her BMW and starts walking in my direction. The rain lashes out on her.

My now-deceased sister's best friend.

The woman who's stared at me for years like I was her favorite sight and who I've fought with myself not to do the same. It's like she's always trying to read my mind whenever she is around.

That's why I've always maintained my distance. I don't like people's attention on me, especially ones I don't trust.

I pretend not to notice her. As she grows closer, I see she's barefoot. That's the first sign she's lost her goddamn mind. No one walks around New York barefoot unless you want to get tetanus.

She stops in front of me. "What really happened to them, Julian?"

I slowly raise my gaze to her, acting as if I were bored. Her dark hair is down, wet strands stuck to her flawless face, and mascara is smeared across her cheek. The fucked-up makeup isn't from the rain.

It's from her tears.

Her heartache.

Her fucking pain.

Unlike me, she doesn't hide her emotions.

She waits, resting her hands on her hips, and she's clearly out of her mind if she thinks I'll answer her.

"Get back in your fucking car," I say, grating the words out.

"No." She furiously shakes her head, and rain flings from her hair. "I want to know what happened to them."

The last person I'll give information to is this rich bitch who thought she was living dangerously by hanging out with my sister.

"That's none of your concern." I crack my neck and slip my Zippo into my pocket. "Go home, Genesis."

"They were murdered, weren't they?" she spits, her anger matching mine. She steps closer, and the sweet scent of her floral perfume floats between us.

"You don't know what you're talking about."

The last thing I need is her going to the cops. I'll deal with the people who killed my family myself. They'll die at my hands, not rot in a prison cell.

"Yes, I—"

I snatch her hand, cutting her off, and yank her toward me.

Her soft body collides into my chest. She blows out a ragged breath, peering up at me through thick lashes. I push her away at the same time I grab her wrist, cupping my hand around it like a shackle.

She attempts to stop me as I drag her away from the sidewalk, through rain puddles, and back to her car.

The driver's door is unlocked, and the dome light beams when I open it. She gasps when I shove her inside. Her eyes are wide as she waits for my next move.

"Go the fuck home." I lower myself to her level, getting in her face. "All connections you had with my family are gone. Go back to your innocent life and stay the fuck away from me." I rise and slam the door shut.

I turn around, mutter, "Good fucking riddance," and walk toward the cathedral.

I stop to punch a random car. A mixture of pleasure and pain radiates up my arm. I wait for the alarm to fire off. When it doesn't, I punch the car again and shake my hand out.

"You know that's not a fair fight, right? Unless that Buick is a Transformer, it can't defend itself."

I whip around to find Genesis standing behind me.

She must not know sass gets you killed.

Maybe I should show her.

I inch toward her, but she doesn't back away, like I hoped. "I told you to go home."

"You aren't my boss."

"No, but I can force you to do things."

She's too brave.

I don't like it.

"Get in your car." I get in her face again, spit flying from my mouth. "Don't make me say it again."

She whips around, and my shoulders relax when she walks away.

They tense back up when she moves in the opposite direction and sits on the cathedral steps.

This girl is fucking mad.

"I'm staying here until you talk to me," she states, full of attitude.

I take three large strides, standing over her. "Sit in the rain for all I care. Warning: This area isn't safe, so try not to get murdered."

She doesn't flinch at my words.

Instead, she holds up a finger. "Speaking of *murder*, the police didn't confirm that as their cause of death."

She pulls her knees to her chest, and I hate that my eyes travel as her dress rises up her thighs. Unfortunately, it stops inches from where I could get a view of her pussy.

"They said it was an accident, but I'm not dumb," she rambles.

"What will you do if it was murder?" I scoff. "You going to solve it, Scooby-Doo?"

Her sweet face hardens. It's not a good look on her.

"Whoever killed them needs to be killed. What's it called? Retribution?"

"Are *you* going to kill them?"

She looks away from me.

"You might've thought you were tough, hanging out with my sister, but you know nothing of our world. If anything, her death should be a warning for you to stay away. This life wasn't made for you."

It wasn't made for any of us.

We were all just shaped into it.

"Julian," she says, staring up at me, her eyes suddenly looking innocent, "will you kill them?"

"You already know the answer." I immediately regret saying that. I don't trust her, so why am I even entertaining this conversation?

"Good." She blows out what sounds like a breath of relief. "I want every person involved to suffer."

Genesis might be different than I thought.

A darkness crawls inside her innocence.

An understanding that I don't get much from the outside world.

But I'll save her from the trauma and stop her before she gets too deep.

I take a step back, scrubbing a hand over my jaw. "And I want you to get back into your car."

She stares at me, wide-eyed, but doesn't move.

"Do you want me to drag you in there again?" I can't believe I'm standing in the rain, having this conversation with her.

"I'd prefer you didn't."

"Have fun sitting out here, alone, in the rain."

"I'll get out of the rain then." She stands, walks up the cathedral steps, and disappears inside.

Taking a second, I debate whether to follow her.

I read people well enough to know that's what she wants.

For some reason, she thinks I'll be the good guy here.

I'm the opposite of the good guy.

Which is why I know I've lost my wits, that my family's deaths have really fucked with my head, when I climb the steps.

I grip the door handle, knowing I'll tell her nothing.

She'll never know she's right.

The Popovs murdered my family over a territory war. They own a casino chain along the Jersey state line and East Coast and decided to expand into New York City. Apart from the holes-in-the-wall, Lucky Kings is the exclusive casino in the city.

When we first found out about their interest, we approached them civilly to offer them a payout to get the fuck out of our city. They declined and purchased land to start the project. In retaliation, we burned down the framework when construction started.

We continued to do that each time they found another location and attempted to rebuild. They needed to know we always eliminated competition, whether it be by money or murder.

The night of my family's murders, we'd burned down their location and killed the two men watching guard. Blowing up my family's home was their revenge.

Now, I'll get mine.

I'll avenge my family and kill every person responsible.

But first, I have to deal with this fucking woman.

What the fuck do I do with her?

I could bail and let her hang out in there alone.

If Melissa were here, she'd get mad if I left Genesis vulnerable.

For my sister's sake, I swing open the cathedral door and step inside. Genesis is hunched forward in a back-row pew, shivering and dripping wet.

I slump down next to her and keep my voice low. "I'll kill them." My tone turns harsh. "Now, will you get your ass in the car and go the fuck home?"

She stares forward. "I'll go home if you go home."

"My home burned down." I don't mean for my response to sound pitying.

Her attention whips to me, the reality of my words hitting her.

While I have my own home, it's never felt like *home*. It doesn't have the warmth of family like my parents' house did. I've never been a people person, but my family was the exception. I enjoyed spending time with them.

You know who I don't enjoy spending time with?

This woman here.

She's pulling up too many memories.

She reminds me of the lightness inside my family.

My sister and mother.

I can't fucking stand that.

To get my mind off problems, I usually do one of two things:

1. Kill someone.
2. Fuck someone.

Melissa would've definitely kicked my ass if I did the first to her friend.

She'd have also kicked my ass if I did the second.

But out of the two, I'd prefer option two.

Genesis's breathing hitches when I lower my hand to her thigh and slowly inch it up her skirt. Goose bumps spread over her skin. She parts her thighs farther, still gazing straight ahead.

I tilt my head down so only she can hear me. "Do you want to go back to my place? Where I lay my head at night?" My eyes are glued to her, and my cock hardens as I sweep my hand closer to her pussy.

Her breathing quickens, and she adjusts how she's sitting to provide me further access into a pussy I know is probably sweeter than anything I deserve.

"Answer me," I demand when my finger feathers along her panty line.

"Yes," she moans.

"Let's go then." I draw my hand back from her pussy, stand, and hold that same hand out to her.

She clears her throat, straightening her dress, and takes my hand.

My jaw tics as I think about all the things I'd love to do to her.

But I won't.

I won't lay a hand on her, not in the way she wants at least.

Something Genesis will learn about me tonight is that I'm not to be trusted.

I walk her outside, back into the rain, and to my Escalade. Unlike when it was her car, she doesn't fight me when I open my passenger door and push her inside.

"Seat belt," I say, shutting her door before walking to my side. I open the back seat door, grab a bag, collect what I need from inside it, and hop into the driver's seat.

As soon as I'm inside, I lock the door. She scoots away from me when she sees what's in my hands.

"Don't be scared," I say calmly.

"Easy for you to say," she replies. "You're the one holding the serial killer accessories."

"You're right." I play with the blindfold in my hand. "Yet you're not running from me. Does that mean you're into this kink?"

"No," she snaps. "I'm just curious what this will lead to."

"You ever heard that curiosity kills the cat?"

"I hope you're not referring to me as the curious cat."

I don't say a word.

"Melissa would hate you."

"Melissa isn't here to hate me any longer."

"She'll hate you from heaven."

"While I agree my sister is in heaven, you're mistaken if you think I'll see her there upon my death. A man with my sins falls straight down to hell."

"The Lord forgives sins."

"Yes, but how many sins does he allow before he stops?"

This might be the most I've talked to her in the years I've known her.

As she waits for my response, I tug the zip tie I grabbed from the bag from my pocket, snatch her wrists, and lock it around them.

"What the hell?" she shrieks.

"You have two options," I tell her. "I can take you home, or we can go back to my place."

"Will your place result in my murder?"

"I have no intention of murdering you tonight, Genesis."

"Un-zip-tie me then."

"No, but I can't let you know where I live." I smirk. "It's a secret." Before she can stop me, I curl my hand around her head, holding her in place, and drop the blindfold over her eyes. "This is only for safety precautions."

"Fucking asshole," she says, struggling against the restraints. "This isn't funny. Get your weird kinks off somewhere else."

"When we're there, I'll take it off." I pull out onto the street. "You keep fighting, I'll drop you off on the side of the road. I'll make sure it's a dark, deserted one too."

Maybe this will be a lesson for her not to trust men like me.

"Right," she whispers when I make my first turn.

"Left," she says when I make another.

I slam on the brakes, and she jolts forward. Her head nearly collides with the dashboard.

"You'd better not be doing what I think you're doing," I say in warning.

"What are you talking about?" she asks, doing a terrible job at playing coy.

"You're counting my turns."

It's smart—I'll give her that.

"You threatened to drop me off in the middle of nowhere. Of course I'm counting your turns."

"Words of wisdom: Next time, don't give yourself up like that."

I make a sudden U-turn.

Then another.

And another.

I drive through a parking lot.

Then a gas station.

Doing everything I can to confuse her.

Her body bumps forward, then to the side, then forward at my swerves.

"Game over," she finally says. "Get this shit off me, Julian." She attempts to wiggle her wrists to break free but can't.

"Oh, Gen, you agreed to play this game. It's not over until *I* say it's over."

She wrinkles her nose. "Who said you make the rules?"

"Considering I'm the one who can easily strangle you, I'd say I do."

I tune out her blabbering about what's fair and unfair.

About how the entire city will investigate her disappearance if I kill her.

She's starting to give me a headache.

Fortunately, we reach our destination not long after.

I stop at the iron gate, lower my window, and hit the Call button on the speaker.

"Hello?" a gruff voice says from the other side. "Astor residence."

I lean forward, resting my arm on the windowsill. "Tell Carlisle I have his daughter."

"What the hell?" Genesis shrieks, returning to her struggle with her tied wrists.

The man clears his throat. "Excuse me, sir?"

"Genesis is in the car with me." When rain drops into my SUV, I inch my window up some. "You have ten seconds to open the gate unless you want me to drop her off here."

I notice a camera in the speaker box turn on. I lean back in my seat to show Genesis. I'm sure it's a great scene—her blindfolded and restrained.

The gate immediately opens, reminding me I'm not dealing with the typical men I'm used to. No one from my world would ever open a gate so easily.

I speed down the drive and flatten my foot against the pedal when we reach the front door.

I jump out of the SUV, swing open Genesis's door, and pull her from her seat. She fights back as I drop her onto the hard concrete and roll her body over with the sole of my foot.

"You motherfucker," she yells, kicking at me. "I'm going to kill you."

"We both know you can't even lay a hand on me." I nudge her farther away from the SUV. "You're welcome for making sure you got home safe."

I squat so we're eye level, grab the pocketknife from my pocket to cut her zip tie, remove the blindfold, and tap her cheek.

Her breathing is noisy, her eyes cold, and she catches me off guard when she pulls back her fist, punching me in the face.

I wince, drawing back, impressed by the sucker punch. "I'll give you that." I cup her face. "Stay away from this world if you know what's best for you." I feel blood against my tongue.

She glares as I step over her body and drive away.

There's only one woman I can never touch, under any circumstances—Genesis Astor.

She's trying to make it damn hard for me though.

The best solution to that is to scare the shit out of her.

Make her fear me.

That's exactly what I did.

16

—————

Genesis

The Past

I ONCE HAD a boyfriend in high school who called his attorney after his friend grabbed my ass at a party. He wanted to *sue* the guy, not punch his lights out. I broke up with him two minutes later.

That was the moment I realized I'd never date a man like him.

I don't want a *my father will sue you* man.

I want a *touch her and die* man.

Loud music booms against as I swing my hips to the beat on the dance floor. Darcy, dressed in a glitter minidress, grabs my hand, twirls across from me, and shakes her ass. Her maroon-dyed hair is sweaty, sticking to the side of her face.

This is our first time at Seven Seconds—the hottest nightclub in the city.

It's also Cristian and Benny Marchetti's club, and Melissa's parents weren't comfortable with her coming to any establishment run by another Mafia family.

I wave my hand in front of my face and mouth, "*Drink break*," to Darcy.

She nods, taking my hand. We weave through the crowd toward the packed bar, where people scream their drink orders to busy bartenders.

Standing on my tiptoes the best I can in my heels, I wave my arm in the air to get one's attention.

No luck.

Ugh.

"Shit. Darcy! Genesis!"

I drop my arm and turn to find Jeff and Kevin—two guys we went to high school with—coming toward us.

"Are you trying to get a drink?" Kevin yells over the music, motioning toward the bar.

"Yep," I shout back.

Kevin grabs my hand, leading me to the opposite end, while Jeff does the same with Darcy. When the bartender sees Kevin, he slides a drink to a patron and heads straight toward us.

Like Darcy and me, Kevin and Jeff are trust-fund babies. I'm sure they spend plenty of money here and tip well. Private sections here alone cost thousands a night.

"Whatever they want," Kevin says to the bartender, signaling toward Darcy and me. "And send two more bottles to our section."

"Got it." The bartender wipes his forehead, cutting his gaze to us.

"Mojitos," Darcy and I say at the same time.

It's been our go-to drink lately.

The bartender salutes us and starts on our drinks.

"Do you come here often?" Kevin asks, resting his arm on the bar.

Darcy slides in closer. "This is actually our first time."

"We have a VIP suite," Kevin says, his glassy eyes on me. "Come hang out."

"Sounds good." I fan myself.

A break from the blaring music and men trying to grind on me sounds amazing.

"Two mojitos," the bartender calls out, handing us glasses.

My lips pucker when I take my first drink.

"Let's go," Kevin says, flicking the tip of my straw when it's out of my mouth.

Darcy pouts her red lips. "I actually wanted to dance more."

Jeff offers his hand to her. "Lead the way then."

Their attention whips to me, as if asking for permission.

Darcy wants to make sure I'm comfortable with being alone with Kevin. We always do that with each other.

"Go dance!" I smack a kiss on her glittery cheek and wave them off.

She grips her drink and disappears through the crowd with Jeff.

"It looks like it's just you and me taking a break from the madness," Kevin says, flashing me a bright white veneered smile. "The suites are better on the ears, I promise."

I return the smile. "*That's* music to my ears."

While I love all music, I tend to lean more toward girlie pop.

Gripping my mojito, I follow Kevin. Eventually, I grab his arm so I don't lose him in the crowd.

When we reach the VIP area, a group of men is huddled near the entrance. Kevin raises his chin in their direction, but none return the gesture. As we get closer, my gaze lands on a recognizable face.

The face of the man I thought could replace my fixation on Julian.

Unsure what to do since it's been years, I keep my head down.

He doesn't let me off that easy, of course. As we pass the men, he snatches my wrist, stopping me.

Kevin halts, peering at me over his broad shoulder.

"I need to talk to this one," Luca says to Kevin.

"Chill out," Luca tells Kevin in irritation. "We own this club, and she knows me. I won't hurt her."

Realization of who he is dawns on Kevin.

Luca Marchetti.

Just like with Damien and Julian, he's dangerous and very much Mafia involved. He's also a killer and a man who only plays by Cristian Marchetti's rules—most of which aren't legal.

"It's okay," I assure Kevin with a smile, tightening my hand on my mojito. "I'll come to your section in a few minutes."

Luca draws me away from the crowd toward a lit area. The other men return to their conversation, and Kevin walks away. When we're around the corner, Luca swings me around to face him.

I smile, taking in his dark hair, beautiful tan face, and strong jawline.

We were only sixteen and at a restaurant when Melissa pointed him out to Darcy and me. She said while all Mafia families are violent, the Marchettis were the worst, and Luca and Benny were just as cruel as the lineage before them. She also told us Luca was very much a noncommittal heartbreaker who swore to stay single forever to prevent himself from being pushed into an arranged marriage.

He was also the Marchetti closest in age to us. I stared at him in fascination, my eyes following his every move, but I didn't think he noticed me.

I found out he very much was when I left the restroom and he pulled me to the side. Shutting my eyes, I remember our first conversation and how sure of himself he was.

"What's your name?" he asked, smirking wickedly.

"Genesis." I could've lied, but I had a feeling he'd know I was.

"Cute name." He crowded me closer. "Where are you from, Genesis?"

I frowned. "Why?"

"I'd like to know how accessible you are to me."

I stood on my tiptoes to better meet his eyes. "Who says I want to be accessible to you?"

"The way you looked at me said it."

"How did I look at you?"

He seemed entertained by my sudden attitude. "Like you wanted to fuck me right then, right there."

"Wow," I said, drawing the word out. "Someone sure is cocky."

He arched a dark brow. "Tell me I'm wrong then."

"You're so wrong."

He dipped his head to mine. "Liar, liar."

I'D GIVEN him my number that day. We texted a few times, no phone calls, and when he asked me out, I was on top of the world. But I learned three things on the few dates we went out on: that Melissa was right, Luca wasn't interested in anything but hookups, he was decently skilled in fingering women in his back seat, and that even though he was hot and fun to spend time with, he wasn't Julian.

It's hard for a woman to forget her first obsession.

The man she fell in love with the moment she saw him.

"Long time no see, babe," he says with a confident smirk.

I playfully roll my eyes at him, and his smirk widens.

Beyond his craziness, Luca can be playful.

"Considering you came into my family's club, does that mean you're looking for me?"

"Cocky much?"

"Miss me much?"

He grabs my hand. "Come on. I'm grabbing you a drink. We need to catch up."

"Fine," I say, faking annoyance as he leads me away from the corner.

Just as we're about to hit the stairs, we stop when someone yells his name.

"Get your ass over here!" the deep, demanding voice adds.

I hold in a breath, expecting Luca to leave me, but he captures my hand, taking me with him.

"Let me have a quick conversation, and then we'll grab that drink," he says, leading me to wherever he wants.

Blowing out a breath, I have no power over my body, so I only nod.

We pass three VIP sections and move toward one with more privacy.

"I have someone with me," he yells before we enter the space.

"Take them the fuck away then," a man replies.

Luca ignores them, dragging me into the VIP section.

My head spins.

Men seated in a U-shaped leather booth, a table in front of them, stop speaking when they notice me.

My focus first gravitates to Benny Marchetti, the Marchetti prince.

His sharp eyes focus on me, his nostrils flaring at my presence.

Knowing it's a bad idea to keep the devil's son's attention on me, I quickly look away. The man beside him stares at me with the same expression.

I drag my gaze to the next two men, and my blood suddenly runs hot.

Julian and Emilio.

I quickly skip Emilio to Julian, who's staring at me in hatred.

I lower my gaze, taking in his black suit jacket. A faint bruise is under one of his eyes, and when he scrubs his hands together, I notice his busted knuckles.

He screams violence.

Always has. Always will.

All these men do.

Why am I not running away?

I pinch my face, sourly glaring at him.

Yeah, asshole. I remember what you did last time I saw you.

He could've at least taken me to *my* home, not my parents'. My father spent the following morning's breakfast lecturing me on choosing the company I kept wisely, claiming people could take photos of me and use them against our family.

Julian relaxes in the booth. "You do know who this is, Luca?"

Luca shifts his attention from a conversation with Benny to Julian and raises a brow. The expression on his face isn't hostile, but it's also not friendly.

Julian lifts his chin in my direction. "Vincent Lombardi's goddaughter."

Say what?

I open my mouth to say that's a bald-faced lie, but Julian speaks over me.

"I'd find another woman in the crowd." Julian's steely gaze cuts back to me. "This one will bring nothing but trouble."

All the men stare me down.

While I know *of* Vincent Lombardi, I've never held a conversation with the man. Nor do I want to.

I'm not sure whether I should tell them Julian is lying.

Will they be mad? See him as untrustworthy?

Freaking kill him?

Julian must not know Luca and I have a history. Luca knows exactly who I am, and my connection with the Lombardis. The man gave me a damn questionnaire on our first date to decide whether I was trustworthy or not. That should've been a huge red flag then.

Benny stands when his phone rings, collecting it from his pocket and pointing it at Luca. "Stay away from her." He motions for his men to get up, and they do. "Let's go. Julian and Emilio, have a drink on me."

Luca shakes his head at Julian, fully knowing he's lying, and lowers his head to my ear. "It seems you've pissed that guy off. You still have my number. Use it." He leaves with Benny without waiting for my response.

"You're such an asshole." I scowl at Julian, fed up with his bullshit, and flip him off. "I'm leaving."

"Stay," he demands, tapping the space beside him. "We need to talk."

"You're right. We do." I charge toward him, standing in front of the table. "What you did the night of the funeral was fucking rude."

I catch a hint of Emilio smirking as he drags his phone from his pocket and pretends to pay attention to the screen.

Julian works his strong jaw. "What are you doing here, Genesis?"

"What are *you* doing here?" I chug the rest of my mojito. "I thought enemies couldn't pass enemy lines without violence."

Emilio shakes his head at my comment.

"The Marchettis and I are discussing business," he replies. "Now, you answer my question."

"Darcy and I came here to dance." I rest my glass on the table.

He motions toward the space around us. "Dance for me then."

I scoff. "Are you asking for a lap dance?"

"Are you offering one?"

"Uh, *no*."

"That's unfortunate."

I turn to Emilio, holding out my hand. "We haven't officially met. I'm Genesis—"

"He knows who you are," Julian says bitterly as Emilio shakes my hand. He shifts out of his suit jacket and rolls his sleeves up.

Emilio's grip is loose, half-assed, as if he's only doing it not to appear rude.

"If you don't want to dance for me, let me take you home," Julian offers.

"Hell no," I say, stretching the word out. "Last time I got in a car with you, you tossed me out on the concrete like a discarded Crunchwrap Supreme wrapper."

Swear to God, I hear a low chuckle from Emilio.

Anger prickles through me, and I harshly tap Emilio on the shoulder, feeling ballsier than I should.

"Do you mind letting me squeeze in here?" I ask him while my attention stays on Julian. "I need to have a little chitty-chat with your friend."

Julian massages his temples, and Emilio slides out of the booth. He waits until I scoot toward Julian before sitting back down. Julian's gaze burns into mine when I reach him, my thigh hitting his.

"What you did was rude," I say, feeling like a broken record.

He cracks his neck. "Someone giving you a ride home isn't rude."

"Don't act like you were some innocent Uber driver." I shove my elbow into his side—a risky move—and turn to better face him. "You zip-freaking-tied and blindfolded me."

"This conversation is growing boring." He reaches across the table, slides my empty glass toward him, and collects an ice cube between his fingers. "That night, I simply treated you like the pain in the ass you were being." He flicks the ice cube toward me, and it smacks me in the face before falling into my lap.

It's cold against my bare thigh, and I pick it up, tossing it onto the floor.

"You took me home because you were too chickenshit." I dip my finger into the glass and drag out my own ice cube. "A man like you tries to act all big and bad, but we both know you can't please a woman."

"You're going to regret challenging me." Julian chuckles as he lowers his hand between my legs.

I whimper as he guides my legs farther apart.

He's hardly touched me, and I've never been more turned on in my life. I grip the edge of the table, tipping my hips up, awaiting his next move.

If he's messing with me, I'm finding a gun and shooting him with it.

Or a knife.

Or a bottle to smash over his head.

Something that'll teach him a lesson.

I don't think my sucker punch last time was punishment enough.

From the corner of my eye, I peer at Emilio when his phone rings. He answers the call, putting his hand over his free ear to block the club noise, and talks to whoever is on the other line.

Julian yanks on my ponytail and shifts me so I'm facing him with my back to Emilio. The ponytail violence was unnecessary, but he did it to prove a point.

That tonight, at this table, all my attention belongs to him.

My eyes feel almost watery as they stare into his, transfixed.

He teasingly runs two fingers along my thong string, and my body is ready to burst when he finally slips two fingers inside me.

Even though I'm wetter than that ice cube, his fingers are so thick that it's a tight fit. He crosses my leg over his in such a skillful way that you'd think my legs were made of Jell-O.

I whimper his name and dig my fingers into his arm as he starts fingering me.

The air is suddenly hotter than it was on the dance floor. My mind is so focused on my pleasure that I can't think of anything else.

Ask me what two plus two is, and I'm saying, *Hot dog*.

Julian groans, slightly breaking me from my trance, and I hear Emilio still on the phone. No longer caring if he's watching, I ride Julian's hand.

It's not a shy ride either.

I ride him like it'll give me the power to live forever.

Ten minutes ago, I was shy at the thought of giving Julian a lap dance in front of Emilio. Now, I'm letting Julian finger fuck me in front of him.

Julian makes me lose all my inhibitions.

He rolls his thumb over my clit, and—*holy freaking shit*.

If someone took a picture of me, it'd ruin my family's reputation.

But right now, I couldn't care less about reputations, or about what's smart, or about how I'm putting my heart on the line. While this might mean just sex for Julian, my heart will for sure feel like it's more.

Julian shoves his face into my hair and whispers, "You like it when my fingers are in your pussy, don't you?"

I moan, not saying a word, and ride the high.

I'm so freaking close to an orgasm.

"Say it." He drags me closer.

My thigh brushes against his, and my breathing hitches at the feel of his hard cock beneath his pants.

I peek over my shoulder, seeing Emilio now texting on his phone.

Julian curls his free hand around my jaw, forcing me to look back at him.

"He can see us," I murmur, Julian stopping me from seeing if Emilio is watching.

"You don't want to give him a show?" He releases my jaw. "I thought you loved attention, Genesis."

His tone is daring, like he's waiting for me to chicken out.

This man's favorite hobby is murder and proving he holds all the power, all the time. It's so easy for men to think that, and it proves how dumb they are.

He's the one about to make *me* orgasm.

I haven't even touched his cock or kissed him.

He fingers me faster, as if no longer having any other rational thoughts, like all that's on his mind is pleasuring me.

I climb onto his lap, giving no fucks about PDA any longer. I do it to get closer to his cock, to rub against it, through his pants. I'm so wrapped up in the moment that I forget there's a crowd around us.

So badly, I want to show Julian what he's missing.

I don't want him to ever forget this night, forget *me*.

I want to ruin him for any other woman.

This man will be mine someday.

My body fires up, pleasure rolling through me like a wave, and I grind on Julian's hand. My heart beats so hard that I'm waiting for it to burst out of my chest and land in Julian's lap.

I shut my eyes, biting into his shoulder, and moan out my orgasm.

I'm still controlling my breathing when he slips his fingers out of me.

"You don't belong here," he hisses in my ear. "Go back to your galas and fundraisers before you get yourself killed."

17

Julian

Present Day

I BUST Slappy in the jaw and then shake out my hand.

Slappy isn't his real name.

Sometimes, when I don't know their names, I give them a nickname. This guy earned the nickname because as soon as I walked in, he started slapping himself on the head and calling himself an idiot.

Slappy's head jerks to the side, and I hear his neck crack.

It doesn't snap, just cracks.

His glasses fly off his nose and hit the wall. He cries out in agony, blood flying from his mouth.

The son of a bitch deserves every hit.

My men caught him trying to rob two women in the parking lot. He had seen them win a few thousand dollars in the casino and found them as easy targets. I have security guards on every corner of the parking lot, so they easily apprehended and brought him inside. We have a secret room next to security, where we deal with imbeciles like him.

I'm glad he chose to be a scumbag here and not follow them home.

"I just wanted some cash," he stutters, blood seeping between his teeth. "I'll never do it again."

"If you want cash at a casino, you gamble. Not rob." I grab my pistol, silencer on the end, and raise it to Slappy's head.

I don't give him the chance to plead for his life before pulling the trigger.

As soon as the bullet strikes his skull, blood and brain matter splatter onto the walls, him, and the floor. His body slumps to the side before collapsing off the chair. Lying there, in a black hoodie and pants, fitting the whole *robber* role, he looks almost like a bunched-up rug.

"Damn, boss," Franko says in disappointment. "You took it easy on him."

"He caught me on the wrong night." I take off the black tee I put on before coming in here and drop it into a basket labeled *F*.

The *F* stands for fire since we burn any clothes with even a speck of someone else's blood on them.

I don't trust washing machines or dry cleaners to get every stain out. The shirt I wore when I killed Genesis's attorney is in there too. I make a mental reminder to have Franko throw them in the fireplace.

Slappy was lucky I was pressed for time and had to make his punishment quick. I could've spent hours torturing him for his stupidity at my business.

Unfortunately, I have a meeting in New York I need to get to.

"Wrong night because your mind is on a dark-haired baddie who counts cards?" He leans down to pick up Slappy's glasses and cracks them in half. "What'd you end up doing with her?"

Franko is more than a mere security guard at the casino. He's one of my closest men, and I trust him. He works strictly for me, not for the Lombardis, and I pay him well for it.

His grandparents owned a casino, and from his teens to his

early twenties, he was their security guard until they sold the business.

"Do with who?" I grab a paper towel and wipe my face.

"Oh, come on. It was only hours ago. I doubt you forgot about her."

I scratch my cheek. "She's having my baby."

"Do you mean currently pregnant with your baby, or you just want her to have your baby in the future?"

"Worry about yourself," I tell him. "But make it clear to security that if they see her on the casino floor, they tell me. No one touches her, or they're dead."

"THERE'S talk about Cernach's family in Ireland being angry over his death," Antonio tells Damien and me.

Cernach Koglin was the Irish mob boss whose murder we staged to prevent Damien from marrying Pippa's cousin, Riona. We thought we'd succeeded and that problem was over.

Seems we were wrong.

The last thing I want to deal with is more Irish assholes.

It's almost five in the morning, and I haven't had a wink of sleep. I hoped to make it home before Genesis woke up, to see her in my bed, but I doubt that'll happen.

I stretch my neck and take a drink of water. "Tell them to take it up with Odhrán, the man who killed him."

Riona murdered Odhrán, so he should no longer be a problem either. It was impressive. She'd played the image of the obedient mob princess so well that no one suspected a thing as she plotted her father's murder. Now, she's the boss of the family, the first woman to do it. So far, she's still alive. I don't know how long men will allow her to stay in charge though.

That further proves my belief that you can't trust anyone.

"This had better not become a problem." Antonio grits his teeth.

He didn't want to kill Cernach, but he did it because my brother loved Pippa. Cernach would've never allowed them to be together.

Like so many bosses, Antonio thinks of the strength and safety of the family first. He grew up with a cruel father who put him through hell. But unlike me, he didn't have a mother who tended to his wounds after. She gave no fucks if he or his brother showed up to dinner, beaten and bruised. When Antonio went to war with his uncle, his mother even sold him out.

He never wanted to be the boss. His brother, Vinny, was the oldest and set to take over. But Vinny was fucking stupid and wanted to be king of New York. He further lost his mind when his girlfriend, Natalia, left him. After Natalia got engaged to Cristian, he kidnapped her, and Cristian killed him for it.

I rest my elbows on the table. "I have another problem to add to the list."

Antonio reclines in his chair and throws his head back. "What now?"

"Dima came to the casino." I can't stop myself from clenching my jaw at the memory of him touching Genesis.

"Please tell me it was only to gamble," Damien says.

Still in a bad mood, I can't stop myself from glaring at my brother. "If he wanted to gamble, I doubt our place is where he'd choose to go."

The two nod in understanding.

"He's watching you," Antonio states, his tone flat.

"Yaroslav will keep him in line," Damien says.

"Yaroslav is getting old," I argue. "Dima knows he'll be in charge soon."

Antonio cuts his glare to me. "I wish you'd run the contract with Yaroslav by me before signing it."

I hold his gaze. "Time was of the essence."

"Yes, but making hurried, last-minute deals are never well thought out." He scowls at me. "I have a meeting." While keeping that scowl on me, he stands and pulls his suit jacket from the back of his chair. "Let's make sure this doesn't turn into a war."

He storms past me and slams the door shut.

Damien stares at me in caution, which pisses me off.

I lean in closer toward him, my face burning. "Look, I've sacrificed my life for his family. Every fucking Bellini has. If Antonio wants to give me trouble for this, I won't help the Lombardis with another goddamn thing."

He blows out a breath, concern lining his face. "You know Antonio always has your back. He just has a lot on his plate right now."

I push my chair out with more force than necessary. "If any of you fail to protect my soon-to-be wife, there'll be problems. If he doesn't want to protect my family, then I'll stop protecting his."

It's suicide for a man to speak about stepping away from the Mafia.

It's seen as betrayal.

Very few men have come out of that decision alive.

Damien shakes his head. "Genesis isn't your wife."

"It appears I need to solve that problem."

Genesis

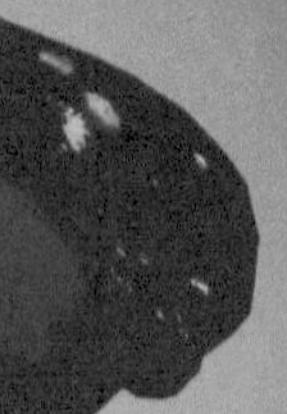

I GROAN, turning off my alarm.

I've been awake for an hour, lying here in disappointment.

Julian didn't come home last night.

It's a further reminder that a conventional relationship with him is out of the question.

He chose me because he saw convenience.

Like I'm a freaking Slurpee at a gas station.

A cold breeze brushes my skin when I slide out of his bed and plod to the bathroom to pee and brush my teeth. When I leave his bedroom, I'm still only wearing his hoodie and my panties.

The house is quiet, and the only noise is the click of a keyboard. As I walk downstairs, I find Emilio working on his MacBook at the island.

He turns in his stool when I reach the bottom of the step, then immediately motions up the stairs. "Go put some clothes on before Julian comes back. I'd prefer not to deal with his jealousy shit this morning."

I walk straight toward him, not listening. "Speaking of Julian, where is he?"

"Working."

I perk up. If Julian isn't here, he can't give me shit about working at the shelter.

"I'll go get dressed," I tell Emilio. "And then you can drive me to work."

"Work?" He draws back and shuts his laptop. "You work?"

"Okay, *rude*. Yes, I work."

"Since when?"

"Since forever."

"You shop, brunch, spa, that type of shit. You having a job is news to me."

All these jerks think they know me so well.

He reopens his laptop, as if done with this conversation.

Unlike other times I've seen Emilio, he's casually dressed today, wearing a black tee and dark jeans. He's wearing blue light glasses, and his black hair is messy.

I spin on my heel and stomp toward the stairs, yelling to him, "We leave in ten minutes."

"Julian would've told me if I needed to take you somewhere. Sorry, but my ass stays here until I get different instructions."

I halt in place, gripping the handrail and hanging over it to glare at him. "Julian *and you* aren't my boss."

"I hate to break it to you, but yes, we are. The faster you get that through your head, the easier your life will become."

I don't think my life will ever be easy again.

I stomp back down the stairs—the goal to steal Emilio's phone and call Damien. Before I make it to the bottom, the door opens, and Julian walks in.

He looks every bit of pissed off when he notices my outfit —or lack thereof. His dissatisfied gaze coasts from me to Emilio.

"Your girl says she needs to go to work," Emilio quickly says, not wanting to make a big deal about what Julian walked in on.

Julian's eyes dart back to me as he tells Emilio, "You can go."

Emilio collects his MacBook and shoves it under his armpit. "Good luck, man," he says to Julian before leaving.

"Take it off," Julian demands as soon as the door closes behind Emilio.

"What?" I stutter, blinking at him.

His face is rigid. "You think it's cute, flirting with other men, wearing *my* shit. You don't deserve to wear my clothes." He crowds me against the wall beside the staircase. "Take. It. The. Fuck. Off."

I gasp when he grabs the bottom of the sweatshirt and rips it over my head in one swift motion.

I shudder, goose bumps crawling over my skin. My nipples harden as the air hits them.

Julian is so close that I can't cover myself. His cold gaze is locked on mine, as if he doesn't even care that my breasts are rubbing against his suit jacket.

"Why are you acting so jealous of Emilio seeing me like this?"

He raises his arms, resting his palms on the wall on each side of my head. "Because you're *mine now*, Genesis. You signed off on it."

A smirk plays at my lips as he lowers his other hand to my stomach.

Tingles spread across every inch of my body.

Inside and out.

My pussy throbs.

God, my body wants him so damn much.

I'm learning the easiest way to manipulate Julian into touching me is by pissing him off.

Making him think he's losing some claim to me.

Like when he saw me with Luca or when I looked at Emilio in the booth at the club. The same with his reaction now.

He loves power, and when I start to take it from him, he touches me to prove it's still there.

I brush my lips over his. "What about when you let him sit in the booth and watch you finger me?" I run my tongue along the seam of his lips. "Was I yours then?"

He bites my lip and curses under his breath. "That night, he heard your moans of pleasure, but he didn't see *your body*." To further drive in his words, he pushes his hand into my panties and cups my pussy. "All he saw was how I played with your pussy so fucking good that you lost control of yourself." He rips my panties off. "It also taught us both that you enjoyed having an audience, don't you?"

I turn my head, looking away from him.

It's true.

If Emilio were still here and Julian had me in this same position, I'd let him do whatever he wanted with my body.

"So wet, just thinking about it," Julian says, hiking my leg up his thigh and thrusting three fingers inside me, stretching me so well.

He loves teasing me and playing games.

I want to do the same with him.

"Where were you all night?" I ask, shutting my eyes.

"Ah, who's the jealous one now?"

"You know where I was. It's only fair." I moan as he plays with my clit.

"I was working."

I grind my hips against his hand, so much pleasure rolling through me that I'm surprised I can speak. "Speaking of work, that's where I need to get to."

He pulls his fingers out and steps back so fast that I almost keel over him. "You don't have a job." He uses the same tone Emilio did when he basically said the same thing.

I huff out a breath as he straightens his suit jacket. "Yes, I do."

"Is that job to fuck me whenever I want?"

"No, the shelter, smart-ass. I'm scheduled to work there today."

"You no longer *volunteer* there." He steps forward, pinning me against the wall and shoving his hand back between my legs.

If his goal is to tease me so I forget about volunteering, he's underestimating me.

I push his shoulder. "It's in the contract, so you have to let me. The shelter is already short-staffed to begin with."

"I'll increase my donation so they can hire more people. Problem solved." He tauntingly smirks at me and presses his hand back against the wall, as if holding me hostage.

"You don't let me go, then you don't get to come inside me." I mock his smirk before ducking underneath his arm. "I'll be ready in ten minutes." I pluck the sweatshirt from the floor and tug it on while walking up the stairs. "The sweatshirt is mine now too."

THE CORONER CALLS on the drive to Safe Hearts Mission. He tells me he can't reach my mother and asks where to send my father's body. His question hurts my heart.

How sad.

My father's body is stranded at the coroner's. I can't believe my mother didn't even have the respect to prepare her husband a proper funeral. I doubt she's even grieving.

We haven't spoken since she told me she was living her best life in Tahiti. She hasn't checked on me once. I really don't have anyone but Julian and my friends.

Another how sad.

I instruct the coroner to send my father's body to the same

funeral home my grandparents went to after their deaths. In his will, he put that he wanted to be buried in the same graveyard as them.

When I get off my shift at Safe Hearts, I'll call the funeral home to set up the arrangements.

Ending the call, I peer at Julian in the driver's seat. "I need my car. That way, you won't have to worry about driving me around."

He shakes his head, braking at a light. "Your car might have trackers."

I slip on my sunglasses. "Who'd put a tracker on my car?"

"The Russians," he states as if it's a known fact. "You were on Dima's radar for weeks. To his understanding, you were locked in as his bride."

I pause, the creeps running through me at the thought of being *anything* to Dima. It takes me a moment to gain my thoughts, and I rest my elbow on the console. "All right then, soon-to-be baby daddy, I need some wheels, sans trackers."

"You have to earn that."

"What's up with you and *earning*?" I glare at him and imitate his voice. "You have to earn your orgasm, earn a car." I level my tone to my normal princess self. "How about *you* earn me?"

For a moment, he stares at me in annoyance.

People don't speak to him like that.

They definitely don't mock him.

Here I am, pushing the psycho killer's buttons.

He tilts his head to the side. "I've earned you *and more*."

I'VE VOLUNTEERED at the Safe Hearts Mission for over a decade.

New York has the highest per capita rate of homelessness in the country.

The first time I really understood homelessness was when my parents took me to see *Cats* on Broadway for my fourteenth birthday. Seeing the people on the streets hurt my heart, and I cried the entire ride home.

The next morning, I asked Sonja to find me ways to help them.

I don't do it for the savior complex.

I do it because it's where my heart led me.

Sonja found Safe Hearts, and every week, we'd volunteer.

Even after growing older, even after losing Sonja, I still volunteer. I will for as long as I can.

I frown, knowing that I'm not only limiting my schedule but also letting them down financially.

Every year, my father donated a substantial amount of money to the mission. He'd also convince clients, friends, and business partners to do the same. Every penny they gave was needed and put to good use.

Now, it's gone.

They already struggle with funding as it is.

I grip the door handle as Julian parks the Escalade. "I'll call when I'm done." Swinging open the door, I jump out of the SUV.

Julian does the same, trailing me as I walk to the entrance.

Troy and Ollie stand guard, blocking the door.

Many of our women are here, escaping domestic violence. Troy and Ollie stayed here with their mother for six months when they were younger, and now, they help keep it safe.

"Hey, guys," I say, waving to them.

"Genesis, it's been a few days." Ollie smiles, moving to the side and opening the door. He freezes when he notices Julian behind me.

I make a *get out of here* gesture toward Julian, but he shakes his head.

This doesn't look good.

Ollie's shoulders tense as Troy steps toward me.

"He's with me," I hurriedly tell them.

Troy—a man who's nearly seven feet tall with muscles galore—levels his blue eyes on me. "Now, Genesis, you know—"

Julian steps to my side. "I'm her fiancé and about to write a major check to this place. I'm no danger to this facility. You have my word."

From the expression on Ollie's face, I know he recognizes Julian.

While men in the mob are known as dangerous, they do help out the community as well. The Lombardis donate millions to charities and organizations to keep their name as clean as they can. They do all their dirty work behind the scenes, though most people know their business isn't legit. I've never heard of them hurting women or children.

"Fiancé?" Ollie's mouth falls open.

I nod. "He's here as a major donor."

Troy slowly nods and opens the door for us.

Julian nods in appreciation as we pass them.

As soon as I walk into the lobby, Lora bursts from her office.

"Genesis!" she calls out, rushing over to hug me. "I saw what happened on the news. I'm so sorry, honey."

I squeeze her tight, and she runs her hand down my back.

Lora is the mission director. Safe Hearts is her life.

As she pulls away, her gaze drifts from me to Julian.

"This is my *fiancé*." I grit my teeth as I say the word. "He wanted to watch me today and give a *very* generous donation."

I'm racking up the lies, but I don't know how else to explain our relationship. It'd be mortifying to say he hired me to have his baby.

Julian extends his hand toward Lora and introduces himself. "It's nice to meet you."

Lora shakes his hand, distrust on her face. She knows I'd never put the mission in harm's way though.

A teenage boy calls Lora's name, and she leaves us.

"All right," I say with an annoyed groan toward Julian. "Time for class."

He scrunches his brows. "Class?"

I motion for him to follow, and he looks around the place as he does. We pass the rec room, where a cartoon is playing, and then reach the classroom.

The room is cramped with only enough space to fit a teacher's desk and ten small ones. Inspirational posters hang on the bright yellow walls, along with sections of crayon scribbles.

I blink, annoyed with the flickering ceiling light. It's been that way for weeks now, and we're waiting for someone to fix it.

"Sit in that corner desk," I direct Julian. "And smile. Jesus, you're going to freak people out."

"That's exactly why I shouldn't be here," he argues, glaring at the desk and then at me.

I point at the door, returning his glare. "Leave then."

"Not without you."

"Let me just teach this class, okay?" I say around a sigh.

He shakes his head, slipping his hands into his pockets, and surprisingly stalks across the room. I use my hand to cover my laugh at the sight of him squeezing into the cramped desk.

He pulls out his phone as four women enter the room.

"Who's he?" Sissy asks when she notices Julian.

"He's job shadowing me," I explain.

There goes another lie.

She nods, her pink slippers sliding across the floor, and plops down in the front row. The other three women pay Julian a quick glance and then sit down, ready to learn.

I teach a variety of classes—a GED prep course, a finance course, as well as reading and math for the children.

It's a great way to put my MBA to use.

Julian lowers his phone when I start class.

Today's lesson is on finance.

I've never seen Julian so focused on me as when I'm teaching. He leans back in the chair and doesn't check his phone once.

For the next hour, he doesn't look away as the women take notes.

I have his full attention.

Maybe this will help him understand why I can't just quit volunteering here.

I'm needed, and he'll need to accept that.

Or it'll cause nothing but chaos between us.

19

Julian

I'VE NEVER BEEN SO ENTERTAINED in a classroom.

Genesis is fucking smart.

Watching her in action is goddamn sexy.

When class ends, my phone rings. Everyone's attention turns to me.

I hurriedly silence the call, like I'm about to get in trouble and Teacher Genesis will confiscate my phone. It takes me two attempts to squeeze out from the desk, and I'm sure it looks ridiculous.

"I need to take this," I whisper to Genesis while leaving the classroom and walking around the corner into a vending machine area.

I lean against the wall and call Paolo back.

"Boss, where are you?" he asks through the speaker.

While I'm not the boss of the Lombardi family, I have men who work exclusively for me. Paolo is one of them.

Paolo works at the casino as well, and it's weird for me not to be there first thing in the morning.

Hell, half the time, I don't even leave, and I sleep there.

"I'm coming in late today," I tell him. "Handle shit for me."

"Everything okay?"

I grip my phone tight and lower my voice. "Keep an eye out for Russians. If you see even one, you call me."

"Got it."

I end the call.

If Genesis hadn't snuck out of my office, I wouldn't have all this Russian anxiety.

Her little antics are why I'm here.

Why she doesn't have much freedom.

She fucked up.

Dima made it clear how easy it was to get to Genesis, and the son of a bitch wanted me to know it.

Per my contract with Yaroslav, I can't marry Genesis until I pay my balance.

Before, I had no problem with that. She needed to give me a baby, and I'd free her from the Russians.

Everything is changing now.

I need to knock her up faster than I thought.

Time for me to start fucking Genesis.

As if the asshole knew I was thinking of him, he calls me.

"Yeah?" I answer.

"You got my money yet?" Yaroslav asks between coughs.

"I'm working on it."

"The clock is ticking. *Ticktock. Ticktock.*"

"I have sixty days."

"Not a long time to come up with that amount of money."

It's not about a lack of funds. I could pay him off today.

"I don't break deals," I say through gritted teeth.

"The same with me, Julian."

"Since I have you on the phone, I want to make something clear."

"What's that?"

"Dima stays away from my casino and Genesis. She's not his wife."

"*Not yet.*"

"*Not ever*," I hiss. "Tell him to stay the fuck away from her. Your son doesn't want the consequences of fucking with me."

I end the call.

"I NEED A FAVOR," I tell Antonio, sitting down in the cognac-brown leather chair seated in front of his desk.

He looks up at me from his office chair, raising a brow.

"Tell Gigi to invite Genesis over for a girls' night," I say, repeating my plan.

Gigi is one of the most protected women in this state. If Genesis is with her, that makes her just as protected.

"Why?" Antonio asks.

"I need her to stay out of trouble while I work."

He sighs, as if understanding my problem. "I'll talk to her."

"Thanks." I slap the arm of the chair and stand. "She's having a rough time with her father's death and now having no family."

"You need to keep her in line and away from the Russians."

"That's my goal and why I'm trying to keep her busy."

He plucks a gold pen from his desk and twirls it between his fingers. "What's your plan with her? Is this a game with her or real?"

His question isn't one from a friend.

It's one from the mob boss of the family I work for.

"I've already paid half a million dollars for her. I think that should answer your question."

20

Genesis

"ARE you ready to explain what's going on with you and Julian?" Darcy asks over FaceTime.

"He said I can crash here since he's at the casino all the time and hardly home." I look away, hating that I'm lying to her.

Lora might not know when I lie, but Darcy does.

"Bullshit," she says, sitting in the living room of her parents' Paris home. "You want to stay there."

I lower my gaze to glare at her. "You're so wrong."

"My door is always open." She holds up a finger. "And before you complain about *lack of room*, stay at my parents' then. They have fifteen guest rooms."

Darcy's condo is in the city, but her parents have a sprawling estate in the suburbs, where I could easily stay. Her parents adore me. Julian would lose his shit if I did because of her brother, Lewi.

Lewi is harmless.

Something men like Julian don't understand is that it's okay to be playful. Your entire personality doesn't have to be brooding and murderous.

Kick off your designer loafers, crack open a beer, and relax.

Switch it up some.

Live a little.

I also haven't told her about Dima and how I'm pretty much unsafe anywhere else. Julian told me it was too dangerous, and I'm also embarrassed about the entire situation. It sucks because Darcy and I have always told each other everything.

Julian calling interrupts our conversation.

"Crap, let me call you back," I say, forcing a chipper tone. "Love ya!"

"Love youuuu," she sings as I switch the call to Julian's.

His is a regular call.

Not a FaceTime.

I can't imagine him FaceTiming.

I can hear him now, already saying FaceTime is risky.

"Yeah?" I answer, imitating his standard answering greeting.

"Pack a bag," he demands. "You're having a sleepover."

"A sleepover with who?"

"Gigi. Pippa. A girls' night."

"You arranged a sleepover for me? What am I, ten?"

"I arranged for you to do something that'll keep your misbehaving ass out of trouble. Now, pack a bag. Emilio will take you."

The jerk hangs up.

EMILIO DRIVES me to Pippa's dance studio, The Ballet Studio, where we're meeting for girls' night.

When we walk in, ballet students are huddled around Pippa, dressed in tutus and tights. She reminds them to practice their routine, and they hug her goodbye before dashing to their waiting parents. Emilio inches away from me, standing near the door, as I walk to Gigi.

"Hey, girl," Gigi says, wearing a fluffy coat and diamond earrings. Her thick hair is halfway pulled back into a bun, the rest of the strands down in curls, and her plump lips are red.

She fits the look of what you'd imagine for a New York Mafia princess.

Even though I knew of Gigi, I didn't officially meet her until she got involved with Antonio and started hanging out with Pippa. I was Pippa's plus-one at Gigi's wedding.

Her and Antonio's love story gives off Romeo and Juliet vibes, minus the whole dying thing. Their families were at war while they were trying to fight their attraction to each other.

Cristian is a no-mercy man, and I thought Antonio would end up dead. But Monster Marchetti now plays nice for the sake of his daughter. It was funny; there were so many bets on whether Cristian would shoot Antonio at their wedding.

Pippa and Amara—Antonio's daughter and Gigi's stepdaughter—head in our direction. Pippa has a zip-up sweatshirt on with the studio's name in glitter on the chest, and her dark hair is pulled back in a tight bun.

"Babe, I'm so sorry for what you're going through." Pippa wraps me in a hug. "I've told Damien I don't know how many times to bring me to Julian's to visit you. I even went on a"—she lowers her voice, so Amara doesn't hear—"S-E-X strike."

"Are you still on the strike?" Gigi asks.

Pippa rolls her eyes. "That's irrelevant."

Gigi tries to keep a straight face but fails.

Pippa flips her off, using her free hand to block Amara from seeing the gesture.

"Really sticking it to him, huh?" I raise a brow.

"He didn't make it easy to say no." Pippa's cheeks burn red. "It was like my threat was a challenge for him. Every morning, he'd join me in the shower, S-T-R-O-K-E himself, and if I tried touching him, he'd remind me of the stupid S-E-X strike."

Gigi laughs.

"I didn't know if I wanted to smack him or F-U-C-K him," Pippa adds.

"I hate when they do that," Gigi says around a groan.

I sigh, a hint of jealousy hitting me.

I'll never have that with Julian.

Never have a husband obsessed with me.

Our relationship will be purely transactional.

"Ready to go?" Amara asks, sliding on a pair of pink Gucci sneakers. She jumps to her feet and smiles. Her hair is in two tight French braids, finished with pink bows.

"Your dad should be here any minute." Gigi pulls her phone from her handbag and checks the screen. "He's taking you out for ice cream."

Amara cheekily grins. "Yay!"

Gigi's phone vibrates in her hand. "And perfect timing."

Emilio walks out of the studio first, and we shuffle out behind him.

I stop in place, Gigi nearly tripping over me, when I see Luca standing in front of a black Escalade, identical to Julian's, looking too confident. His lips twist into a wide smirk when our eyes meet, and he twirls the key ring around his finger.

"That's my cousin, Luca," Gigi explains. "He's driving us."

Oh shit.

Pippa covers her mouth, shaking her head. "Julian will lose his shit over this. I can't wait." She knows about my history with Luca.

Gigi? I'm not so sure.

Luca's and Julian's fingers earned me the nickname Finger Queen.

At least, according to Pippa, who loves reminding me of my hookups.

Julian knows about Luca and me. He made it clear at Gigi's wedding that he wasn't very happy about it either. He texted me later that night, and I told him if he was so worried about Luca in my panties, he should've stepped up and touched me first. He never replied to that text. I was almost positive the jerk had blocked me.

"Nope." Emilio grabs my wrist to stop me from moving closer to Luca. "Not fucking happening."

Welp. It seems Emilio also knows something.

Luca's amused attention travels from me to Emilio. "Sup, man?"

"He's taking us to my dad's," Gigi explains to Emilio, not catching on to the tension.

She and Amara walk away when a black Mercedes stops. The windows roll down, and Antonio comes into view. Gigi helps Amara into the car as Pippa slides into the back seat of Luca's Escalade.

Luca opens the driver's door. "Genesis, I'll let you have the front seat."

"You're not leaving with him," Emilio says, still holding me.

I break out of his hold, but don't walk toward Luca.

Luca cocks his head. "She won't be alone with me in the car. It's not like I'm going to try to fuck her." He immediately stops to add, "Unless she asks for it."

I glare at Luca, trying my hardest to look scary. "Really?"

He throws out his arms. "I'm only helping you make your case, babe."

"What's the problem, Emilio?" Gigi asks, rejoining us after Antonio leaves with Amara. "Luca is a safe driver, I promise. Genesis is in good hands." She hops into the back seat with Pippa.

"She's most definitely in good hands," Luca says, his voice smug with confidence.

"I'll drive her," Emilio states, tugging me toward his Mercedes. "We'll follow."

"No way in hell will Cristian allow you to drive onto the property." Luca shakes his head. "If you insist on being a pain in the ass, you can drive her most of the way. Then I'll pull over and drive her the rest of the way."

Luca slides into the driver's seat and slams the door shut.

"He doesn't like playing chaperone," Gigi shouts through the open window. "He's always like this. Don't take it personally!"

Right now, I'd rather agree to Julian's rules than Luca's.

Luca isn't the one saving my life right now, and I doubt Cristian would let him anyway. From what I've heard, Cristian doesn't like outsiders. The whole *Emilio not allowed on his property* thing further proves that point.

I follow Emilio back to his car that's parked a few cars back from Luca.

As soon as we're in the vehicle, Emilio tugs his phone from his suit jacket. "Did you know she's going to the Marchetti mansion?" he asks into the speaker.

He nods a few times, listening.

My guess is, to Julian.

"Did you know Luca would be her Uber driver there?" Emilio stresses.

"So dramatic," I grumble under my breath.

What does he think I'll do with Luca?

Let him finger me in front of my friends?

I mean, I did let *him* watch Julian and me.

Emilio extends his phone to me.

I huff, taking it from him.

"Every time I let you out of the house, you cause trouble," Julian says on the other end of the line.

"You're the one who arranged girls' night," I argue. "It's not my fault you have subpar event planning skills. Going forward, I'd suggest you allow me to arrange these."

"I have a better idea. You don't leave the house."

"You caused this trouble. Not me."

"Wrong," he bites out. "You created this trouble when you caught Luca's attention."

"I can't help it that my charm brings all the boys to the yard."

Julian curses under his breath.

"Are you feeling a little insecure there, Julian?"

"Nah, I'm feeling a little murderous, and you're making your way onto the list of possible victims."

"Those aren't words to get on my good side."

There's a brief silence before he says, "Being on your good side is of no concern to me."

"I don't care about being on your good side." I end the call and toss the phone in Emilio's lap. "Let's go."

He grabs his phone from his lap when it rings again, checks the caller ID, and answers while extending the phone to me.

Julian's face is suddenly in front of me.

He glares into the screen like some villain.

I guess I was wrong there.

The man does FaceTime.

"Say one more smart-ass word, and I'll instruct Emilio to take you home and lock you in my bedroom." His voice turns icier than I ever thought possible for someone. "Don't fucking test me on this. Keep misbehaving, and I'll tie you to my bed and spend all night fingering you but stopping right before *you're fucking there*. I'll keep doing that, like a loop, making you suffer."

Jesus.

My jaw drops, and I look at Emilio.

He's pretending he didn't hear Julian.

"Eyes fucking on me," Julian grinds out. "Don't look at him."

"Why are you even concerned about Luca?" I snap.

"You let that man finger fuck you. Going forward, you so

much as allow a man to touch your arm, I'll cut his goddamn finger off."

"That's a little drastic, don't you think?" I roll my eyes slowly, so he doesn't miss me doing it.

"Gen, baby, that's letting someone off easy. Keep talking, and I'll connect that finger to a chain and force you to wear it as a necklace."

I stare at him, unsure of how to reply to that.

Where does he even come up with this bullshit?

He should really be on the writing team for the Saw franchise.

I'm sure he has endless torture and murder ideas in that psycho brain of his.

"I don't appreciate being bossed around." With one hand, I jerk the seat belt around my body. It looks awkward, and I almost drop the phone in the process.

He waits until I'm settled before narrowing his eyes at me. "Be a good girl or suffer the consequences later."

He hangs up on me.

"Asshole," I hiss, handing the phone back to Emilio.

I'VE BEEN to the Marchetti mansion.

Not many can say that.

I officially can now.

Every woman in this room with me has ties to the Mafia.

It seems I've now joined the club.

Neomi and her sisters, Bria and Isabella, who everyone calls Bella, joined us an hour ago. Technically, Neomi lives on the property, just in a separate house with Benny and their baby girl.

The aroma of buttery popcorn fills the air as we hang out in the theater room in Gigi's wing of the mansion. She may live with Antonio now, but according to Natalia, Cristian has left her space untouched, just in case she ever decides to come home.

"Listen, someone other than me needs to choose a movie," Natalia says, handing me a popcorn bowl before plopping down in the recliner beside mine. "That way, if it's terrible, no one can blame me."

"What kind of monster blames someone for picking a bad movie?" I ask.

"Monster Marchetti," Natalia, Neomi, and Gigi say simultaneously.

"It's cute blame," Natalia says. "Like *I'll punish you in the bedroom for your crappy choice*."

Gigi flings popcorn at Natalia's head. "Um, gross! That's my dad, weirdo."

"Benny does the same with me," Neomi says from the recliner behind me. "I *always* pick bad ones because I like being punished."

She and Natalia burst out in laughter.

Gigi heaves a pillow toward Neomi's head from across the room. "I hate both of you." She does a motion of the entire theater. "From now on, no one sleeping with *any* of my family members is allowed at girls' night. You losers go pick sucky movies and hang out with your husbands."

I've always wondered how Gigi felt about her father marrying her best friend. From what I've heard, it was her idea after she learned Vinny put out a hit on her. If Darcy married my father, I'd literally have to flee the country—à la my mother's style.

But most fathers and Cristian Marchetti are not the same.

Cristian is a total DILF.

He does not give dad vibes at all.

Natalia digs the popcorn from her hair, drops it into her mouth, and smiles.

Had she chosen a different career than mob wife, she could've easily had a modeling career. Her wavy black hair is layered and reaches her ass, and she has curves I'd die for. It's no mystery why she started a war between two men. A man died for her, and a man killed for her.

"Does it count if we *want* to sleep with one of your family members?" Isabella asks, pulling her black curls into a high ponytail before shoving a handful of Skittles into her mouth.

Gigi snuggles into her blanket, making herself comfortable, and gives Isabella a pointed look. "If you and Luca ever start bumping uglies and you decide to talk about it, you'll join the banned list."

"Then that's the last you'll see of me," Isabella says. "I shall sacrifice girls' nights for the D."

"Lame!" Natalia shouts.

"Wait." I shift, turning in my recliner to peer back at Isabella. "You and Luca are …"

"Are nothing," she cries out, dramatically throwing her arms and head back. Skittles fly out of the package in every direction.

"In case the dramatics don't make it obvious, she has a crush on Luca," Bria explains, leaning toward me. "Last year, she bought *a freaking wishing well* on eBay with all intentions of installing it in our backyard. Her plan was to throw pennies into it every night and wish to marry Luca until it came true."

"Our mother watched too many Disney movies when pregnant with her," Neomi explains.

"It was *The Princess Bride*, thank you very much," Isabella argues. "And don't be jealous because Mother spent her pregnancy with you watching *Jerry Springer*. It's why I'm a romantic and you compare every bald man to Steve, the bodyguard."

Neomi throws her hands up. "Oh, I'm sorry I compared the *one* boyfriend you had to him."

"Was he a boyfriend though?" Bria asks. "You met him online and never in person."

"I stopped talking to him because you said he looked like he had a condom on his head!"

"It should be written into law that bald men aren't allowed to wear spandex beanies," Neomi says with a shrug.

"Not this conversation again," Gigi groans.

"I agree," Natalia says. "Let's have Genesis tell us about her and Julian."

I choke on the popcorn and hurriedly wash it down with a sip of Dr Pepper. "You know, I watched this *Jerry Springer* episode once—"

"Nice try!" Pippa says, walking into the room, holding a sleeping Alessia in her arms. "We want all the details."

The women stare at me hungrily, waiting for me to feed them juicy gossip.

"There's nothing to tell," I say slowly before clearing my throat. "You all know about my father. I'm pretty much homeless, poor, and possibly in legal trouble. Julian is helping me so I'm not sleeping on the street. 'Tis all."

"Sorry to break it to you, but Julian doesn't just *help someone out*," Gigi states matter-of-factly. "None of the men in our world do. There's always a price for something."

My mouth turns dry.

I know I can trust Pippa, but I don't know the others as well.

Gigi has unwavering loyalty to Antonio, so I can't see her betraying me. If anyone wanted to cross me, it'd be Neomi or her sisters.

A few years ago, Vincent Lombardi called a hit on Benny. The bullet hit Neomi instead, and the Cavallaros then joined the war against the Lombardis.

I once heard that unlike many other Mafia bosses, Severino never got angry with his wife when she birthed daughters. Daughters gave him contracts, which gave him power, and he already had an heir to the throne. That was, until his son was murdered a few years ago. Now, Severino has no one to take over his throne, and the Cavallaro name might die with him.

Chills vibrate through my body.

That must be how Julian feels.

While Pippa and Damien have Alessia, there's no Bellini boy to continue their name through generations.

What if I get pregnant and have a girl?

Will we keep trying until I have a boy?

There was nothing regarding the sex of the baby in the contract.

Bria snapping her fingers in my face breaks me out of my thoughts. "Earth to Genesis!"

"Shoot, sorry." I brush my fingers through my hair, suddenly feeling a sense of sadness. "We just … a baby."

Yes, while unable to come up with an explanation, I just said it with one word.

"Baby?" Pippa gasps. "You're pregnant?" She glances around at everyone. "Someone grab me my phone, so I can tell Damien he's about to be an uncle!"

"Whoa!" I quickly shout. "I'm not pregnant."

"Then, spill, or I'm organizing a meeting to plan a baby shower," Gigi says.

I snatch a Twizzlers from the package beside me. "I'm not pregnant … *yet*."

If anyone can understand the logic behind this insanity, it'll be these ladies.

Marriage contracts are their way of life.

And I *think* I can trust them.

"We signed a contract," I add, biting off the edge of the Twizzler.

"A marriage one?" Natalia asks, giving me her full attention.

I shake my head. "A baby one."

Julian and I discussed marriage, but it wasn't the sole purpose of the contract.

It was all about a baby.

Bria whistles. "The baby contracts are always the most complicated."

Neomi snorts. "Okay, *Elle Woods*."

"What's Julian holding over your head?" Natalia asks me.

I take another bite of the Twizzler.

How do I explain to them that my family thought the best way to pay off a debt was to hand over their daughter?

A flush creeps over my cheeks in embarrassment. All along, I believed I came from a good name. I was so wrong. I came from a family of corruption, lies, and ruin.

"You were friends with his sister before her passing, right?" Gigi asks, her voice soft and composed.

I nod.

"Cute," Isabella comments, holding up a Skittles. "The *best friend's brother* trope is my favorite." She stops, a thought hitting her. "Actually, my second favorite. I'm all about enemies to lovers, baby."

"Ignore her," Neomi says, kicking her feet out from the blanket to show off her fuzzy white socks. "What does Julian have on you, Genesis?"

I blink at her. "What do you mean?"

Natalia presses her hand against her chest. "When I agreed to marry Cristian, it was because my ex wanted to kill me. I married him in exchange for protection."

"I married Benny because of a marriage contract," Neomi adds.

"When I agreed to marry Antonio, it was because he held a gun to my head … and a priest's," Gigi says.

"What the women who are lucky enough to be married are saying is that in every contract in this world, there's a weakness and a solution to solve that weakness," Isabella explains.

Bria nods in agreement. "Julian's vulnerability is he wants a child. What's yours, Genesis? Why are you agreeing to something as precious as having someone's child? What do you get in exchange?"

I go still for a moment, not meeting anyone's gaze.

Before my father's death, I was never someone with trust issues, but now, I am. I trust *no* one, not even Julian.

"Do you know who Dima Morozova is?" I ask, disgust hitting my throat from just saying his name.

"The Russian Bratva boss's son?" Neomi immediately asks.

"The *psycho* Russian Bratva boss's son," Gigi says, as if that correction is necessary for the story.

I inhale three breaths and start telling them my situation.

None of them mutters a word as they listen with full attention. I don't tell them everything, only what happened in my father's office. Every one of them grins when I tell them about Julian barging into the room and basically plucking me straight out of Dima's hands.

Getting it off my chest feels good.

"Dima is hot, but Julian is definitely hotter," Neomi says. "He also gives less murder vibes, you know? Men who give off those vibes are total red flags."

"Says the girl who's married to Benny Marchetti," Natalia comments with a laugh.

"Says the girl who's married to the man who created him," Neomi argues with a playful grin. "I've never worried about Benny hurting me." Her dark-eyed gaze slips back to me. "But if I were marrying Dima? I'd always be looking over my shoulder. The Russians offered my father a marriage union years ago for Bella. He told them to kick rocks."

"Trust me, in the moment, a contract seems like the craziest thing in the world," Bria says. "The men like to talk about it, throw it in your face, but then it'll blow over."

"That depends," Gigi chimes in. "Dima is batshit crazy, and

coming from a Marchetti, that's saying a lot. Julian showing up at your father's office was a blessing."

Pippa kisses the top of Alessia's head. "This girl would love to have a baby cousin, so we're all for another Bellini baby. Plus, I'd love to have you as a sister-in-law."

"That's the problem," I mutter, frowning. "Julian doesn't want a wife. He wants a uterus."

Gigi shakes her head. "Julian may want you to believe that because Mafia men equate talking about feelings to death. Julian chose *you* for the contract because he wants *you*. Even if you weren't able to have his baby, he'd have figured out another way to save you and make sure you were his. The Russian thing is his excuse."

Neomi nods. "These men want you to believe it's all about contracts and loyalty." She raises her hand to make a *yapping* gesture. "Meanwhile, they're buying you puppies, coming home to you every night, and risking their lives for you. Eventually, reality will smack them in the face."

"Seeing it when it happens is fun as hell," Natalia says, winking at me.

I wish I could believe them, but just like at the ballet studio, my gut tells me that Julian and I will never be like them.

He made that clear.

I'M HOMESICK.

Or rather, homesick for Julian.

I don't know what to call it.

It's past midnight, and I'm in Gigi's bedroom with her, Pippa, and Alessia.

Neomi and her sisters went home, and Natalia left for her

wing of the mansion an hour ago. My plan was to stay overnight, but I miss Julian.

I want to be there, in his home, with him.

He said it was mine for the time being anyway.

I'm halfway paying attention to an old *Euphoria* episode playing in the background. Pippa is beside me, Alessia is cooing from the bassinet beside the bed, and Gigi is sprawled across the ottoman in the corner, talking on her phone.

She's whispering, but I've heard her tell Antonio, "Good night," and, "I love you," at least six times.

I grab my phone, get out of bed, and walk to the attached bathroom. I blink against the bright light and unlock my phone. My finger tingles, hovering over Julian's name.

The Marchetti mansion may be the safest home in New York, but there's one flaw—no Julian. And like a kid at a sleepover, I miss home.

Out of nowhere, Julian has become my comfort.

He answers on the second ring.

"Come get me," I say.

"What happened?" he immediately asks, his voice laced with a hint of panic.

"Nothing," I sigh. "I just … never mind."

"I can't pick you up right now," he says before I hang up. "I'll send Emilio."

I can't explain why, but I sense he's sporting a pleased smile, like he knows I miss him.

"Are you coming home tonight?" I ask.

"It wasn't in my plans."

I frown, leaning against the marble countertop.

"But I'll come home for you, baby."

A pleasant hum fills my blood, a rush of energy hitting me.

"I'll call Emilio, and we'll get you home. Okay?"

"Okay," I whisper.

For a change, he says goodbye before hanging up.

I check myself in the mirror, splash some water on my face, and leave the bathroom. Gigi isn't on the phone, but she's looking at her screen.

"Do you mind if I go home?" I ask her.

She lowers her phone. "This isn't some teenage slumber party. You can stay overnight, go home, or stay the whole week." She leans in closer. "To be honest, I'm considering the same."

"Thank God," Pippa says. "I've been waiting for someone to say they missed their man."

I whip around to look at her. "Julian isn't *my man*."

She bends down, scooping Alessia up into her arms. "Yet you want to go home *to him*."

"I'll see if Antonio can pick us up," Gigi says. "Otherwise, I'll get one of my father's men to do it."

My phone vibrates with a text from Julian.

> Julian: Emilio will pick you up in 25 minutes.

I reply to him.

> Me: Gigi is asking Antonio for a ride.

> Julian: Keep me updated.

> Me: Will you be home before me?

> Julian: Probably not.

I make a sour face.

> Julian: I fully expect you to be in my bed when I do though.

"Can we stop at a coffee shop?" I ask Emilio from his passenger seat.

Antonio picked us up from the mansion, then met Emilio at the gas station. I felt like a child being shuttled between divorced parents as I moved from one car to the other.

Emilio checks the time on the car's dashboard. "It's one in the morning."

"Do you have a bedtime?" I ask. "I seriously doubt you plan to go home, do your skin care routine, and binge-watch *Gilmore Girls* until you fall asleep. We have plenty of time."

"I have no idea what the hell you're talking about," he mutters. "We just left the gas station. Why didn't you get coffee there?"

"Last time I checked, that gas station doesn't have an espresso machine, or oat milk, or my favorite hazelnut syrup."

He stops at a red light. "When was the last time *you checked*?"

I was a regular at the gas station when I was underage. The old clerk would sell me alcohol, and back then, I loved their blue slushies, mixed with vodka.

"Oh, come on, Emilio," I groan. "You should get one for yourself, too, since you'll probably be up all night, right?"

When the light turns green, he signals and turns left, ignoring me.

We're so close to my favorite coffee shop that's open twenty-four seven that I can practically smell the coffee.

I sit up straight, hands folded in my lap. "Believe me, it's way less annoying to get me a coffee than listen to me complain about needing one." I point at the upcoming streetlight. "Make a left. Brew Delights will be on your right."

A grin spreads across my face when he follows my directions and parks in front of the coffee shop.

He releases his seat belt. "What's your order?"

I do the same. "I'm going in with you."

He shakes his head. "You'll stay in here. I'm already going out of my way for this."

I fight the urge to roll my eyes, nervous he'll cancel our coffee stop and leave. "I prefer ordering my own coffee."

He grabs his phone to send a text.

A few seconds later, my phone buzzes, and Julian's name flashes on the screen.

I hold up the phone and narrow my eyes at Emilio. "Are you seriously causing this much trouble over a cup of joe?"

He doesn't reply, and this time, I allow myself to roll my eyes.

"Hello?" I huff into the speaker.

"What are you trying to do?" Julian asks in irritation.

"Get a coffee, duh." I scoff. "Don't you want me awake when you get home?"

"We have an espresso machine there."

"I want an espresso from Brew Delights." I pout my lip out even though he can't see me. "It's my favorite."

Emilio curses, rubbing his forehead.

"Give Emilio the phone," Julian says.

I hand him the phone, all smiles.

Emilio takes it and nods while listening to Julian on the other line.

After ending the call, he tosses my phone in the cupholder. "Come on," he says around a grunt, opening his door. "Let's make this fucking fast."

I grin, happy to get my way, and jump out of the car. "By the way, you're paying," I call out to him. "In case you didn't hear the news, I'm broke."

"Of fucking course," Emilio says, pushing the door open to Brew Delights. "I'm charging Julian double for this shit."

I just love getting my way.

I don't know how long that'll last though.

I also don't know what'll happen when Julian gets home.

MY CAFFEINE BUZZ IS FADING.

Even the extra shots didn't help.

It's been a long day.

Girls' day/night.

Telling them my secret.

Admitting I missed Julian.

Two a.m. hits, and he still isn't home.

Lying in his bed, I text him.

No response.

I yawn as three a.m. passes and text him again.

He leaves me on Read.

Asshole.

I send him one final text.

> Me: I don't sleep in men's beds who leave me on Read.

If you can't text back, then I forget how to open my legs.

It's the rule of law.

One problem with my *I don't sleep in men's beds* warning: I'm too comfortable to get up and stomp to the guest room.

I'm cozy and warm, and while the guest bed is comfy, Julian's is heavenly.

Soft, smells of him, and I don't know where he got these sheets, but I want them in every color.

"Just one more second," I whisper to myself. "Then, I'll get up."

That second turns into two.

Then three.

When it hits four, I'm snoring.

THE CLICK of the bedroom door wakes me.

A hint of sunlight peeks through the blinds. I blink, watching Julian shut the door behind him.

Since the jerk couldn't text back, I shut my eyes, pretending to sleep.

Swear to God, I hear him chuckle on his walk to the bathroom. He at least has the decency to shut the door before switching on the light. I huff, roll onto my side, and face away from the bathroom.

As I yawn, I hear the shower start. Reaching for my phone, I check the time.

Five a.m.

A bright light suddenly cuts across the room, and the shower gets louder. I scream when I'm dragged out of bed, across the room, and shoved into the shower.

21

Genesis

"WHAT THE HELL?" I scream as freezing water pours down my skin.

The bastard could've at least waited for the water to warm up first.

Julian stands outside the shower, wearing only black boxer briefs. The glass door is open, and his large frame blocks me from leaving. A large bruise is on his left pec, and I notice a smear of blood along his neck.

I glare at him, my teeth chattering. "Let me out."

He slowly shakes his head, his gaze silently roaming down my body. My black nightie is soaked to my body like a second skin. He halts, his stare intense when it reaches the base of my thighs, where my short nightie ends.

Uncaring I'm freezing my ass off, he takes his sweet little time raising his gaze. It doesn't move far, stopping at my breasts. His face burns as my nipples pucker beneath the black lace, and I cross my arms.

When he reaches forward, I stumble back a step, my back hitting the chilly tiled wall. It was an overreaction. All he does is turn another handle, and water cascades from two more showerheads.

I watch him, captivated, when he drops his briefs. A *very impressive* hard cock springs free. Unlike him, I attempt not to make it obvious I'm staring, but I'm doing a crappy job at it. He steps inside the shower as the water warms, shutting the door behind him.

The shower has enough room to fit four people comfortably, but with him, it feels claustrophobic.

I can't stop myself from taking another peek at his cock.

Tonight's my first time seeing him naked.

I've thought about it plenty of times.

Touched myself to those thoughts aplenty.

Facing me sideways, he collects a handful of water and splashes it over his face, not muttering a word to me. He does it again to his neck, washing away the blood.

I inch forward to get better beneath the water.

"I don't take well to threats," he says sharply, turning to face me.

"What?" I ask, water sprinkling my face.

He steps closer, coming toe to toe with me. "Your little text. I don't reward those who like to play games." Lowering his head, he gets closer to my face. "I *punish* them."

Are you kidding?

The big, bad Mafia man is upset about a text?

He literally slaughters people for looking at him the wrong way.

I lift my chin in defiance. "Maybe if you'd sent a *little text back*, I wouldn't have threatened to leave your bed." I roll my eyes. "And seriously, my threat was the lamest of all threats."

I attempt to step back, but he circles his arm around my waist, stopping me.

"Shall we compare my threats to yours?" I go on as he digs his fingers through my nightie. It's a warning, another *threat*, but

I can't stop my big mouth from blabbering. "You've threatened to hand me over to Dima countless times, and if anyone should be mad, *it's me*, especially after *this*." I motion toward my wet body and then the shower.

Narrowing his eyes, he watches me coolly as water splashes off his jaw, hitting me in the face.

And because I'm not the best decision maker when I'm tired, I continue running my mouth. "I should've stayed at the Marchettis'. Luca would've at least warmed the water for me first."

His icy stare immediately grows hot.

His strong jaw tics.

The shower and he suddenly feel scorching.

I gasp when he shoves me backward, my back colliding with the shower wall. He stalks a step forward, and I lose a breath when his rough hand wraps around my neck.

He smirks, as if he loves that he stole that breath.

I stare straight into his eyes, refusing him the satisfaction of seeing my fear as he keeps me trapped against the wall.

Keeping his hand around my neck, he collects water in his other one, similar to how he did earlier, and tosses it in my face. Water lands in my mouth, and he clasps his hand over my lips, stopping me from spitting it out.

He squeezes my neck tighter, preventing me from swallowing the water, and I choke.

Lowering his head, he smooths his nose along my jawline as I fight for breaths. My eyes feel too heavy, and I swear I'm close to passing out.

I heave forward, spitting the water out and gasping for breaths when he finally moves his hand from my mouth. He doesn't give me time to recover before his lips are on mine, and I wince in pain when he bites my lip with his canine.

"You ever speak another man's name when you're naked with me, there will be severe consequences." He bites into it so rough that I know it's drawing blood. "I swear to you, Genesis, that isn't a fucking *threat*." He shoves more water down my throat, doing the same thing again. "And when I'm done with your punishment, I'll hold a gun to your head and make you drown that motherfucker."

I anchor my hand around his wrist, attempting to pull his hand away from my neck, but I'm not strong enough.

He grins in satisfaction, loving that he's outpowering me, but loosens it an inch.

Most likely so he doesn't kill me.

My eyes water, and my limbs shake.

"Do I make myself clear?" he hisses.

"Yes," I attempt to squeak out, and some of the water spews from my lips.

"That's my good girl."

He steps back, his hand falling from my neck, and I hunch forward, gasping for air. But he doesn't stay away for long, only long enough to make sure I don't choke to death in his shower.

My mind speeds as he jerks my legs open, stepping between them.

His wet body is against mine.

When his gaze finds mine again, he stares at me wildly.

This is so fucking hot.

I'm so insane for thinking that too.

I've never wanted sex like this.

Deranged, mental, desperate sex.

He lowers his hand between my legs, his lips finding my ear. "Is this why you wanted me to come home?"

I moan.

He savagely thrusts a thick finger inside me.

"You ruined the mood," I lie. "Get out, and I'm going to the guest room."

A threatening chuckle leaves him. "No, I'm staying *right here*. You asked me to come home and fell asleep in my bed.

This is what you wanted." He shoves two more fingers inside me, hooking my leg around his waist. "I came home to fuck you against this wall and fill you with my cum."

His eyes are crazed.

His lips pursed together.

I want to kiss him, but I'm scared.

Am I allowed to do that?

He's not gentle as he finger fucks me.

I'd never expect tenderness from a man like him.

It's rough and fast, and my body slams against the wall.

The shower feels like it's heated to a million degrees.

Steam surrounds us, coating the glass.

"I want to feel you," I moan. "*All* of you."

"Take off your fucking nightie," he demands.

He inches back, his gaze intense as I pull the wet fabric off my body. As soon as it drops to our feet, his mouth finds my neck, his thumb massaging my clit.

I shut my eyes, losing the energy to keep them open when he sucks on my nipple. Pleasure overcomes me, and my orgasm radiates through my entire body. He digs his fingers into my thigh, keeping me in place as my limbs loosen. If he wasn't holding me up, I'd fall like a noodle on the floor.

He squats, shoving his thick cock inside me with no warning.

It fills my pussy perfectly.

My body becomes alive again as he wraps my legs around his waist, holding me in place.

Now that I've felt his cock, I'll never just want his fingers again.

I'm not afraid of this man because he's a brutal killer.

I'm afraid of him because I know if I let myself get too close, he'll break my heart. He'll break all of me, whether he realizes it or not.

Men like him don't have enough good heart to give away.

Theirs are black, and bruised, and damaged.

Who wants a damaged heart?

That doesn't entail a happily ever after.

All thoughts of how he'll destroy me leave me with his first thrust.

Sooo good.

Years in the making.

Time stands still yet flies by at the same time.

I want to remember every moment, but my mind can't keep up as he roughly fucks me against the wall.

It's hot, and wet, and wild.

He bites my lip again, then my neck. "You're so fucking tight, Gen, baby." His teeth move to my ear, biting into the cartilage, as if causing pain is always necessary for him.

I decide to return the favor and run my sharp nails down his back.

He doesn't even wince. "Harder," he whisper-hisses. "If you want to cause me pain, you'd better fucking do it harder."

His hips slap against mine so hard that I'm surprised my hip bone doesn't break.

I moan, sinking my nails into his skin, using them as an anchor to hold him as he fucks me senseless.

"Yessss," I moan. "Oh my God, don't stop, don't stop, don't you dare fucking stop."

For the first time ever, he listens.

He doesn't stop, only fucks me harder.

His strokes quicken, and seconds later, I'm falling apart again.

I cry out his name as he continues to fuck me.

With each stroke, he grunts.

"This pussy is mine and only mine," he sneers as I try to catch my breath. "Say it."

"Only yours," I moan, wanting it to be true.

Two more strokes, and his body stills.

He throws his head back, his arms shaking, and when he

raises it, his eyes are heavy and half shut. It's the most relaxed I've ever seen him.

It doesn't last long though.

He jerks his hips forward one last time. "Don't you fucking lose a drop of that cum."

"Aye aye, captain," I reply with a shaky breath because words are apparently hard for me to come up with at the moment.

My response doesn't make him laugh.

He's actually completely emotionless to it.

"Don't ignore my texts again," I finally say. "And you need to come home earlier."

He draws back a few inches, his eyes wicked. "If I get to come home to this every night, that won't be a problem."

22

Julian

I'M NOT EASILY DISTRACTED.

When I was seventeen, Vincent Lombardi told my father he'd never seen a more focused man at my age. I don't believe in mindless distractions or casual conversation.

Everything I say and do has a purpose.

I'm a workaholic with no personal life.

Genesis is fucking with that.

My focus has been shit all day. I've reread this report ten times, and I still don't know what it says.

She's consumed my every thought.

Her in the shower, wearing only a nightie.

Her naked body.

Thrusting inside her tight pussy.

The taste of her lips—a flavor I'll never forget.

Genesis promised to stay home today and behave herself. But knowing her, I could lock her away and throw away the key, and she'd find a way to cause trouble. I left my credit card on the nightstand, hoping that'd keep her busy.

After our shower this morning, she curled up in my bed and fell asleep. I returned to the casino without getting any sleep.

My bed is now her bed because, damn it, no fucking way can I sleep, knowing she's in the same house yet sleeping in the guest room.

I haven't heard from her, but the constant credit card alerts on my phone tell me she's awake. I don't know what she's buying, nor do I have the time to give a shit.

My father taught me early on to always spoil your woman. They shoulder our life's burdens. Mob wives deserve medals, rainbows, and hell, their own islands for what they do, yet they receive very little credit. My mother was a saint and earned the same respect from my father.

I toss my pen onto the desk and push my paperwork aside when my phone rings.

"Julian," Caesar says when I answer, "it appears one of your accounts was hit by fraud. This morning, there's been a string of charges from bulk food and bedding companies, like Costco and Pottery Barn, and toy stores."

"No fraud," I say.

"Are you opening a homeless shelter?"

"No, it appears I'm just financing one. All charges on that card are approved."

23

Genesis

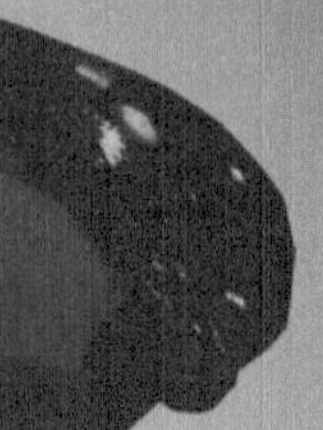

AFTER THE FEW days of hell I'd had, I woke up this morning to something to smile about.

Fresh pink peonies in a pink vase were on the nightstand.

A note written in Julian's handwriting was beside them, making my heart fuzzy.

> YOU'RE USED TO PEONIES BEING DELIVERED DAILY.
> HERE'S MY CREDIT CARD. BUY YOURSELF SOMETHING NICE.
> BE GOOD.

Julian said to never expect romance from him, but flowers sound pretty romantic to me.

I've spent the day carrying the peonies around with me everywhere.

In the bathroom when I showered.

In the closet when I got dressed.

And now, they're next to me as I sit at the island, shopping on my MacBook.

I'm not shopping for myself.

The shelter needs supplies, and usually, I spend a few thousand dollars a month buying them. Just because I'm broke now doesn't mean those necessities disappear.

A smart person would probably use the credit card to buy a plane ticket or flee the country. But I refuse to spend my life running, and I signed a contract. My father might've ruined our family name, but I'm still an Astor who keeps her word.

I'm also almost positive Dima would hunt me down.

That man seems adamant I'll be his wife.

So, uterus, buckle up and start doing your thing, please.

Dima surely won't want a wife knocked up by another man.

When I finish shopping, I open a new browser tab to a grocery delivery service, place an order, and then text Julian.

> Me: Come home tonight. I have a surprise for you.

Julian made a big mistake.

He proved to me that he *could* be romantic.

I'm going to make him realize it.

Show him his heart isn't as black and wicked as he thinks.

Maybe, just maybe, I can get this murderous Mafia man to fall in love with me.

Wish me luck.

24

Julian

I had no intention of going home today.

I'm behind on work and have two meetings scheduled.

But after Genesis's text?

Fuck work and fuck those meetings.

I scrub a hand over my face.

Her text should make me *not* want to go home.

It should make me want to sit behind my desk all night long.

Surprises aren't good.

I'd rather have someone shoot me in the damn foot than have a surprise.

But here I am, driving home, for Genesis's *surprise*.

Driving over the damn speed limit at that.

I texted Emilio when I left the casino and told him he could leave. Genesis should be able to stay out of trouble for at least a few hours before I get there. I also don't want him to know what this *surprise* is before me.

I park in the garage, and before I step out of the Escalade, my phone rings.

Franko's name flashes across my screen.

"Yeah," I say, answering the call.

"We caught another one of Yaroslav's men in the casino," he tells me. "I have him tied up in the back room. What do you want me to do with him?"

Shit.

Terrible timing.

I can either leave and deal with the fucking Russian, disappointing Genesis, or handle it later. I take a second, weighing my options.

I don't even make it to second two before my decision is made.

I'll go in and see what Genesis's surprise is. If it's something ridiculous—like bringing the entire shelter to my home—I'll leave and deal with the Russian.

This is unlike me.

I've always been a *business first* man.

"Keep him there. I'll call you in an hour and tell you what to do," I say into the phone before ending the call.

As I walk inside, I have a strange urge to say, *Honey, I'm home.*

It's what my father would announce every evening when he came home to my mother. It was a ritual with them. Whether he'd had a good day or walked in, beaten and bruised, he always said it.

Always kissed her on the cheek and said he loved her.

Always said dinner smelled good.

But I'm not my father.

I'm not a husband.

I'm not a family man, and I don't want Genesis to view me as one.

She doesn't need that attachment to me.

My father loved my mother, and her, him, but he put her in dangerous situations.

She handled them well, but ultimately, they killed her.

I shut my mouth, holding myself back from saying those three words. As soon as I step inside, the aroma of garlic and olive oil drifts up my nostrils. My mouth waters, and I sniff the air.

Genesis is in the kitchen, parked in front of the stove, stirring something inside a pot. She's dressed in black pants that look like they belong to a businessman about to make a deal and a tight, almost-spandex-looking tank.

I sniff again, picking up the smell of fresh tomatoes. An open bottle of red wine is on the counter with two glasses beside it. One of them is half full and the other is empty.

She looks over at me with a friendly smile, holding up the spoon half covered with tomato sauce. "Oh, hey." A hint of shyness is in her voice. "I wasn't sure if you'd come home or not …" She pauses, chewing on her bottom lip, and her shoulders droop. "Seriously, is it so hard to text back? Or, hell, you don't even have to physically text. Just tell Siri to confirm you'll be home for dinner."

I unbuckle my suit jacket, strolling deeper into the kitchen. "What if I say *my* surprise to you was showing up to see yours?"

"Nope." She waves the spoon in the air, and I'm surprised sauce doesn't fall from it. "I'm able to smell bullshit from a mile away."

I step closer. "And I'm able to smell my mother's spaghetti sauce from a mile away." I sniff again, walking straight to the stove to look in the pot.

She sets the spoon down and backs away from the stove.

Not only does the sauce smell like my mother's recipe, but it also looks like it.

A thickness forms in my throat as I stare down at it, remembering all the time my mother spent in the kitchen, making this very sauce.

Plenty of people asked for the recipe for this sauce, but she was particular about who she shared it with. It's nearly identical with chunks of tomato, mushrooms, carrots, pancetta, and sausage.

Genesis stands a few inches away, awkwardly moving from one foot to the other when my gaze snaps to her.

The sauce was a family favorite, but since it took four hours to make, my mother would only make it on Sundays.

Millions of memories rush through my mind.

Good ones.

Bad ones.

Sad ones.

I'm reminded that I'll never share a meal with my family again.

There was a point when I accepted I'd never have my mother's sauce again since I didn't know anyone alive who knew how to make it. I thought her recipes had gone to the grave with her.

Damien and I aren't the cooking type.

"How did you …" I ask, staring at her, stunned. My words trail off, like I'm unable to finish the question.

Her cheeks redden. "Your mother taught Melissa and me. It's my first time making it by myself, so I can't promise it'll taste as good as hers since she was a sauce genius, but I tried my best." Her tone is a fusion of hope and worry.

Hope that I'll love it.

Worry that I'll hate it.

What do I feel?

How do I react to this?

Other than my mother and sister, I've never had someone do something like this for me. It's fucking weird.

But there's also this warmth that spreads through my chest.

A feeling I've never experienced.

What is Genesis doing to me?

First, she has me saving her ass, then coming home because she misses me, and now *this*?

She didn't do this for me out of calculation.

Unlike me, Genesis doesn't do favors because she wants something back for them.

She did this for me because she cares.

"Julian," she breathes out, breaking me from my thoughts.

I clear my throat. "It smells delicious, and I'm sure it tastes just as amazing."

She inches closer, picks up the spoon, drags it through the sauce, and scoops some into it.

"Taste test it for me." She holds it out for me to taste.

I debate doing what she asked.

But with the way she's looking at me, there's no damn way I can deny her. Leaning in, I taste the sauce and can't stop myself from groaning. She leaves the spoon in my mouth for a moment, standing on her tiptoes so the spoon doesn't fall from her hand.

It tastes goddamn amazing.

So similar to my mother's, like she was making it alongside her.

When my mother did teach someone to cook—and she was picky with who she did it with—she always took her time. She'd show them step by step with patience.

"What do you think?" she asks, falling back on her heels as the spoon leaves my mouth.

"Delicious." I lick my lips. "My mother would have been fucking proud."

Genesis beams at the compliment.

Like I told her she was beautiful in a million different ways.

"Oh shit," she says, rushing over to the opposite side of me.

Spaghetti is in another pot, about to boil over. I hurriedly grab the handle and take the pot, moving it to a cool burner, as she turns off the flame.

She's the first to ever cook in this kitchen since I bought the place.

I only have pots and pans because the interior designer insisted on it.

I've never sat down and enjoyed a home-cooked meal here.

Most of my meals are either eaten out or in my office.

"Thank you," she says shyly as I pull away from the stove.

I curl my lips.

It's not a full smile but halfway there.

"I'm going to run upstairs and change," I tell her.

Her lips curl up, matching mine for a moment before turning into a full-on smile.

I jog upstairs to change into gray sweats and a sweatshirt.

As I wash my face, I stare at myself in the mirror. Little by little, I finally release the smile that started building in the kitchen.

But then I suddenly drop it.

This dark heart of mine isn't supposed to warm like this.

I can't fall in love with Genesis.

I'm not capable of being a good partner.

I'm selfish.

Business is always my main priority.

I disappear for days sometimes.

I'd also be putting Genesis more in harm's way.

Enemies don't give a shit about wives when their husbands hate them.

But when husbands love their wives?

They become the biggest target.

There's no way to ruin a man like taking the woman he loves.

Right now, she's on Dima's radar, but I'm hoping that'll change once I pay off Yaroslav. Then, I need to make it a point to Antonio that she deserves the same protection as the other women.

Genesis is sacrificing a life of love for me.

The least I can do is make sure she's always protected.

I feel my stomach growl, already thinking about the pasta.

I never imagined I'd get a surprise like this.

Morning peonies aren't enough in return for something this sweet.

She deserves more.

Genesis is fucking with my head, and I'm nervous she'll find a way to do the same with this cold heart of mine.

25

Genesis

I was so nervous for Julian to try the sauce.

It was more than just tasting a simple spaghetti sauce.

It was a memory.

A memory that could have gone one of two ways—he'd enjoy it or hate it.

I had to stop myself from jumping up and down and doing a damn cartwheel when he said his mother would have been proud.

He wasn't lying either.

Julian might not have realized it, but I saw the pleasure on his face.

His eyes shut, his shoulders relaxing, as he tasted the sauce.

Earlier, I'd ordered groceries, and as soon as they were delivered, I started making the sauce. It was done for thirty minutes, and I kept the flame on low with high hopes that he'd come home.

If he didn't, I doubted I'd cook for him again.

Cooking is a labor of love.

The oven beeps, the heat temperature met, and I slide the

garlic bread onto a shelf. Then, I grab the pot of spaghetti and drain it.

Making tonight's dinner was fun.

It took my mind away from my problems.

Marta said it did the same with her.

Man, how I miss her and Melissa.

I swipe away a tear from my cheek at the same time I hear Julian returning downstairs, now dressed in gray sweats and a NY Yankees sweatshirt. He's hot as hell in suits but seeing him casual is just as attractive. It also makes him seem more approachable.

"Oh, and thank you for the flowers," I say, motioning toward the vase on the island. "How'd you know I love peonies and am used to getting them every day?"

He grabs the bottle of wine, tops off my glass, and fills the other. "I know everything." Taking the glass with him, he settles on a stool.

I roll my eyes. "Okay, *why'd* you get me peonies?"

"You've had so much taken away from you suddenly. Your normal life gone. I hoped something as simple as your favorite flower would make you feel like your life could become a little bit more normal again."

Oh my God.

Speaking of normal ... who is this man?

This isn't my normal Julian.

The one I've known for nearly a decade.

If sauce makes him this nice, I'll keep the stuff in stock.

Can it up and fill the cabinets with it.

"Dinner is almost finished," I tell him.

He looks around, scanning our surroundings, and his gaze stops on the dining room table. It's already set, and four candles are lit in the center.

I hate that his eyes narrow in on it.

Like the candles did something to personally piss him off.

His attention slips back to me, the friendliness in them from earlier dimming. "Are we playing house?"

I glare at him, grab the tongs, and open and close them in front of him. "Don't ruin this night."

He rears back, cocking his head to the side, and pushes the tongs away from his face. "Just asking a question, Gen."

"What would you do if I said yes?"

He rests his elbow on the counter and runs his thumb over his strong chin. "Then, I'll repeat what I told you last night. If I get this every night, coming home won't be a problem."

My cheeks burn as I not only remember his words from last night but also what happened. It takes everything in me not to beg him to say those words again.

Some might not consider them romantic, but they're like a love song in my ears.

Cherished words I want to remember forever.

Julian might not realize it, but his response doesn't come out as cold or indifferent as he thinks it does.

It's brimmed with emotion and evidence that even though he's fighting it, this is more than just an arrangement for him too.

He can try to deny it all he wants, but he was waiting for a moment to claim me without having to admit his feelings. He wanted me before he learned about what my father did and the plan for me to marry Dima.

Julian was waiting for an excuse to make me his.

"When did you get more butterflies?" he asks out of nowhere. "From what I remember, you only had one."

I hold up my arm, displaying the three purple butterfly tattoos along my right forearm.

"How'd you know I only had one?" I ask, a self-satisfied smile on my face. "Did you secretly check me out all those years you pretended I didn't exist?"

He stares at me, stone-faced, not as entertained by my joke. "What do the butterflies stand for?"

"They're for people I've loved and lost." I point at a butterfly. "This first one is for my nanny."

He raises a brow. "The one who taught you how to illegally count cards?"

"Hey," I say with full offense. "I never did it illegally until the night at Lucky Kings with you."

"Smart. You can get in a lot of trouble for that."

I know this, which is *why* I never did it before. Sonya's nephew died as a result of card counting. Though he did it with an illegal gambling ring with the Chicago Mafia, which was just asking for trouble.

"We only did it for fun … when I couldn't sleep," I explain. "After her death, I got my first butterfly *for her*. She was obsessed with butterflies and would always take me to butterfly gardens. I gained a love for them too. We always said, one day, we'd have a beautiful butterfly garden."

"Did you get one?"

I shake my head. "I asked my mom, and she said no. According to her, she doesn't like *bugs*." I roll my eyes.

His full attention is on me. "If you had a garden, what butterflies would you put in there?"

"*All* of them."

"Do you have a favorite?"

"Monarchs." I sigh, a hint of sadness hitting me. "But sadly, their population is in decline." I scrunch up my face. "I wish I could save them."

"You'd save the entire planet if you could, it seems." He takes a drink of wine.

"Yeah, well, minus the bad guys, obvi."

He raises a brow, showing he's clearly a *bad guy*.

"Not *you*," I quickly correct. "I'm talking Jeffrey Dahmer, King Joffrey bad guys. You're just morally gray." I spin on my heel, turning to the stove to stir the sauce.

"Morally gray?" he asks my back.

I turn on my heel to face him again. "Men who aren't clearly bad or evil. Complex men who make you question whether their motives are pure or not."

He licks his lips, rearing back in amusement. "Do *you* think my motives are pure?"

"Undecided, hence, the *morally gray*."

"You let me know when you decide then."

The oven timer beeping interrupts our conversation. Julian stands, circling the island and grabbing the potholder on his way to the stove. He bumps his hip against mine—more playful than I've ever seen him in my life—and beats me to opening the oven.

"You ready for our first dinner date?" I ask as he draws out the bread and sets it on the counter.

"This isn't a dinner date," he states matter-of-factly, closing the oven door.

I rest my hands on my waist. "This is *so* a dinner date. Admit it, or no pasta for you."

26

Julian

My father used to say that the way to a man's heart was through his stomach.

I always told him he was full of shit.

There was no way to my heart.

No meal. No woman. No fucking gestures that could reach it.

My heart? There's no route to it.

Hell, it hardly exists.

It's tortured and decayed.

Just like my soul.

Yet right now, as Genesis waits for me to give in, I think of him.

His sayings and advice.

Then, I think of my mother.

The time and love she put into cooking for us.

Genesis put that same time and care into making dinner, just for me.

It's more than just a simple dinner.

I blow out a raspy breath. "Get your ass to the table for our dinner date."

There.

I said it.

I caved.

A smile beams on her face.

I glare at her in return.

I'm supposed to be the master manipulator.

The one in charge.

Not this butterfly-loving woman who wants to save the world.

She isn't supposed to be bringing me to my knees like this.

Genesis pours the sauce over the spaghetti and scoops it into a serving bowl, and my cock jerks as I watch her move around the kitchen like she owns it.

Like it's hers and she's here to stay.

I follow her with the bread to the dining room. Just like cooking in the kitchen, I've never eaten a meal in here. The dinner table seats eight, like it belongs in a home where home-cooked meals are served regularly.

The walls are an earthy green—a must that I gave the interior designer. It was my mother's favorite color. Tall windows line one wall, and rain pings against them as a roll of thunder echoes around us.

As Genesis situates everything, I return to the kitchen for the wine bottle and glasses. Realizing the bottle is only half full, I snag another from the wine fridge and uncork it.

When I return, Genesis dims the lights and sits. She's created this intimate, romantic ambience that's melting all the unhappiness of the day off me.

I take the chair beside her at the head of the table. My focus stays on her as she makes herself comfortable, and the candles flicker between us.

She's so damn breathtaking.

I'm not speaking just physically beautiful either.

Her beauty radiates from the inside out. I've never witnessed such a compassionate heart.

Here she is, having dinner with a man who's the complete opposite.

Granted, she didn't have much choice, but she hasn't tried to run once.

In fact, she's done nothing but try to get closer through the years we've known each other. I don't know if the good person in her thinks she can rub that humanity off on me, but she's wrong. She could cut out half her heart and hand it to me, and it still wouldn't be enough to fill the void in my chest.

I'm ruined.

I've been that way since childhood, when my future was decided for me.

I tip my head forward, motioning for her to serve herself. She fills her plate with spaghetti and grabs a slice of bread as I fill our glasses.

"Thank you," I say as she grabs my plate and does the same. "No one has ever done something like this for me."

Not that I've given anyone the chance to.

She's the first woman I've ever let step foot into my home.

"You're welcome." She smiles, wrapping a noodle around her fork. "No one has ever paid a million dollars for me before. It's kind of hard to pay someone back for that, but food is a nice start."

I take a bite, moaning as I swallow it down, and point at my plate. "This right here makes up for that and more."

The small taste test I did earlier didn't do the sauce justice.

It has the perfect ratio of tomatoes, garlic, and seasoning with a touch of sweetness. My mother always added a dash of sugar to everything.

She grins, just like she did in the kitchen when I broke down and declared this a dinner date.

This is a reminder of home, of my family, of what I've lost.

But I'm not sad about it this time.

The nostalgia is nice.

"What did you do today?" she asks me, biting into her bread.

"Worked at the casino." I take another bite.

"What all did you do there?"

This woman loves to ask questions.

Again, it reminds me so much of my family dinners.

My mother would ask my father similar questions, and he'd usually tell her some bullshit story because he'd never break down the gruesome details of how we really spent our time.

"I had a few business meetings," I state, my voice serious. "We discussed retraining our dealers on spotting card counters."

I give her a stern look, and she throws her head back, laughing.

"I'm sure *no one* would dare have the balls to do that in a Lucky Kings Casino," she says around giggles.

"No one in their right mind," I correct, waggling my fork at her. "It seems I've found the one who would dare."

She gasps, feigning offense. "You can't blame a girl for trying to win some cash."

"Point made." I lean back in my chair and take a swig of my wine. "I'd ask what you did today, but it seems I already know. Cooking and spending money."

She wipes sauce off the side of her lip. "The shelter needed supplies."

"What if I said I'll double my monthly donation if you agree to stay home instead of volunteering?"

She violently shakes her head. "The shelter is my place." She mirrors my posture in her chair, grabbing her glass and taking a sip. "Earlier, you said I'd save the entire planet if I could. I know that's not possible, but I can and *have* helped change lives at the shelter. It means a lot to me."

The softness in her tone and face has me giving up my power.

I'll let her have this—*for now.*

I point my glass at her. "When you get pregnant, we're revisiting this conversation."

"*If* I get pregnant," she corrects, sighing.

I have to stop myself from grinding my teeth, showing her it'd devastate me if it didn't happen. "You will get pregnant."

She wrinkles her nose, pressing her lips to the rim of her glass and looking at me over it. "How can you be so certain?"

I set down my glass and shift in my chair to collect her face in my hands. Her lower lip trembles, and she nearly drops her glass as she slides it on the table.

Smoothing my thumb over her warm cheek, I dip my head, our lips only inches apart. "Gen, baby, when a man sees the most beautiful woman on this earth—one who brings him to his knees, even if he fights it—he'll want to fuck her every second of the day. Add in that woman having the biggest heart he's ever seen, he'll do anything to make that woman the mother of his child."

27

Genesis

 "My mother must've really loved you," Julian says. "She was greedy with her cannoli recipe."

Dinner went better than I'd hoped.

Hell, I wasn't even sure he'd come home.

After we finished eating, I told him to keep his butt in the chair and dashed to the kitchen. Earlier, when the sauce was on the stove, I made his mother's cannoli. I had to call three markets and have a special delivery to get the same hazelnuts and mini dark chocolate chips she used. Tonight, I wanted to remind Julian of all the things he loved.

I have the cannoli recipe memorized. I make them every Christmas for gifts and mail them to large shelter donors. People have told me they look forward to receiving them every year.

So far, the night has gone perfectly.

We're on our second bottle of wine, and conversation has felt normal.

Well, normal for what you get with Julian.

He's speaking more than six words in an hour, period, so that's progress.

When he said he saw me as the most beautiful woman on this

earth, I wanted to throw everything off the table, climb over it, and straddle him. I'd never heard him say anything so nice to *anyone*.

My reserved Julian broke out of his dark cocoon tonight for me.

Day by day, he's unraveling his layers, letting me see more of who he really is deep down.

His compliment about his mother loving me adds to my joy of the night.

He helps me clear the table after dessert. I'm shocked at how much he's helping me. I always had dinner at his parents' home, and the men never helped the women clean up. He stands beside me at the counter, handing me dishes as I load them into the dishwasher.

Everything feels so domesticated.

So, unlike everything he swore he'd never give me.

As I arch forward to shut the dishwasher, I feel a sharp sting on my ass. I whip around to find Julian standing a few inches away, twirling the dish towel in his hand.

"You jerk!" I yelp, hopping back and covering my ass with my hands. "That hurt!"

He twirls the towel in his hand again, a devious smirk on his face. "Oh, come on. That was a love tap."

Just like his behavior tonight, I'm getting such a different man from Julian Bellini, murderous, high-ranking man in the Mafia.

No suit, only casual sweats.

No serial killer demeanor, instead playful.

I love this side of him, and if he keeps it up, I'll keep wanting more.

I match his amusement. "A love tap, huh?" Opening the small drawer beside the sink, I snatch another dish towel. "How about I return the love tap then?"

He drops back a step, walking backward, but doesn't stop

spinning the towel. I wildly whip my towel in the air, stepping closer, as if preparing to spar with someone. Though if this were a real spar, the audience would for sure be laughing at my theatrics.

Julian laughs.

The first one I've ever heard from him.

It's the sexiest laugh in the world, swear to God.

A husky laugh, coming straight from his stomach, though a bit hoarse, like it was lying dormant there for years.

He stretches out his arm, catching me off guard, and easily snatches my towel from me.

Well, shit.

My shoulders slump, and I pout.

He tosses both towels over his shoulder, and they land on the floor. "As much as I love spanking, I'd much rather do it when we're naked."

It takes him one step to reach me. His movement is so fast that I yelp again when he throws me over his shoulder, keeping his hold on my ass so I don't fall.

"How about we try to make a baby, huh?" he says, darting up the stairs, and my body bounces against his with each step he takes.

My heart beats wildly as I anticipate what's to come.

Time to fuck this man so well that he doesn't only give me his orgasm.

He gives me his everything.

And I'm not stopping until it happens.

What do I have to lose anyway?

28

Julian

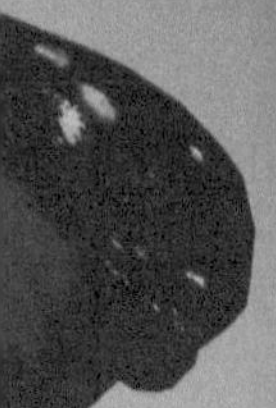

I DROP Genesis to her feet when we reach the bedroom and flip on the light.

Tonight, it won't be a quickie in the shower or after I've dealt with a night of chaos.

It's after one of the best nights of my life in years.

All that's on my mind is her and everything she did for me tonight.

Her calling it a surprise was an understatement.

It was more than just dinner and dessert.

Her plump red lips arch into an angelic smile as she stares at me, awaiting my next move.

The room is quiet. The only sounds I hear are her heavy breathing. I unzip my sweatshirt, push it off my arms, and stroll across the room to drape it over the arm of the chair in the corner.

Her eyes stay on me, watching my every move. As I come up behind her, she peers over her shoulder at me. Her body quivers when I unclasp her hair clip.

Her thick hair cascades down her shoulders in waves. Licking my lips, I play with the strap of her tank. Her breathing hitches. It's raspy, half a moan, and my cock twitches in my pants.

The room suddenly feels like it's a million degrees.

Lowering my head, I rain kisses down her bare shoulder and whisper against her skin, "There are so many ways I want to touch you, *to fuck you* tonight, but I can't seem to make up my mind on *how* I should." I suck on her skin. "Let me ask you. How do you want me to fuck you tonight, Genesis?"

She blows out a series of breaths and is nearly out of them when she says, "However you want, Julian."

I draw back a few inches, not expecting that response.

Not expecting her to give me free rein to her body.

That's fucking dangerous, baby.

"Let's start with this." I tug at the hem of her tank. "I want this off."

I help her pull the tank over her head. Our movements are fast but almost seem like they're in slow motion. I want her so bad.

I toss the tank across the room, and it lands on the chair, on top of my sweatshirt.

"And the pants," I whisper-hiss in her ear.

As she unzips them, I move to stand in front of her. I settle all my attention on her as she slides the pants down her legs and steps out of them, kicking them to the side with her bare foot.

My mouth waters so much that I'm shocked I don't choke on my own spit as I stare at her perfect body.

I saw her naked in the shower, but everything was so fast that I didn't get the time to truly appreciate her beauty and take in every inch.

Genesis looks like the sexiest fucking centerfold, dressed in only a strapless red bra and matching lace panties.

I bite my lip as my eyes zero in on the rhinestone heart in the middle of her panties, right over her pussy.

While I've never been in a relationship, I've had fuck buddies.

Women I've called when I was lonely and wanted to fuck.

Only a few though because I'm a picky man who keeps to himself most of the time. I'd meet with them a few nights a week, never staying overnight and never sharing anything personal. All of those are over now.

Some of them didn't even know what I did for a living.

I sure as hell never allowed them into my personal space, like I have with Genesis.

I slowly advance closer, like a predator would their prey.

A patient predator who won't risk losing their kill.

I lick my upper and then lower lip before pressing them against hers.

I've never kissed a woman so damn soft.

Wait, now that I'm thinking about it, I've never kissed a woman on the lips before, period. I've never been a fan of intimacy, and I always saw kissing as that.

She immediately opens her mouth, allowing me to slip my tongue between her lips. Lowering my hand to her panties, I trace the rhinestone heart with my thumb, feeling her knees go weak as her tongue dances with mine.

Biting into her lip, I shove my hand into her panties and swear I hear a moan of relief from her.

I match her moan as I slide my fingers along her slit, feeling how wet her pussy is for me. My heart is on fire as I back her up until her thighs hit the bed. My hand leaves her panties to press against her chest and push her on the bed.

When she attempts to sit up, I grip her ankles and pull her down the bed until her ass is on the edge. I jerk her thighs apart while sliding to my knees.

Tipping my head forward, I press my nose against her pussy over her panties and trace the heart with my tongue.

She's quiet, panting above me while keeping her eyes on me, not blinking once.

"Your pussy smells amazing," I groan, nudging the panties to the side with my nose and smelling it bare.

"Please," she whimpers before repeating the word, only more pleading this time.

"You want more, baby?" I ask, my gaze sharpening on her as I drag my hands up her soft thighs.

"Yes," she begs. "More. Everything. I want it *all*, Julian."

She says my name in a pant.

The sexiest sound in the motherfucking world.

Leaning back, I pull her panties down her legs, balling them in my fist before holding them out in front of me. I stare at them, almost in a daze, and run my finger over the heart again.

Is she reminding me that we all have one?

Or that I can have hers?

Fuck. I shouldn't be thinking about this like I am.

All that should be on my mind is fucking this incredible woman, legs spread out, pussy right in front of my face for me to feast on.

God, she fucks with my brain, causing me to overthink shit.

I shove the panties into my pocket and slide closer, my knees rubbing against the rug, and make myself comfortable. I grin as I make one quick lick up her pussy slit.

Her body comes alive, nearly pushing off the bed.

Yes, give me that reaction, baby.

"Show me how much you love me pleasuring your body, Gen, baby," I tell her. "I want to hear every emotion and feeling inside you as I eat this sweet pussy." I thrust a finger inside her. "Do you hear me?"

"Yes," she moans as I slip my finger in and out of her.

I do it slowly.

Torturously as she wriggles on the bed.

"More," she demands. "That's my emotion … fucking more,

Julian." She's panting so hard that it takes her five times longer than normal to finish her statement.

Leaning forward, I brush my tongue over her clit, sucking gently before dragging it down her slit.

I groan, loving this.

She tastes delicious.

The best meal ever.

She's the dream woman I never thought I'd have.

Like I told her before, if I get to come home every night to what she's been giving me, I'll hardly ever want to leave the house. She'll never have to worry about her man not coming home at night because I'll be addicted to everything about her.

I shake away those thoughts, telling myself it's my dick that's so transfixed with everything that's Genesis.

Nothing more than physical.

Just lust with her.

Her body starts shaking as I thrust three fingers inside her.

I finger her, taste her, and play with her clit, all in different rhythms.

Whenever I see she's close, I stop and switch them up.

I want to play mind games with her, want to play with her body like an instrument I want to master.

The moans and sounds she makes are sexy as fuck.

She writhes against the bed. One of her hands grips the blanket beneath her, and the other lowers to my head, pulling at my hair so tight that I'm worried I'll be bald by the time she orgasms.

She extends her legs and rests them on my shoulders, giving me a better angle to pleasure her sweet pussy.

"I'm close," she cries out. "For the love of God, do not stop!"

The heels of her feet dig into my back, putting so much pressure on my body that I'm surprised she's not cracking my spine. I add another finger, upping my pace, and suck on her clit.

Seconds later, she moans my name as her entire body shakes.

Her legs fall limp, and she gasps for breaths. I give her a moment, pressing kisses up her thighs, to come down from her high. As I stare up at her, watching as pleasure crosses her face, I wish I could take a picture and keep it as my screen saver.

"Climb up the bed, Gen," I say as she comes down. "Let me own you."

I won't ask her for anything in return.

She doesn't need to suck my cock or jerk me off.

Tasting her pussy was enough foreplay for me.

Now, my cock wants inside her.

She does as I said, climbing up the bed, and situates herself so she's lying naturally, as if ready for bed. I push my pants and briefs down, my cock springing forward.

It's hard as a fucking rock, throbbing for her.

The bed shifts, and she lifts herself as I join her in bed. As if on instinct, as if she's thought about this before, she opens her legs, giving me room to kneel between her toned thighs.

I stroke my cock, staring straight into her deep eyes, and play with her clit. "Tell me you want me."

"I want you, Julian," she says, sounding almost desperate. "*All* of you."

With one thrust, I'm completely inside her.

I throw my head back in complete delight.

At the top of the world.

No revenge, no kill, no amount of money is better than this.

I'm not patient enough to give her time to adjust to my size.

She whimpers as I pull out and immediately push back inside her. Her hand shoots out to the headboard, stopping her head from hitting it.

I've never fucked a woman bare like I do with her.

Never felt a pussy feel so damn good.

I fuck her hard.

Soft.

Then hard.

I lose my breath.

Lose my mind.

As I fill her up over and over again.

I'm in heaven, and I want this to last forever.

I moan her name like it's the only word that I want to leave my mouth again.

Genesis lifts herself, clinging to me, and sinks her nails into my skin like she wants to anchor herself to my body for the rest of our lives.

I slow my pace, grabbing each of her wrists and slamming them down on the mattress to each side of her head. I lower my waist, thrusting inside her deep, and interlace our fingers.

She moans my name, raising her hips to meet my thrusts, and I up my speed. I'm fucking her so hard that I'm shocked I'm not pushing her through the mattress. Our bodies drip in sweat, like we've been in the sauna for hours.

I tip my head to drag my lips over hers.

"I've never felt anything so amazing," I hiss out, my sweat falling onto her shoulders, mixing with hers.

I kiss her.

It's passionate—so damn passionate.

It's one that makes two people come together.

I fuck Genesis like a man would with a woman he wants to keep forever.

"I'm ..." she moans, breaking our kiss to move her head from side to side, struggling to fight her orgasm so this will last longer.

"Yes, take this cock raw and come all over it," I groan, sucking on her neck and licking her sweat. "Give me all your cum like I'm about to give you all mine."

Not even a second later, she falls apart beneath me.

I grip the flare of her hips, throw her legs back over my shoulders, and pound into her hard.

I lose any rhythm I had, getting lost in her pussy.

In everything she is.

Her entire waist is off the bed as I hold it up and fuck her ruthlessly.

No more giving it to her slow.

My cock grows harder, pulsing inside her soft pussy. I can feel my pulse in my spine as I give her three final strokes, and pleasure shoots through my entire body.

I tightly grip her hips, holding her in place, and come inside her so hard, hoping this is the night I put a baby inside her.

I COLLAPSE ON MY BACK, and Genesis and I lie there, catching our breaths.

Draping my arm over my face, I try to calm myself, to come down from the best sex I've ever had in my life.

It was so fucking vanilla too.

Missionary, on a bed, with—dare I say it—an emotional connection?

Oh, fuck me.

Our breathing creates the perfect melody, and neither of us says a word.

Minutes pass until she turns on her side, holding herself up on her elbow, and she smiles down at me. Her face is red and sweaty, and her red lipstick is smeared across her face. Black remnants of mascara are on her cheeks.

I like knowing I messed up her makeup.

That I was the only one able to do something like that.

Her eyes are tired and dreamy, and I can tell I fucked nearly all the energy out of her.

Even with all that, she's so damn beautiful.

This might sound bad, but deep down, I'm almost happy her parents fucked her over. If they hadn't, she wouldn't be in my bed right now.

I needed that push that told me if I didn't act then, I'd lose her forever.

My gaze shifts from her face to where she's holding herself up. I blink, zeroing in on the butterfly tattoos, trying to get the best view of them I can.

When that isn't enough, I snatch her wrist and pull it closer. She topples forward, resting her other hand on my chest so she doesn't fall. I can't stop myself from planting a kiss on the butterflies.

Each one is different.

"There's writing in them," I say, staring at them like I'm looking at a sacred piece of art.

She nods, resting her chin on my chest and gazing up at me. "The initials of people I've loved and lost."

I trace my finger along the initials of a purple butterfly.

SW.

"Sonya Whitton," she explains. "My nanny."

I move my fingers, doing the same with the other two, which have *MB.*

There's no question who they're for.

Melissa Bellini.

Marta Bellini.

I run my thumb over one *MB* and then the other. "When did you get these?"

"The day after the funeral," she whispers. "Twelve hours after you threw me out of your car and onto my parents' driveway." She pokes her nail into my chest. "I actually considered having your initials tattooed on my ass with devil horns above them."

I smack her ass, holding myself back from laughing at her comment.

"At least I took you home," I say, faking offense. "That should have earned me a butterfly."

She runs her nails across my chest. "You most definitely didn't deserve a butterfly."

"Fair. I'm not exactly butterfly material."

"I could put you as a moth."

I run my finger down her spine, and her body shakes.

"You can tattoo my initials *anywhere* and *anyhow* you want. I'd love to show my ownership on this perfect body. Though"—I give her ass a light squeeze—"I'd prefer no devil horns or moths."

She lays her head on my chest, as if running out of all her energy. "Your turn to tell me about your tattoos."

"I'll tell you about *one*," I say, faking to be more annoyed than I am.

"Can I choose it?"

I perform a *have at it* gesture.

She taps her lip. "Technically, I gave you two since I told you about the butterflies *and* initials."

"You drive a hard bargain. Take your pick."

"The praying hands on your neck." She runs her fingers along my neck, over my Adam's apple.

"They're praying hands." Praying hands with light emitting from them.

"Yessss," she drawls out, shooting me an annoyed look. "But when and why did you get them?"

"All the men in my family were raised not to fear death. When I was ten, my grandmother told me she was never afraid to die. When I asked her why, she gave me a necklace with prayer hands similar to this." I place my hand over hers on my throat. "She said she didn't fear death because she knew when it happened, she'd go somewhere beautiful. While I'm not sure what awaits me in death, I like to give myself a little hope."

My grandmother was the only person who knows this story.

She went with me to get the tattoo when I was fifteen. It was my first tat, and my mother nearly lost her shit when she saw it. I got grounded for a week, and when I refused to tell her *why* I chose the praying hands, she grounded me for another.

Genesis strokes my skin, tracing the lines of the tattoo. "That's beautiful." She rises up to press her lips against the edge of mine. "And, Julian, you're going somewhere beautiful when you die … when you're *old as fuck* and you need a cane."

I offer her a soft smile, not believing a word she said.

Men in the Mafia don't live long. Most don't make it past their forties.

I've never expected to live a long life.

"You're literally tatted everywhere," she comments, looking over my skin as if reading a script. "Your arms, your hands, your fingers, *everywhere*. When I got the butterflies, they hurt like hell."

"I've been through far worse pain than getting some ink, baby."

"Why the Cupid?" she asks, moving her attention to the tattoo on the side of my neck. "For someone so anti-love, that sure says the opposite."

"That's for my parents. Cupid was the son of the love goddess, Venus, and the god of war, Mars. It's how I saw them. My mother as love and my father as war."

Lowering her head, she presses a kiss to Cupid and then runs her finger along my jawline. "I have one last request."

I stare up into her eager eyes. "You're sure asking for a lot of those tonight."

She grabs my hand again and lowers it to my chest, right over my heart—one small section of my skin that isn't inked. For some reason, I've always felt like I needed to save that space.

"Here's where I want you to have a tattoo for me," she says, her voice so light and tender. "Then, next to it, I want one for our child."

I WAIT until Genesis has been asleep for an hour before slipping out of bed and driving to the casino.

During the drive, I realize something.

My entire time with Genesis, I didn't once think about the Russians, or Lucky Kings, or the chaotic shit happening in my life.

My mind was present and there with her.

She picked a movie for us to watch, which I hardly paid attention to because she chattered the entire time, foreshadowing what'd happen in the movie. Not that she made it to the end. She'd yawned nearly a hundred times before dozing off.

While she slept, I checked my phone, seeing the text from Franko, telling me where he'd taken the Russian who came to the casino.

I arrive at the warehouse we lease, located thirty minutes from the New York casino, shortly after two in the morning. When I walk in, I'm disappointed it's not Dima.

Though I didn't get my hopes up.

I know Franko would've told me if it was.

Since I've been doing my research on the Russians, I know the man tied to the chair is Marlen. Franko shoved a rag, which I know has drain cleaner on it, into his mouth, which means he probably wouldn't shut the fuck up and Franko grew tired of it.

Franko is in the corner, sitting on a stool, eating Taco Bell and reading a *Maxim* magazine. He tips his chin toward me, dropping the magazine on the table, and sits back to enjoy the show.

Marlen jerks his head up when he hears me click the door shut. Drool falls from his mouth, landing onto his scuffed sneaker and the floor.

Both of his eyes are bruised, and they widen when he sees me.

Did the dumb fuck not know this would happen?

Marlen is a soldier with the Russians. He holds hardly any rank, but I know he answers mainly to Dima. I also know Dima fucks his girlfriend while Marlen is out, killing for his family.

What great loyalty they have there.

Walking straight to him, I backhand him across the face. "What the fuck were you doing in my casino, Marlen?"

Marlen flinches not only from the slap but I think from my knowledge of his name as well. He whips his head from side to side, attempting to speak, and I drag leather gloves from my pocket before tugging the rag from his mouth.

I punch him in the face. "Answer me, or I'll knock every damn tooth out of your mouth and shove them up your girlfriend's asshole. The asshole Dima fucks while you're jerking his other men off."

Marlen snarls at me, showing off his gold front tooth. "I was gambling." His Russian accent isn't as thick as Yaroslav's other men.

I can't wait to knock that tooth out.

Maybe I'll mail it to Dima.

Let him know I'm not fucking playing.

"Bullshit." I punch him again, hoping it loosens his teeth.

No teeth fly, so this time, I put more force into my punch.

Marlen takes it like a man, not cowering once.

I stand tall in front of him, drawing my switchblade from the jeans I changed into before leaving, and hold it up. "I don't have much patience for men who don't talk." I open the switchblade.

"Fuck you," he screams.

I stand behind him and stick the blade against his throat.

He's playing cool, but I can feel his Adam's apple bobbing.

Can feel his jugular tighten.

"You kill me, you're asking for a war," he bites out.

"Nah, you're a soldier." I dig the blade into his skin until I see blood. "No one cares about you. They'll pick another stupid motherfucker to take your place in seconds."

"That's where you're wrong," he says with a snarl. "I'm being promoted to capo."

Franko busts out in laughter, lighting a cigarette and taking a long hit of it. "You're not capo material, you dumb motherfucker. Whoever told you that was lying out of their Russian asshole."

"Yaroslav is dying," he blurts out.

I lower the blade to his chest, waiting for him to continue.

"Colon cancer," he says as I walk around his chair to face him, slipping the switchblade back into my pocket. "He won't be boss for much longer. Soon, Dima will be in charge, and he's already promised me a promotion."

I reach my hand into my other pocket. Marlen pulls his shoulder back, gaining more confidence, as if I give two fucks about his rank.

He grins and spits at my feet. "Here soon, that pretty girl of yours will be his. *Ours* because I'll convince him to share. I'll fuck her from behind first—"

I draw out my gun and shoot him in the head.

Consequences be damned.

His dead eyes stare straight into my soul as blood gushes from his head.

Seeing him dead is fucking beautiful.

So damn gratifying and only adds to the enjoyment of my night. I'd been waiting too damn long to kill one of Dima's men.

Marlen's body slumps to the side, the blood pouring out of his head, and his body then falls forward.

I spit on his body, kick it, and then tell Franko to put his head in a bowling ball bag and deliver it to Dima's front porch. The fucker owns a bowling alley, and I want him to know, next time, I'll replace every bowling ball with a Russian head.

As I walk to the Escalade, I call the local florist and order pink peonies.

BENNY MARCHETTI CALLS me before the sun meets the earth.

"Marchetti," I say as I answer.

"I'm going to kill your ass, Bellini." That's how he starts the call.

Those aren't the words I like to hear from the next in line in the country's most dangerous Mafia family, but I don't let it affect me.

"Why's that?" I reply, my voice calm.

"My wife has suddenly decided she wants to volunteer at a shelter now since your girl mentioned it to her and her sisters."

I can't help but smirk as I sit behind the steering wheel of the Escalade.

That's exactly what I wanted when I suggested girls' night. I knew if Neomi, Gigi, or Natalia volunteered with Genesis, she'd be protected. Those men give their wives the best security. If she's with them, she's also offered that prime security, and I don't have to be there.

"Why's that my problem?" I ask.

"One of my men will have to accompany them."

"Good."

"Joke's on you because that man is Luca."

I clench my hand around the phone, not expecting that bullshit.

Plan backfired in my fucking face.

"Consider it my day to watch them at the shelter," I say, gritting out each word.

No fucking way am I having Luca around Genesis.

I'm not jealous of him, but I don't like him. If he does one thing to piss me off, I'll happily put a bullet in his head. And then I'll be unleashing the worst Marchetti beast if I kill Cristian's nephew.

I hate that another man has touched what's mine.

I'll make sure it never happens again.

29

Genesis

I WAKE up to peonies on the nightstand again.

But no Julian.

I'd rather have him than flowers.

I'd rather have him than *any* man, even a guy who could give me a safe life, a 401(k), and a white picket fence.

It's always been Julian from the time he walked into his parents' kitchen.

I check my phone, noticing I've almost overslept, and roll out of bed. I was so exhausted last night that I don't even remember falling asleep as we watched the movie.

Deciding to take a quick shower, I step in to turn on the water, noticing all my shower essentials have been moved from the guest bathroom and are in here now. As I shower, the glass steams, blocking the view of the rest of the bathroom.

I think about Julian and about the last time I was in here.

How he touched me.

Fucked me.

How amazing it was with him in here.

My thoughts drift to when he told me about his tattoos last night.

He's been sharing his thoughts, his life, with me.

I never thought I'd be able to chip away at his thick skin and reveal the real Julian. So far, I'm loving it. It's better than I even imagined, but now, like an addict, I want more.

After showering, I turn the faucet handle and open the door. I nearly fall back when I find Julian standing in front of me, holding a towel out in my direction.

He's dressed, looking like he had more sleep than I did even though that's not true.

I take the towel from him, draping it around my body. "It's warm."

He nods. "I put it in the dryer to warm it up so you wouldn't be freezing."

"Look at you," I say in a cooing voice. "All romantic."

"Not romantic." He narrows his eyes at me and reaches out to confiscate the towel, but I swat his hand away. "Fine, I did it because if there's a baby in your stomach, I want him or her to stay warm. Can't have them getting hypothermia."

I can't stop myself from throwing my head back and laughing. "If you think that's how it works in a woman's uterus, you have some serious research to do before I give you the benefit of being *baby daddy* on the birth certificate."

He steps in closer, his shoes getting wet, as he's nearly in the shower with me. "I'm the only *baby daddy* option for you. Don't make that mistake."

I kiss his lips. "Who's my chaperone today?"

"Me," he says sharply, as if I asked him to head to the hospital and donate a lung to me.

"You're lying."

"I wish." He snatches the towel from me, giving me a mischievous smirk, and wipes the water off the bottom of his shoes before tossing it back to me. "How's that for romantic?"

"Did you really just do that?" I throw the towel at him and

stomp out of the shower, shivering and trailing water along the tiled floor. "How rude."

"Neomi and her friends are tagging along with you at the shelter." He opens a cabinet, collects a folded towel, and tosses it to me.

This one, unfortunately, isn't warm.

"You have ten minutes," he says before leaving the bathroom.

Julian

"I HEARD about your deal with Yaroslav," Benny says as we follow the women into Safe Hearts Mission.

I glare at him, crossing my arms.

He takes off his Ray-Bans and slides them into his pocket. "You fall in love with one of these women, prepare to hear the gossip."

I shake my head, still glaring. "That's the difference between us, Marchetti. I'm not in love with anyone except my casino and money."

"We all go through that denial phase." He scratches his cheek, watching Neomi out of the corner of his eye.

My glare still doesn't leave my face.

"Let me just say this."

"I'd rather you not say shit," I fire back.

He doesn't listen. "I've never heard of a man willing to pay a million dollars for a woman he doesn't care about. Most men wouldn't even do that for their own wives."

My glare drops, and I raise a brow. "You wouldn't for yours?"

"I'd pay *millions*—motherfucking plural—for Neomi." He

cuts a look from her to me. "You're in that same club." He scrubs his hands together. "Though words of advice: get that balance paid. I have never and will never trust Yaroslav and his weird-ass son. Never trust *anyone* when it comes to the woman you love, let alone them."

I motion toward the door. "You can leave. I got this covered."

He chuckles. "I can't wait for the reality to bite you in the ass." He pats me on the back. "Have fun babysitting. Something happens to my wife, you won't be alive long enough to worry about the Russians."

THERE SHOULD BE a research study done on how I went from Mafia capo to playing babysitter at a women's and children's shelter.

I stand to the side, watching as Genesis introduces Neomi and her sisters to the shelter staff and then leads them into the kitchen. Three other people are working, preparing breakfast, while another sets out a row of chocolate milk cartons.

I take a look around the kitchen, realizing Genesis was right when she said they needed all the funding they could get. From the number of residents I've seen staying here, this amount of food won't last them long.

The bananas are on their last few days.

I'll have to fix that.

Behind the scenes, of course.

Genesis can't know I'm doing shit out of the kindness of my heart.

She'll try to pull some *aw, romantic* shit, like she did this morning. She's lucky I didn't catch that towel on fire and throw it at her.

Neomi and her sisters start cutting fruits and veggies while I follow Genesis back into the classroom we went in before. She unlocks a desk drawer and drags out a thick binder, dropping it onto the desk with a thud.

I stroll across the room, sit in a chair, and drum my fingers along my chin. "I'm ready for class, Miss Astor."

I have to bite my tongue from calling her *Mrs. Bellini.*

She opens the binder, her eyes serious as they train on me. "Today's class will be different. It's a kids' day."

I cock my head to the side, not understanding.

"My students are children," she says slowly, as if I need an extra moment to comprehend.

Before I can reply, kids start walking in, consuming the classroom.

If I have my guess, most of them are preteen to teenagers.

"Yo, Ms. Genesis!" one kid says, throwing a hacky sack in the air. "I saw you on TV. Don't worry; I ain't believing shit that comes out of those old-ass newscasters' mouths."

"Nate!" Genesis scolds. "Language."

"You want me to beat them up?" a blonde girl asks. "I've been working on my right hook."

"No, you should let me write a story about them," another girl says, wearing a Looney Tunes T-shirt. "Show them how real journalism is done."

Genesis motions for them to take their seats. "While I appreciate all the support, I am fine, and no violence or stories about them, okay? They're just doing their job."

"Who's this sucker?" a kid with a Mohawk asks, pointing at me while taking the seat beside me. "Aren't you a little old to be learning your ABCs, bro?"

Another girl snorts while three other kids burst out laughing.

Genesis covers her mouth, like she's trying her hardest not to laugh.

What the fuck?

She didn't tell me I'd come to the shelter and volunteer to be bullied.

I lean into the armrest, closer to the boy who called me a sucker. "I'll give you twenty bucks if you convince the class they don't want to learn today, and you guys leave." I pull out a crisp twenty from my jacket pocket and hold it up.

"Whoa!" the kid says, jumping out of his chair. "This dude is trying to bribe me." He snatches the twenty from my hand. "Thanks, man, but I take my education seriously."

"All right, everyone," Genesis says, finally taking control of these bad-ass kids, "let's all be nice. This is my friend, Julian. He's going to hang out with me while I teach today."

"Friend or *boyfriend*?" one girl, who looks to be the youngest, asks, turning in her chair to give me a thumbs-up. "He's sooooo cute."

"Friend," Genesis clarifies, motioning for her to turn back around.

"Listen," the one who stole my twenty says. "We love Ms. Genesis. She's the coolest, and she spends extra time with us. If you break her heart, we will not be happy around here. Got it?"

I salute him. "Won't happen."

He holds out his fist, and I fist-bump him.

Then I make a grab for the twenty on his desk, but he swipes it before I can.

"Don't think you're faster than me," he says with a childish smirk. "I can hear your old bones sounding creaky way over here."

I draw back, shocked that this kid is talking to me like this.

Hell, is this how kids are?

Will mine come out talking shit and swiping cash?

With Bellini blood, who knows?

Genesis snaps her fingers. "Alllll right, everyone. Pay attention, or everyone gets an extra essay to write."

I hear groans, and moans, and ughs coming from every

corner of the classroom with one exception of a girl saying she loves homework with a squeal.

As she starts her class, I lean back and kick my foot on the desk.

The kid beside me does the same.

That results in a glare from Genesis, and I drop my foot, feeling like a student scolded.

I watch Genesis teach them about World War II.

Then tell them about Shakespeare.

It's the most random class of stray knowledge I've ever heard. It's like she just throws out whatever's on her mind. Not only are the kids fully engaged with her, but so am I. They listen and answer her questions.

Watching her teach and have patience with these kids relaxes me.

Puts me in a trance where I can't take my eyes off her.

She'll be a phenomenal mother.

I chose well.

But did I only choose her for a child … or did I also choose her for me?

31

Genesis

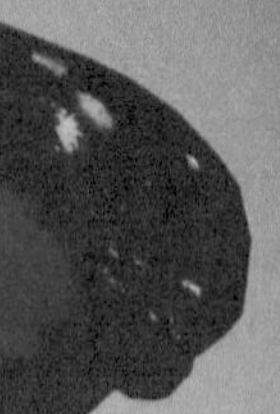

Even though I tried to hide it, I was worried about Neomi and her sisters coming to Safe Hearts today.

We normally have the same staff and volunteers.

Since we're in the city, we get the occasional celebrity volunteer, mostly on holidays, but it's typically a publicity stunt for photo ops, and they don't stay long.

When class is over and it's time for lunch, I return to the kitchen. Julian follows close. At first, I thought about putting up a fight about him escorting me to the shelter.

He surprised me in class today, and I couldn't hold back my smiles when he actually participated with them. He answered questions, and he and Karson kept giving each other hell about missed answers. Sometimes, I think Julian was purposely missing, so Karson, the kid next to him, would crack a joke.

Karson and his mother have been with us for four months now. In the beginning, he was difficult in my class, always giving me hell and interrupting my teachings. Until one day, I asked him to stay after class and talked to him about his favorite comic book. He was shocked I'd read it.

I like helping people, enjoy making them feel better, and I always want everyone to know that they matter.

Situations come and go.

Money is earned and lost.

But people are still people.

They still have hearts, and feelings, and needs.

Sometimes, I think the world forgets that.

In the kitchen, I find Isabella arranging trays of food. Bria dumps French fries on the trays, and Neomi adds a scoopful of fruit alongside the turkey sandwiches.

They came fully dressed for the job, all wearing jeans, sneakers, and T-shirts.

Everyone says the Cavallaro sisters are always easy to point out with their similarities. While all different lengths, they all have dark hair. Bria's is short, Isabella's is long, and Neomi's hits her shoulders.

"How's it going?" I ask.

"Great!" Isabella says, grinning over at me. "I talked to Lora, and she's setting up a schedule for us to volunteer once a week."

Bria nods, shooting me a similar smile to Isabella's. "Thank you for letting us tag along with you. I'm sure getting us started was kind of a headache, but I'm glad we got to hang out in a space that means so much to you."

"If there's anything more we can do, please let us know," Neomi adds, setting down the fruit bowl. "I can tell this place does a lot for these women and children."

Mary, the head of the kitchen, comes up behind them. "You're welcome anytime."

Since help in the kitchen is limited, Mary is thankful whenever she has extra hands, but I know she's picky about them. So, for her to give the okay for the girls to return tells me they left a really good impression on her.

It's nice to have people share their love of the shelter with me. While Darcy volunteers with me sometimes, she's so busy with her family's business and traveling that she can't make a commitment. The shelter has always been a personal thing. My father always wrote checks, so that was enough in his eyes, and my mother refused to volunteer.

Julian stays in the kitchen, making phone calls, while the girls and I serve lunch. As we're finishing up, Benny returns to take them home.

I thank them for coming and hug them before looking at Benny.

"Thank you for bringing them," I say.

He nods and shrugs, and I hear him mutter, "Next time, convince them to just let me write a check."

"Hey," Neomi warns, slapping his shoulder. "For that comment, I'm making you come with me the next three times."

"We have a dog and child to take care of," Benny says. "We agreed once a week. Be happy with that."

Neomi rolls her eyes and mimics his voice as they leave.

Julian stops at my side, waiting for me so we can walk out behind them.

"Genesis," Lora says, rushing out of her office, as if she didn't want to miss me. She waves me toward her. "Can I speak with you for a moment?"

"Of course," I say, following her into her office, and she shuts the door behind us.

"Thank you for bringing your friends." She takes a seat behind her desk. "We always appreciate the extra help." A stretch of concern crosses her face. "I need to ask you a favor."

I nod, knowing I'll do it unless it's something extreme.

"We have a new woman, Sage, who came here for help. She told us she was scared for her life, but other than that, she has hardly said a word to anyone. I think it was a domestic situation, but she refuses to talk with the therapist. She spends nearly every minute in her bed, either writing or reading." Lora adjusts her glasses. "You're the youngest woman on staff here. Think you can try talking to her?"

"If she hasn't talked to you, you think she'll open up *to me*?"

Lora is one of the easiest people to talk to. It's why she's so good at her job and has been director of the shelter for two decades.

"Don't sell yourself short, Genesis. You've had many women and children open up to you who haven't with anyone else."

"All right." I nod. "I'll try to talk to her."

"Thank you."

I leave her office, her following me, and she points me toward a dark-haired girl sitting on a bottom bunk, writing in a journal. No one else is in the room. This is typically snack and arts and crafts time.

The woman is wearing headphones and bobbing her head, lip-syncing to the music. Her gaze flicks over to us, and she slowly lowers the headphones, knowing she's the focus of attention.

Lora stays behind as I walk over to the woman.

She glances at each side of the room, like she's looking for a quick exit.

"Hi," I say, approaching her. "Sage, right?"

She drops the journal, not saying a word, staring at me like I'm the villain in her story.

Like she already doesn't trust me.

Did she see me on the news?

My students did, so there's a high possibility that answer is a yes.

Will that reputation follow me everywhere now?

I motion toward her bed. "Do you mind if I sit?"

She directs her gaze downward and shrugs.

"I'm Genesis," I introduce myself, slowly sitting on the edge of the bed. "I teach classes here if you ever want to drop in. I'd love to have you."

She lifts her gaze, flicking her bangs away from her eyes. "I'm good." Snatching her journal, she shoves it into a brown backpack.

"All right," I say, my voice soft and understanding. "The offer is always open."

Here, you let people come to you on their own time.

Safe Hearts has taught me patience.

She abruptly stands from the bed and hoists the backpack over her shoulder. "I'm not stupid, and I don't need stupid classes."

I feel like a failure as I watch her storm off.

Julian is waiting for me at the entrance, on his phone, when I leave the room.

"You ready to go?" he asks.

I can't stop myself from hugging him.

He inches back, not pushing me away, but I can feel the way his body tenses in surprise.

"Thank you," I whisper into his chest.

"WE NEED TO TALK ABOUT SOMETHING," Julian tells me on the drive home.

I glance up from my phone, raising a brow. "Yeah?"

"What do you want to do with your dad's body?"

I wince, shrinking back in the seat. "Geesh, can you say it any colder?"

He works his jaw. "You can't expect me to respect a man who did what he did."

I squeeze my eyes shut, understanding his feelings. I should feel the same way, but deep down, I keep remembering my father's good traits.

"If we have a funeral, will it be a shit show?" I ask.

"Most likely, yes."

"Can we do a private one then?"

"Genesis, welcome to your new world. Where, for the right price, you can do anything you want."

IT'S NOT VERY OFTEN that you turn on the local news, and you're the topic of conversation.

"The FBI brought Genesis Astor in for questioning, and she's fully cooperated with us," Cliff Sikes, New York's top prosecutor, states, looking deep into the camera. "We've investigated her, and we can confidently say she knew nothing about her father's fraud. She's also offered to turn over personal belongings to repay the victims Carlisle Astor stole from."

Derrick stands behind Cliff, clad in the same FBI jacket and hat, and nods along with his every word. Cliff had introduced him as Agent Green at the beginning of his speech.

Reporters scream question after question at him.

"What about her mother?" one asks. "Does Genesis know where she is?"

"We've yet to locate Diana Astor," Cliff replies.

"Doesn't that prove she's guilty?" the same reporter questions.

"That proves she needs to get in touch with us ASAP before we start assuming that."

I can tell from the cynical expression on his face that he fully believes my mother is guilty.

I turn down the volume on the TV and immediately call my mother.

"Hello?" she answers, surprising me.

Though, since I recently got a new number so reporters would stop calling me, she probably didn't know it was me.

"Mom," I breathe out. "Have you been watching the news? You *need* to talk to the Feds before you get arrested."

"I'll do no such thing," she huffs out.

"Do you *want* to go to prison?"

"Oh, sweetie." Her tone turns so patronizing that I debate hanging up on her. "I have no intention of returning to the United States."

"How do you plan to live out of the country with no money?" After the question leaves my mouth, I realize how stupid it was.

"You don't think we made sure I was situated financially before I fled?"

A sour taste fills my mouth, and I cover my mouth, forcing bile back down. "What about making sure *I* was okay?" I hold in a breath, fighting back a sob so she doesn't hear it leave me.

Fuck that.

"Oh shoot, what's that?" She starts to talk to someone in the background. "Oh, honey, my massage therapist is here. I'll need to call you back." She hangs up.

What a joke.

32

Julian

"YAROSLAV, ANSWER YOUR FUCKING PHONE," I say to his voicemail. "I have your fucking money."

What man doesn't answer his phone for half a million dollars?

Yaroslav is usually known for easy contact and taking calls. If he doesn't have his phone, one of his men does, and they immediately hand it over to him.

The fucker doesn't like missing deals.

Fire burns through my veins as I slide my phone into my pocket and stare through the Escalade windshield at the Moro Bowling Alley.

I'm not a man who takes kindly to being ignored.

If he doesn't want to answer my calls, then I'll go to his place of business and shove my fucking phone down his throat.

His bowling alley sits on a desolate road, surrounded by failing businesses with similar Russian names. I'd bet my Escalade they don't make a dime, and the businesses are simply there to launder dirty money through.

I crack the tension in my neck, grab my Glock from the

glove compartment, and stroll through the nearly empty parking lot and into the building.

It reeks of cigarettes and stale pizza. A group of senior citizen bowlers are in one of the eight lanes.

A young guy is slouched forward on the front counter, focused on his phone, not even noticing my presence.

He doesn't look up from his phone until I'm directly in front of him and fisting his shirt. He grunts, dropping his phone.

With my free hand, I press my Glock against his forehead. "Get me Yaroslav."

He attempts to pull away, but I apply more pressure with the Glock.

"He's not …" The guy holds up his arms, stumbling back, and trips against the stool, all while still in my hold. "He's not here."

"Where is he?" I ask, spitting in his face.

"I don't know, man," he squeaks out. "I only work here part-time."

He's a fucking liar.

Yaroslav wouldn't have any run-of-the-mill part-timer working here.

I release the guy, pushing him backward, noticing a camera in the corner. With my Glock still pointed at the guy's forehead, I raise my middle finger to the camera.

"Yaroslav never comes here," the guy goes on. "His wife runs this place."

I jerk back, lowering my Glock, and he bends at the waist, catching his breath.

"Tell whoever the fuck will get the message to Yaroslav that he needs to call Julian before I set this fucking place on fire."

I hoped for a better ending for this trip.

I need to get Yaroslav his fucking money, so I don't have to worry about him or his fucking son again. Unfortunately, I don't have enough time to tear the entire bowling alley to shreds. I have to get back to Genesis for her father's service.

We're burying the asshole that's Carlisle Astor today.

A fucking headache, if you ask me. I'd prefer to throw him in a hole and let him rot, but Genesis wants a service.

Like with everything lately, Genesis gets what Genesis wants.

Pleasing her seems to be the theme of my life lately.

Since I have *a little* time to kill and want to send a message, I snatch a bowling ball and throw it through the large window. The glass shatters, but I don't take a second to admire the damage before grabbing another ball. I keep my grip in the three finger holes and hurl it behind the counter. The guy ducks, the ball only missing his head by seconds.

Damn.

I always thought I had good aim.

My nerves skyrocket as I charge out of the bowling alley.

Regret settles inside me like a heavy weight.

I should've paid Yaroslav the million at the beginning and got this over with.

Instead, I chose to play games, and now, I'm paying for it.

But with how stubborn Genesis was, I was worried she wouldn't go with my plan if there was nothing for her to lose.

I slam my fist against the steering wheel when I'm back in the Escalade.

If Yaroslav doesn't call me back soon, I'll consider the contract null and void and then drag Genesis to the altar and marry her.

Genesis is dressed in a black dress and heels when I return to the house.

All I hear is the click of her heels as she paces the kitchen in front of the island.

"I can't believe my mom isn't at least coming home for his funeral," she says, throwing her arms up. "She and my father were married for thirty years, and that's how she treats him? Like he didn't even matter to her."

Lowering her head, she stops pacing and sniffles.

I hold back the urge to tell her she shouldn't give a shit about her mother.

I also have to refrain from saying fuck her mother and dead-ass father.

She doesn't need anything from them.

She needs someone who cares.

Me.

I'll protect her at all costs.

It's what Melissa and my mother would've wanted.

If Genesis needs someone to hold her hand as she grieves, I'll hold it tight.

Sit by her side for as long as she needs.

Like me, she has no one.

We're two broken souls.

"You ready?" I ask.

She raises her head, her sorrowful eyes hitting mine. "As ready as I'll ever be." Her shoulders slump as she walks toward me.

Grabbing her hand, I walk her to the Escalade, open the door for her, and wait until she's buckled in before slipping into the driver's side.

She's quiet during the short drive to the funeral home.

We kept the service details private, not wanting to deal with protestors or trouble. If Carlisle wasn't rotting in a casket at the moment, he'd have plenty of death threats against him.

No one likes selfish fuckers who steal their money, good person or not. People lost their entire life savings because of him.

A few cars are in the parking lot. I asked Darcy, Pippa, and Gigi to come so Genesis wouldn't feel so alone.

I'm happy they're here, giving her support.

When we walk into the funeral home, there's a picture of Carlisle in the lobby. I guess the coroner didn't go with my suggestion of putting Satan's fucking picture there.

I made most of the funeral plans, and there were multiple reasons I chose a closed casket.

Carlisle shot himself in the head. No matter how good the mortician, it's hard to cover that shit up.

Second, I saw how horrified Genesis was at her dad's dead body in the office. I didn't want her to feel that same pain again.

And last, I knew it'd give me the temptation to shoot him in the head because I never got the chance to. The fucker deserves a bullet from me after what he did to Genesis.

The room is eerily quiet, with the exception of Frank Sinatra's "My Way" playing through the speakers. The same picture that's in the lobby is displayed on an easel beside the black casket.

The women are inside the room, seated in the second row, with Damien and Antonio in the row behind them. As soon as they notice Genesis and me, they jump up from the chairs and rush toward her.

Darcy hugs her first, apologizing for being gone for too long.

Pippa wraps her in her arms tight, telling her she's sorry for her loss.

When it's Gigi's turn, she simply plants a soft kiss on her cheek.

Surprisingly, I haven't seen Genesis cry once today.

She's sniffled a few times, but that's it.

It's so different from my family's funeral.

She bawled in the front row, sobbing, with red eyes and a handful of tissues.

Genesis sits in the front row, and I take the seat beside her as the priest enters the room. He doesn't speak long, just goes on with his speech about Carlisle making his gateway to heaven, to which I have to hold myself back from correcting him to say that it was a fast track straight to motherfucking hell.

When he asks if anyone would like to say a word, no one volunteers. He apologizes for our loss once more before leaving the same way he came in.

This is the shortest funeral I've ever gone to.

And I've attended plenty.

I wish I could say I hadn't since my family's, but unfortunately, there have been so many that I've lost count.

Death will always be inevitable.

One day, all of us will die.

In this life, the men die younger.

There's one in ten odds of us living until we're gray and old.

As I peer over at Genesis, who hasn't said a word since we sat, a thick reality hits me.

I want to beat those odds.

Want to be that one man out of ten.

I want to live for her.

For us. For our future.

"Hey, Lora," I say, knocking on her office door. "Do you have a moment?"

When I asked Genesis what she wanted to do after her father's funeral, she told me she scheduled herself to teach at Safe Hearts. She instructed me to take her home to change, and then we made a pit stop at Brew Delights for her favorite coffee and a croissant.

Like me with the casino, Safe Hearts is her safe space.

Her escape.

Where she can go and not think about her problems.

I respect that, but I also wish she'd find another *escape*.

Ideally, a room in our home.

She can pick up any damn hobby, just do it at fucking home so I don't have to play chaperone all the damn time.

Normally, I'd hassle her about coming to the shelter, especially when she's done more than the agreed-upon days in our contract, but today, I'll give her a pass.

That still doesn't make me happy about it.

She's putting herself in danger every time she's at the shelter.

Not only from possible enemies of mine but also from people who want to hurt another woman here. Genesis knows this though. She's been aware that the shelter is dangerous for years, but it's never stopped her from coming here.

She once told me she'd rather die for a good cause than act like it didn't exist.

I join Lora in her office, and she gestures for me to shut the door if I'd like.

I do but hesitate to sit when she motions for me to do that next.

I'm typically a stander, especially when in other people's offices, but I don't want to seem threatening, so I take a seat in the uncomfortable chair that was most likely made before the damn Trojan War started.

It creaks as I adjust myself in the seat, and I hope I don't break it.

I rest my arm on the chair. "I'd like to fund additional security here."

Call it funding, a donation—I don't give a shit.

Concern floods her tired face. "Is there a reason we'd need additional security?"

I shake my head, trying my best to put her at ease. "I'm sure you're aware of what Genesis's father did. She's received death threats, and I want to make sure she's as safe as possible."

It's somewhat true.

She received three death threats.

I returned those threats to the men who'd sent them by putting bullets in their heads.

Lora adjusts her sleeves, tugging on one, thinking.

"I'll set up everything," I go on, trying to sound as casual as possible. "I'd just hate for Genesis to have to leave here because she doesn't feel safe." I shake my head in fake disappointment. "It'd just break her poor heart." I place my hand against my chest. "*Everyone's* heart."

"Oh … all right," Lora says. "We'll need to provide background checks on everyone."

"Not a problem."

"If you can get female security, that'd be best. It'd make the women feel more comfortable."

"Background check. Females. Keep everyone protected." I stand, salute, and then wink at Lora. "I got it covered."

After leaving her office, I check to make sure Genesis is still in class and then retreat outside to call Yaroslav again.

Voicemail.

"Yaroslav, you have *two fucking days*," I say, then end the call.

33

Genesis

"Hɪ, Sᴀɢᴇ," I say, collecting my folders as she stops in front of my desk. "Thank you for coming to class today."

Today was her second class.

During the first one, she hadn't said a word or volunteered one answer.

Today, she answered one question.

Progress is progress.

She trails her fingers over the desk, her brown bangs falling in front of her eyes. "I saw you on the news." She doesn't look up. "A story about your father."

I'm getting better at dealing with comments about him.

Improving on not suddenly feeling this intense anxiety.

What my father did will haunt me for the rest of my life.

I stand, shoving my folder into my bag, and not knowing what to say, I stay quiet. Unlike with the teens who came barreling into my classroom, talking shit, her situation is different.

We don't have a relationship where I can tell her to cool it.

Attending my classes is optional for her, not mandatory, like with the children.

"My dad is dead too," she says, finally looking up at me and blowing the bangs away from her face.

"I'm so sorry," I say, my voice soft as I try to control my emotions. "I know it's hard."

I don't want to talk about losing my father on the day of his funeral.

It's why I came here.

But I don't want to blow her off.

According to Lora, Sage still refuses to talk with a shelter therapist and isolates herself from the other women. She plays Go Fish with the children sometimes, but that's the only time she speaks.

No one knows why she's here, who she is, or where she came from. There are no physical signs of abuse that we can see, but that doesn't always mean anything. Abuse isn't only scars and bruises. Many people suffer severe mental and emotional abuse here as well.

Sage is one big mystery, but sooner or later, she'll have to answer questions. Therapy and a psych evaluation are mandatory at the shelter. They need to know who they're housing.

"Did he pass away recently?" I ask her.

She retreats a few steps, and I fully expect her to leave. Surprising me, she grabs a chair from the front row and jerks it away from the desk. It scrapes across the floor, making a loud screeching sound that hurts my ears.

I watch, eyes wide, as she sits beside me.

"About a month ago." She suddenly flicks her attention to the doorway, as if someone were watching.

I peek a glance, making sure it's not Julian.

The man loves to sneak into my class.

There's no one.

She runs her hand over her floral tank. "He killed himself."

"Is that why you're here?" I ask, softening my voice. "You have nowhere else to go? No family?"

She plays with her hands on the desk. "My mother is still alive. She and my father were never married, and then she married my stepfather when I was eight. I have a younger sister."

"You can't stay with them?"

"They kicked me out." Her attention slips to her chipped nails, and she bites at them. "She said since I was twenty, they didn't owe me anything. My stepfather handed me a hundred dollars and told me to get started on living my 'adult life.'" She says the last two words in air quotes.

"You came to the right place, Sage," I say, resting my hand on her shoulder. "Safe Hearts will help you every step of the way in moving into your *adult life*." I don't use air quotes. "Please talk to our therapist and tell Lora your situation. They'll help you find a job, get on your feet, and find you a program for housing assistance. And anytime I'm here, feel free to come to me. I'm always here to talk about *anything*. It doesn't even have to be serious all the time."

"Thank you," she whispers, a tear falling down her cheek before she slowly lifts her gaze back to mine. "I'm glad I came to your class today."

I smile at her. "I'm glad you did too."

IT'S BEEN A ROUGH WEEK, but I've made it.

I've made it because of the people I have around me.

Julian has cut his time at the casino in half. When I talked to Pippa, she mentioned Damien and Antonio weren't happy about it. I bite my lip, holding back from telling her that maybe it was Julian's time for happiness.

He's always fought for other people's relationships and safety. It's time he does the same for himself.

As usual, a vase of peonies is on the nightstand when I wake up.

Sometimes there's a note to go with them, but it's not always consistent.

Today, there is one.

I'M TAKING YOU OUT TONIGHT. DON'T WEAR BLACK.

His notes are always short and straight to the point.

Never longer than a few sentences.

Opening my nightstand drawer, I grab the pile of his other notes I've saved and flip through them.

ORDER SOMETHING NICE FOR YOURSELF ON YOUR CARD.

I ordered a new pair of heels.

WILL BE HOME LATE. SLEEP NAKED, PLS.

That night, he woke me up, and we pretty much had sex for three hours straight.

YOU LOOK GORGEOUS WHEN YOU SLEEP. DON'T THINK THAT'S CREEPY.

I laugh because, a few times, I've caught him staring when I wake up in the middle of the night and tell him the creep-meter is firing off at a ten.

I smile wide, the biggest smirk of my life, when I hit my favorite note.

I CAN'T WAIT TO PUT A BABY IN YOU TONIGHT.

Unless he's the best actor in the world, Julian is falling for me.

I'm sure of it.

I, Genesis Astor, will make history as the one woman who was able to steal Julian Bellini's heart.

It'll be a victory for all of us women who want to tame the bad boys.

Julian refuses to tell me where we're going.

Because of that, I *almost* wear black.

But since I'm one to always honor dress codes, I don't.

The last thing I want to do is attend someone's event, not on theme.

I'm in our closet—yes, it's our closet now since Julian grabbed all my stuff one day and moved it in here, like he had with my shower stuff—when Julian walks in.

He stops in step, his deep eyes darkening as they travel down my body, and he licks his lips. I squeeze my thighs together, a zing of excitement rushing through me.

His movements are so fluid as he drops his suit jacket on the floor and advances toward me like a man on a mission. I don't even have a chance to ask questions before he drops to his knees in front of me. He slides my panties down my legs in seconds and drapes my leg over his shoulder.

In true Julian fashion, he doesn't say a word as he presses his face against my pussy. I moan his name. I lower one hand to his hair, pulling at the roots when he makes the first lick down my slit.

My other hand moves to his shoulder, and I dig my fingers

into his shirt while he spreads me deeper to thrust two fingers inside me.

"So damn delicious," he says, staring up at me. "I wish I could have this pussy for every meal of my life."

"You can," I breathe out.

He slaps my pussy. "That's right." *Another lick.* "Because I own it."

When I shudder, he covers my entire pussy with his mouth.

I run my fingers through his hair, relaxing myself, and rest my back against the wall. I'm growing addicted to how it feels with him there.

The scrape of his facial hair on my thighs.

It's rough, but it feels so damn good.

How it feels when he places kisses on my skin, softer than what you'd imagine from a man like him.

The way he'll take short breaks, run his hands up my thighs, and praise me when I'm close, but he isn't finished with me yet. He loves to torture me with his tongue.

He moans my name between flicks of his tongue before sucking gently on my clit.

"Sooo good," I moan.

"So mine," he says, circling his tongue around my clit and then making a sweep so deep down my pussy that I swear it's close to my ass.

Julian loves eating me out.

He doesn't do it to go through the motions before sex.

Some nights, when I'm tired, he'll eat me out until I fall asleep, never expecting anything in return.

My muscles twitch, my spine tingling, and pressure builds inside my body.

I'm shaking.

"Yes, give me that orgasm," Julian groans, licking me three more times. "Drip your pussy juice all over my face. Drown me with it. I want to taste it on my lips and tongue for the rest of the fucking night."

And that does it.

I forget every thought in my head as waves of warmth and pleasure flow through my veins. My pussy pulsates against his fingers, and as my orgasm shatters through, he harshly plunges three fingers inside me, fingering me fast.

When I'm done coming down from my Julian-induced high, I realize he's literally holding me up because my shaking legs are useless. He waits until I'm stable, giving me time to catch my breath, before inching back a step.

"All right, get dressed." He kisses my forehead, grabs my panties, and helps me put them back on. "We don't want to be late."

I place my hand on my chest, still fighting for breaths. "That was so fucking hot."

"Hot for you. Fucking delicious for me." He collects my juices from his wet lips, sucks on his fingers, and winks at me.

I watch him as he strips out of his clothes and quickly changes before I can return the favor. He's attentive, helping me with my shoes, before we walk downstairs.

If he's not falling in love with me, I'm so screwed.

Because I'm already there.

I'm so in love with this man that I'm ready to hand him my heart.

I hope he doesn't give it back to me broken.

WHEN WE'RE FINALLY in the car, I peer over at Julian while buckling my seat belt. "Will you tell me where we're going now?"

He adjusts the rearview mirror while backing out of the garage. "To get married."

"Har har, funny," I grumble.

He shifts to look over at me. "Don't believe me?"

I shake my head, laughing. "I absolutely do not believe you."

A smirk spreads across his face, and he makes a show of locking my door. "By the end of the night, you'll be Mrs. Bellini."

Julian

GENESIS GAPES at me from the leather passenger seat when I parallel park in front of the cathedral.

The sun is setting, the sky darkening.

A few stars are already making their presence.

I stare out the window at the cathedral.

The same one where we had my family's service.

Where Genesis made me promise to get revenge on the men who'd killed my family.

This is where we first argued and I first touched her.

And now, we're making a new memory—where we marry.

Genesis leans toward me, resting her bare elbow on the console. "Have you lost your mind, Julian Bellini?"

"I sure as fuck have." I unbuckle my seat belt, and the wind hits me when I step out of the Escalade. I speed walk around the SUV to her side.

I've lost the small ounce of sanity I had before signing the deal with Yaroslav. Breaking contracts is a rarity for me because it can be a death sentence.

Your word is one of the strongest things you have in this world.

You break it once, and that crack will be there forever, following you around.

But at this point, all my fucks are out the window.

I'm shattering my word to Yaroslav to keep mine to Genesis —that I'll keep her safe.

This could've been a simple close of a deal. I've given Yaroslav plenty of time to return my calls. He's been dodging them for a reason, and no way in hell will I allow that reasoning to hit me by surprise. No man, especially in our world, delays getting half a million dollars unless there's an ulterior motive.

When I *do* finally get in contact with him, I'll inform him that Genesis is now a married woman and transfer the money into his account, and the deal will be done.

No more fucking with the Russians.

Good fucking riddance.

At this point, if for some reason Genesis can't have a baby, we'll deal with that later. Her safety is my highest priority.

Now, all I need is for her to comply with the plan.

A few people pass me on the sidewalk as I open Genesis's door.

Her eyes widen as she stares at me in confusion.

I place a foot on the running board, offering her my hand. "Let's go get married, Gen."

"Ring those wedding bells," she says, singing out the words and taking my hand.

She releases a yelp when I help her out of the SUV, and then she adjusts her red dress.

It feels good that I didn't have to force her.

Not that I'll admit it to her, but I would've. Had she tried to be difficult, I'd have thrown her over my shoulder and carried her right into the cathedral.

"Oh my God!"

I turn on my heel to find Darcy rushing over to us, her handbag swinging through the air and between her fingers.

"It's true!" She bends at the waist when she reaches us, catching her breath. "I swore I thought Julian was messing with me."

"Trust me, I'm still trying to figure out he isn't," Genesis says, staring up at me.

"It's real," I tell her, jerking my head toward the cathedral steps.

While I didn't plan a large ceremony, I did arrange for a priest and Darcy. I wanted Genesis to have her best friend as her maid of honor.

I scrub a hand over my sweaty forehead, disappointed Damien won't be here as my best man, but I won't risk him or Antonio trying to stop me. They'd demand I wait until I heard back from Yaroslav before marrying Genesis.

They'd tell me to think logically.

Like they can trust Yaroslav.

But me? I don't trust any of them.

That's why there's no changing my mind.

They could hold a gun to my head and tell me not to, and I'd still say my vows to Genesis, not giving a shit if they pulled the trigger.

Darcy pulls Genesis into a tight hug. She dressed for the occasion in a light-pink dress, and her maroon-colored hair is pulled into some kind of updo. I asked her to keep this on the down-low and not to even tell Pippa.

"You look gorg, babe," Darcy tells Genesis, holding her at arm's length and eyeing her knee-length dress and sparkly heels.

"Thank you," Genesis whispers to her before pinching her lips and shooting me a quick look. "Though I wish *someone* had told me I was tying the knot. I'd definitely have chosen something else."

"We'll have another wedding," I assure her. "This one is just paperwork."

She raises a brow. "A contract type of paperwork? Tell me this one gets me out of the one my father signed."

"This one makes you mine." I grab her hand and lead her into the cathedral.

Darcy is behind us, chattering about the lack of a bachelorette party and how disappointed she is that she can't throw Genesis one.

Low classical music drifts through the air when we enter the cathedral. The aroma of rich, sweet incense surrounds us. Lit candles line the altar and are situated on the piano, where a man is playing.

The lights are dimmed, giving off a Gothic vibe.

I've attended other weddings here.

They're usually more cheerful, more alive, and brighter.

I didn't want that.

I directed Father Jerome, saying that I wanted an intimate ceremony.

I'm not a man of cheer.

Darkness gives us monsters our peace.

Father Jerome stands tall at the base of the altar, waiting for us.

"Do we wait for 'Here Comes the Bride'?" Darcy asks.

This is why I've always been drawn more to Genesis.

Darcy has a bad case of can-never-keep-her-mouth-shut-itis.

I ignore her and lead Genesis forward.

"Guess not," Darcy mutters beneath her breath.

Genesis hasn't said a word, and her attention sweeps our surroundings. She suddenly halts for a moment to run her hand over the pew we sat at the night of the funeral.

I'd buy that one if I could.

Maybe if I write the church a hefty check, they'll let me have it.

There's a price for everything.

My heart is dully thudding in my chest for a million reasons.

This is final, the last chapter of my personal life.

I'll be stuck with Genesis forever since divorces are frowned upon in this life.

She'll also be stuck with me.

Then comes the reminder that saying *I do* to her tonight could ultimately lead me to my death.

Yaroslav or Dima could kill me for voiding the contract.

Antonio could for my bringing danger onto the family for not fulfilling my word or asking for permission.

But unlike other men who serve Antonio Lombardi, I'm not afraid to suffer the consequences of my actions. I also have my own fucking mind and won't kneel to any man, mob boss or not.

All for a woman, some may say.

To which I'd probably say yes and shoot them in the face.

Genesis deserves a safe home and a husband who cares about her, not some fucking abusive Russian prick. Hell, she deserves better than me, but I'm the hand of cards she was dealt.

I bet she didn't count these cards.

Father Jerome clears his throat when we reach him.

Genesis's hand grows clammy in mine, and I give it a tight squeeze.

"Father," I say with a slow nod, dropping Genesis's hand and turning to face her.

He peers at Genesis, noticing her outfit is not one of a typical bride, and looks at me skeptically. "She's agreed to this, correct?" He straightens his clerical collar, as if suddenly questioning telling me yes to this.

Genesis's attention sweeps from me to the priest. She wrinkles her nose, puzzled at his comment.

"The last wedding he did for the Lombardis was forced," I explain, as if no big deal.

"Gigi's?" Genesis asks Father Jerome.

The priest nods, his eyes looking at the floor before rising back to hers. "I swore I wouldn't do another, uh"—he clears his throat, as if he's struggling to finish his sentence—"*wedding* for them, but for Julian, I'll do this." He gives me a respectful nod. "I was there when we buried your family. You're a good man."

A good man?

I have to hold myself back from laughing.

If he knew the horrors I could confess in his confessional, I doubt he'd say that. He'd probably pour a bucket of holy water on me, then set me on fire.

But, hey, if he wants to think my heart is pure, then have at it.

Genesis gives Father Jerome a red-lipped smile. "I want this, Father." Her beautiful smile moves to me, growing, and nearly takes over her entire face. "I want to be his wife."

I lick my lips, giving her a smile that doesn't reach my eyes, but is still bigger than one I've given in years.

I gulp, tapping my pocket as reality seeps inside me.

I've lied to myself all night.

I'm not marrying Genesis to save her or because I want her to have my baby.

I'm marrying Genesis so she'll be mine forever.

35

Genesis

I DON'T CARE what anyone says.

This is romantic.

The hazy air, the surprise, Julian arranging all this.

He didn't have to do it, but he did.

I glance over my shoulder at Darcy, who gives me a thumbs-up.

This is why she's my best friend. From the moment I hugged her back, she knew I was okay with this. She may ask me questions later, but she'd never ruin a moment like this by going into interrogation mode.

The priest begins speaking.

He stutters at the beginning, his cheeks reddening as he peers at me.

I offer him a reassuring smile, confirming I'm okay with this.

Poor guy.

I'm sure crazy-ass Antonio put him through the wringer when he kidnapped him, held him at gunpoint, and forced him to officiate their wedding.

It wasn't the wedding *I* attended.

No, that one was better organized and legal with another priest, who was lucky enough not to have the looming threat of death over his head.

I say my vows with Julian, surprised I can even form words.

This weird mixture of shock and excitement zips through my veins as I stare at Julian across from me. He's dressed in a fitted black tux, a black suit vest, and a tie. With his outfit, I assumed we were going to a nice dinner, an event, or a wedding.

But not *our* wedding.

He hasn't looked anywhere but at me since Father Jerome began.

His eyes are glued to me, as if he doesn't want to miss a beat of this.

He stares as if I'm all that matters to him and he'll deal with whatever consequences will come later.

I've fallen in love with those blue eyes—the rarity and beauty of them.

How they're just as unique and wild as he is.

My heart rate picks up when Julian fishes two black velvet ring boxes from his pocket.

His hand is warm when he grabs mine, slowly slipping a diamond ring on my finger. The ring is cold, a contrast to his warmth. I don't look at it yet, since I can't look away from him. I want to see every expression on his face throughout this ceremony.

I take his hand next, take the diamond band from him, and slip it onto his thick finger.

This man is taken by me.

My ownership is branded on him in a loop of diamonds.

"You may kiss the bride," Father Jerome finally says.

Julian wraps his arm around my waist, tugging me toward him, and his lips are instantly on mine.

While we've kissed plenty of times, it feels more real this time.

Intimate.

It feels like a hug you've wanted for lifetimes.

As his tongue slides into my mouth, I know this will last forever.

That he's taking my soul as I take his name.

When he finally pulls away, I stare down at the huge, glistening diamond on my hand.

"I'm a Bellini," I whisper to him.

Julian kisses me again. "You're a Bellini."

Is lust different when you're married?

I know we're technically newlyweds, but after hearing Julian say his vows to be mine forever, it's upped my desire for him tenfold.

The same with him.

We can hardly keep our hands off each other when we walk through the front door. Shoot, it was a struggle not to straddle him while we sat in traffic on the ride here.

I *did* tease him, though.

As he drove, I turned into a little temptress, massaging his thigh, so close to his cock, until he groaned my name. He grabbed my wrist, returning my hand to my lap and shaking his head, as if I was nothing but trouble.

That didn't stop me.

I reached out again, fully placing my palm on his cock and rubbing it.

It got harder and harder within seconds.

My mouth watered, and I knew, tonight, I'd have his cock in my mouth.

"I'm going to fuck you so hard for teasing me," Julian warns, turning me around and unzipping my dress in one swift movement.

I step out of the dress and kick it to the side. He hisses under his breath, his gaze sweeping down my body, just like his eyes always do.

If I'm naked, Julian is staring at every inch of my skin.

As I take his hand and lead him into the living room, I get a flashback of him doing the same with me tonight, straight to the altar. I wish we'd taped it so I could watch it over and over, like my favorite movie.

I try to act like I'm in control, though I know Julian *always* is, but he allows me to play along as I push him onto the couch. The cushions indent as he makes himself comfortable and stretches his arms along the back.

He waggles his finger in a *come here* motion, but I ignore it.

Instead, I fall to my knees and slowly separate his.

He stops me. "Tonight is about you."

"Every night is about me," I whine, pouting out my lip and then licking the bottom one, hoping it'll help my case.

His thighs tense, and I smile.

He raises a brow. "Are you complaining about that?"

"No." I wiggle forward on my knees, thankful for the rug, and settle myself comfortably between his legs. "Let me suck your dick, *husband*." Lowering my head, I nuzzle my nose against his dick over his pants.

Groaning, he throws his head back. "When you say it like that, how can I deny you?"

He tips his head forward, watching me as I unzip his pants.

I'm pretty much a rookie at blow jobs. I've been lucky in that, with my selection of hookup partners, they've always been more interested in giving *me* oral than the other way around.

Not that I've ever had a problem with that.

But I want to pleasure Julian.

His eyes are soft, focused on me as I tug down his pants and boxer briefs. They bunch up at his Gucci loafers when I lower them all the way down.

My mouth waters as his erection springs forward.

It's hard, and throbbing, and purple at the end. Thick veins protrude from it.

My beautiful husband has a beautiful cock.

I stare, closing one eye, and it twitches, as if knowing the spotlight's on it.

"Gen, baby," Julian rasps, his eyes locked on mine, "while I appreciate you eyeing my cock like it's your favorite snack, I'd appreciate your lips on it more." He jerks his hips forward. "I want to feel that mouth wrapped around this dick that's so fucking hard for you." Lowering his hand, he strokes himself once.

All that's on my mind is pleasing him as I bob my head forward and slowly lower my mouth onto his cock, inch by inch. He sucks in a thick breath through his teeth, resting his hands on the top of my head.

I suck him up and down while stroking him in the process.

And while I've always been told I have a big mouth, it's not large enough to take all of Julian without gagging. When I do gag, he winds my hair around his wrist and slightly tugs me back, helping me.

He doesn't make a comment, or wince, or make a big deal about it.

"Relax your throat, baby," he whispers in praise. "You can do it. Just go slow and take as much as you can."

I wiggle closer, improving on my deep-throating skills, and feel his cock jerk inside my mouth. It's growing harder and harder, and beads of pre-cum drip onto my tongue.

It tastes salty.

Delicious.

I moan, growing more excited because I'm getting *him* excited.

I know he's getting close when he pumps his hips forward, fucking my face, and he loses all the gentleness he had when I first dropped to my knees.

My ruthless husband has reemerged.

The monster not staying in for long.

He grunts, lifting me by my hair to get a better angle, and his thighs tense as he lifts them.

"Smack my chest if it's too much," he groans, ramming his cock so deep in my throat that I can hardly breathe … and I love it.

It's exactly the response I want from him.

I wanted him to gag me, to make me breathless with his cock, to make him lose control.

"Fuuuuuck," he moans, cupping the back of my head to hold me in place. He gives me two more harsh thrusts inside my mouth.

His cock pulsates against my tongue, and I moan as he comes in my mouth.

"Yeah, take that cum in your sweet mouth," he sneers, and as I attempt to stare up at him, his face is scrunched together. He looks the most focused I've ever seen him in his life.

His entire body shakes as his cum fills my mouth.

He doesn't release me until every drop is out of his cock and in my mouth.

When he releases me, he's relaxed, his shoulders somewhat droopy. His eyes are intense as they lock on my face.

"Open your mouth," he orders.

I do, and he drags his thumb across my lips.

"My wife, swallowing my cum. What a beautiful sight."

To show him I'm a good little wife, I slip my finger in my mouth and moan.

I nearly fall on my ass when he stands, pulling his pants back up but leaving them unbuttoned.

"Your turn, baby," he says, catching me, tossing me over his shoulder, and carrying me up the steps newlywed style.

I'm panting, lost in my thoughts, and I thread my fingers through his hair as he opens the bedroom door. I lose a breath when he tosses me on the bed.

Grabbing my ankles, he drags me to the edge of the bed.

Julian's signature move.

The man loves me on the edge of the bed. He once said it was the perfect spot to spread out his perfect meal. He impressively unclasps my heels, faster than I do, and tosses them over his shoulder.

Then, my panties are gone, and his mouth is on my pussy.

He eats me fast and then slow, and he fingers me, all while calling me his good little wife.

My body spasms.

My heart is ready to fly out of my chest.

It takes him *maybe* ten seconds until I'm moaning his name.

Giving him head and then him eating me out is the perfect combo for me to come quickly, it seems.

"Crawl up the bed," he says, stripping out of his clothes.

I scoot my ass up the bed, shoving off throw pillows and pulling the duvet back.

Julian stares at me in admiration as he climbs up my body.

His eyes soften as he lines his cock up with my opening. But before he thrusts inside me, he leans in closer, runs his thumb along my jawline, and whispers, "I'd ruin any deal for you."

I gasp as he pushes himself inside me.

He fucks me the slowest he's ever fucked me.

No, he makes love to me … or his version of love.

Our eyes don't leave each other's.

I watch the emotion pass through them.

His sweat lands on my body.

His grunts match my moans.

We move our bodies so in sync.

My heart is on fire, taking every drip of emotion he provides me.

I'm going to prove to this man he has a heart, and then I'll convince him to hand it over to me to take care of it.

36

Julian

"You'll never believe it," I say, holding up the glass, which is half filled with whiskey. "I'm a married man."

Sitting on a stool, I toast the air and take a long drag of the liquid.

When I brought Genesis into my life, I didn't expect her to change it so much.

Didn't expect her to change *me* so much.

Every night, I come home early, not spending every hour working.

I call in and check on her throughout the day.

Genesis consumes most of my thoughts.

It reminds me of my parents' marriage.

I almost feel like my father.

He always looked forward to going home to my mother. He said it was nice knowing someone cared that you *did* come home.

Men in our lifestyle not coming home was common.

Death is even more common.

It was a fact I accepted a long time ago.

If I died, then I died.

But now, I care more than I ever have.

I care because I want to come home to Genesis, knowing she does give a damn I'm home.

I chuckle, shaking my head. "On top of that, I'm married to Genesis." I down the rest of my drink and lower the glass to the garage workbench.

The car I'm speaking to doesn't reply to me.

It never does.

Not that I'm insane enough to *expect* it to.

I visit my family's graves regularly, but this is where I go when I want to talk to my father alone.

Sitting here, talking to this car, is my source of therapy.

I don't do it often since I'm busy and I prefer not to talk much, but anytime I've opened up about *any* of my feelings, it's here.

I look away from the car at the sound of the garage door that leads into the house opening. Genesis appears in the doorway, and I lean back in the stool to get a better look as she walks toward me.

She's dressed in a cashmere robe and fluffy pink slippers. "You weren't in bed," she says around a yawn, her eyes sleepy.

I check my watch, realizing it's four in the morning. I snuck out a few hours ago. "I couldn't sleep and didn't want to wake you." I take a sip of my drink, hoping she'll go back to bed.

In true Genesis style, she doesn't.

She walks closer, running her fingers along the '67 Chevy Chevelle. It's blue with a white stripe on the hood.

"It's just like your father's," she comments, looking inside through the window.

I nod. "It is."

It took me a year to find the same make and model in decent condition. I had it repainted and reupholstered, making it an exact replica of the car my father had cherished. When Damien and I were kids, he'd make us stay up late and help him fix it up.

The car meant so much to him.

Now, it means so much to me.

Genesis sits on a mechanic stool with wheels, and I drag her toward me.

She stares at the car, as if recollecting her own memories from it. "I remember Melissa used to beg him to drive it, and he'd always say no." A smile forms on her face. "One time, he grounded her because she was inside, *fake* driving, and he said even that was dangerous with her."

I brush a hand across my cheek. "She did wreck her car a good ten times. One of those times, she crashed into my father's SUV. He didn't trust her behind the wheel much."

"Did he let you drive it?"

"Hell no. He didn't let *anyone* drive it. It was his pride and joy. He'd only take it out for date nights with my mother."

She slides off the stool, standing, and squeezes herself between my legs. "Telling me that was dangerous." She plants a tender kiss to my cheek, resting her hand on my thigh.

"Why?" I close my arm around her waist, dragging her closer.

"Because tomorrow, you're taking me out for a date night and driving this."

37

Genesis

THE CAR MATCHES Julian's father, Carlo's, car to a T.

The blue leather seats, the AM/FM radio and 8-track, and the black-cherry air freshener that hangs from the rearview mirror.

I only know what an 8-track is because I asked his father when he was working on the car, and I looked inside.

"Where are we going?" I ask Julian.

"You'll see," he replies from behind the large vintage steering wheel.

It looks almost comical, watching him drive it.

I'm so used to him looking all intimidating in the Escalade.

It's three in the afternoon. He was gone for most of the day, working at the casino, while I hung out at home. A few days ago, I asked Lora if she had any shelter work I could do from home. She suggested I help with social media, so I've been spending my free time doing that and writing up lesson plans.

Other than Darcy and the priest, no one knows about our marriage.

It sucks because I want to scream it from the rooftops, but I understand why I have to keep quiet.

"Can I have a hint?" I whine.

"Food." That's the lame hint he gives me.

My face falls. "Can I get another?"

"Don't be greedy, Gen."

"You're the one being greedy with the hints, mister."

Shaking his head, he fights back a smile. It's a regular move from him. Lord forbid, he smiles once in a while.

These Mafia men think they'll burst into flames if they show any emotion other than rage.

"How about you control the music?" He leans forward to tap the console.

I gape at the radio. "On *that* thing?"

"Yes, on *that* thing."

I grab my phone, shaking it in the air. "There's nowhere to sync or plug in my phone."

"Play the radio or 8-track."

"All right, let me just grab my most current 8-track." I fetch my purse from the floorboard, making a show of sifting through it.

"They're called tapes, and open the glove compartment."

"Didn't know you were such a music-thingy specialist," I grumble, tossing my purse back on the floorboard.

When I open the glove compartment, I find a stack of 8-track *tapes*.

A full-on *told you so* expression is on his face.

I give him the finger.

He shakes his head again.

I flip through the tapes. "Where'd you even get these? The extinct store?"

"It's wild, the things you can find on the internet."

I look through the options.

The Beatles, The Rolling Stones, Jimi Hendrix, and Adriano Celentano.

"All Marta's favorites," I comment.

Julian nods. "The same tapes my father kept in his glove

compartment."

I love this nostalgia trip.

"Let's go with The Beatles." I lean in closer to the 8-track. "Now, how the heck do I work this thing?"

"Slide the tape in, album side up."

"Got it."

I feel like I've just solved the mystery of the Alcatraz escape when the tape slides in, and "Hey Jude" flows through the speakers.

I sing along, swaying my shoulders to the music.

Had it not been for Marta, I wouldn't know this song.

She taught me so much—how to cook, an appreciation for new music, and how a real mother loves. She was who I needed after losing Sonya.

Julian taps his thumb against the steering wheel to the beat.

A few more songs play until Julian pulls into the parking lot of a small pizzeria.

I've never been here before, but as I read the sign, I instantly recognize it.

Il Migliore Pizzeria.

Marta's sister's pizzeria.

I peer over at Julian, slack jawed.

"I figured we'd stay on theme of following in my parents' date-night traditions." He kills the engine. "They came here frequently."

"Pizza sounds amazing." I open my door, stepping out, and the sun is setting in the background.

I love that he brought me to a place that meant so much to his family.

Julian's opening the door into his life for me.

I'm his wife now, and he's my husband.

Even if he said the opposite before, this is a true marriage.

We will make it one.

I'll also make date night a regular for us too.

Traditions are made to be passed down, and we'll do that.

Julian rests his hand on the base of my back while leading me toward the entrance. The sweet aroma of pizza hits me as soon as the door opens.

It's a Thursday, and the place is packed.

Nearly all the booths are taken, and the tables in the middle are full. People are laughing, eating, and drinking.

"Oh my freaking God!" a teenage girl's voice says. "Julian? Is that you?"

My attention slides to the hostess stand as a girl skips around it. Her black hair is in two French braids, and she's wearing a black shirt with the pizzeria's logo.

"I can't believe you're here!" she says when she reaches us.

"Hi, Betty," Julian says, a trace of unease on his face.

She grins, not catching on to his apprehension, and hugs him. He taps her back a few times, and she pulls away.

"This is my cousin," Julian introduces to me.

Betty immediately hugs me.

"This is my wife, Genesis," Julian continues when Betty pulls back.

Betty gasps.

I nearly do the same, shocked he told her that.

"It's so nice to meet you, Genesis! Let me get you guys a booth." She turns to grab menus but stops. "Do you need menus?"

Julian shakes his head.

"Perfect." She waves us forward. "Nothing has changed on it."

As I walk past, a few heads turn in our direction.

Since we're on the outskirts of the city, more in a small town, not as many gape as they see Julian. His Mafia-related reputation hasn't followed him here.

Framed photos and newspaper stories are hung on the brick

walls. Red-and-white checkered cloths cover the tables but not the booths though.

"Here ya go!" Betty says. "Aunt Marta's favorite booth."

Julian's gaze drifts over his shoulder toward the door.

"Thank you, Betty," I say, rushing out the words.

I push Julian closer to the booth, stopping him from changing his mind. The uncertainty on his face tells me he's wondering if this was a mistake.

"What can I get you to drink?" Betty asks.

"I'll have a water," I say with a smile.

Julian holds up two fingers. "Make that two."

"Got it!" Betty skips away.

Julian makes himself comfortable, and I slide into the booth, across from him. He's quiet as I glance to the right, noticing the photos.

The largest one is of his family. They're sitting in this same booth with a deep-dish pizza in front of them. In the photo, Julian is squeezed in the booth with Melissa, Damien, and a boy I don't recognize.

I tap the photo. "Who's that?"

"My cousin Nuncio. Betty's older brother." He shifts in his seat uncomfortably, smoothing his hand over his jaw. "He's dead."

My heart drops in sadness. "I'm so sorry."

"His death is what broke my mother and Aunt Belinda's relationship. It's why we're no longer the large family we used to be."

"Can I ask what happened?"

"He died on my sixteenth birthday." His Adam's apple bobs. "Vincent threw me a party at some club. Nuncio and I snuck in the back alley to smoke a cigarette. Out of nowhere, a car pulled into the alley and started shooting. I jumped behind the dumpster, but Nuncio was too slow. A bullet hit him in the chest, and he died three hours later."

Reaching out, I rest my hand over his. His arm tenses, as if he's debating pulling away, but he doesn't.

"Did they find out who did it?" I ask.

"Some asshole my father had banned from the casino. Fucker is dead now." He squares his shoulders back in the booth. "After Nuncio's death, my aunt Belinda begged my mother and father to leave the Mafia life. When my father refused, she told my mother to leave him. Not that she disliked my father—she loved him—but because she was scared for their lives. They offered him a stake in the pizzeria even, but he would never turn his back on the Lombardis. My aunt said she'd no longer put her family in harm's way and stopped coming around. The only time my mother saw her was when she and my father came here. Other than that, it was like they no longer existed in each other's world." His face turns almost vacant. "The rest of my mother's family walked away from her too. It was either she chose them or my father. She chose him."

Her choice was her death.

I know that's what Julian is thinking.

I lean in closer, softening my tone. "How long has it been since you've been here?"

"Eight years."

"It really is you!"

I look away from Julian to find a petite woman, with frizzy hair and bright purple lipstick, strolling toward us.

"When Betty told me you were here, I almost didn't believe it," she adds when she reaches us. She motions for Julian to stand. "Now, you get your butt up and give me a hug."

Julian isn't even all the way to his feet when she wraps him in a tight hug.

"There he is!" A man comes up behind them, wearing an apron with a pizza wearing headphones on it, and slaps Julian on the back. "About time you came here. We've missed you and your brother coming up here, eating all the pizza and telling me how I could make pizzas better." He shakes his head and winks. "Smart-mouthed kids."

Julian shakes his head, a crack of a smile on his lips. "It's nice to see you, Aunt Belinda and Uncle Mick."

"And who is this pretty thing?" Belinda scoots in closer to me, resting her hip against the table.

"My wife," Julian says, laying his soft eyes on me, "Genesis."

His shoulders have eased.

His jaw is unclenched.

He's growing comfortable here.

"Wife? Now, that's what I like to hear!" Belinda's expression is similar to Betty's. "A beautiful wife."

I stand and hug Belinda, feeling that same warmth from her as I used to get from Marta.

"Did you have a wedding?" Betty asks, coming up behind her parents with our waters.

"No," I say with a hint of a frown. "It was a quick thing."

"Are you pregnant?" Betty asks, setting down the waters.

"Betty!" Belinda smacks her arm.

"No," I say around a laugh. "We're not pregnant."

"Not yet," Julian corrects. "We're going to have a wedding."

"And we'll be sure to send you an invite," I add.

Mick rubs his hands together. "Congrats to the newlyweds! I'll send out my favorite pizza."

"You two enjoy your meal," Belinda says with a smile. "You let us know if you need anything, and don't you leave before saying goodbye!"

"We won't," I say, returning the smile.

"I love them," I say as soon as they're out of earshot.

"They're good people." Julian rubs his face. "Sometimes, I wish my father had taken their offer. Our lives would've been different."

"I could totally see you tossing pizzas in the air, looking all hot." I smirk, settling one elbow on the table.

He forces a smile.

"You could always do that, you know? Leave that world behind and start a new one. There's plenty of places we could go."

He leans back in the booth, an unsettling expression on his face. "The only way I leave the Lombardi family is when I die. My parents signed me up for life, no exceptions."

"But wouldn't Damien …" My words trail off.

"Damien isn't the boss. Even he's stuck in this life. He's just lucky enough to be at the top of the totem pole." He stops, grabs his water, and scoffs. "Though I wouldn't consider him lucky."

I drag my hand along the hem of my tank.

I'm having a love-hate relationship with our conversation.

I love that I'm getting to know Julian better, meeting his family and learning the secrets of his life. But I hate that some of those secrets are so dark.

I want to fix that for him.

Shine some light.

Show him there is good out here.

The proof is right in front of him—me, the family who was so excited to see him tonight, our future.

"Garlic bread is here," Betty says, dropping the bread and two plates off at our table. "Let me know if you need anything. Otherwise, Dad has your pizza in the oven." She shoots a glance at Julian. "Skyline still your favorite?"

"Skyline is still my favorite," he confirms with a nod.

"I'm happy we came here," Julian says, watching me. "I wasn't sure I ever would again."

"Thank you for bringing me." I smile over at him. "I think we just started a new tradition. Date nights, just like your parents."

"I'll be sure to always pencil you in."

I push myself forward and peck a kiss on his lips. "You'd better, *husband*."

AFTER WE FINISH the most amazing pizza I've had in my life—I'm not even kidding, and this is coming from a New York girlie—Belinda and Mick come to our table to tell us goodbye.

A tear slips down Belinda's cheek as she makes us promise to come again soon and not to forget their wedding invites.

"Genesis, you're changing my life," Julian says when we're back in the car. He stares straight ahead through the windshield, as if he isn't sure whether he likes it or not.

I scoot in closer—a plus of not having a center console—and rest my head against his shoulder. "You saved mine, so it's only fair."

He takes my hand, tenderly kissing it. "You want to know why I want a baby so bad?"

"Why?" I whisper.

"Other than Damien, I have no one else. No other Bellinis exist in this world. My mom, she wanted a big family, grandchildren. I still want to give her that."

"You have me." I squeeze his hand. "And soon, we'll have a baby."

38

———

Julian

"You fucking married her?" Antonio yells, charging into my office.

Damien is right behind him, and he slams the door shut.

"Knock next time," I grit out, tossing my pen on my desk and standing.

"How'd you find out?" I ask them.

"I find *everything* out," Antonio snarls.

I should give all the fucks at this moment, but I don't.

I'm disrespecting the boss.

Antonio could pull out his gun and shoot me in the head for it.

I've seen him kill for less.

I don't regret marrying Genesis, and I stand behind my decision.

If he wants to shoot me for it, then he can.

But now that Genesis is my wife, even with me buried in the ground, the family has to protect and take care of her.

Damien strolls closer to my desk, rubbing his brow. "Please tell us you paid Yaroslav off before you said *I do*."

When his eyes land on me, there's a twinge of hurt in them because I didn't tell him.

We're brothers.

Best friends.

Have always stuck together.

I'm just as hurt he wasn't there.

Antonio clears his throat, the cords showing in his neck. "Did you?"

I shake my head. "I've tried calling the bastard for days, and he's not answering my calls. I have his money."

"Fuck!" Antonio slams his hand against the table.

"One of his men told me he's dying of cancer," I say, failing to add that it was one of his men *I killed*.

Damien's nostrils flare. "If that's the case, then Dima is either in charge or will be soon."

I clench my fist and jaw at the thought.

"You've thoroughly fucked us," Antonio says, aiming his finger in my direction. "I was already pissed you'd signed a contract with another family without my knowledge, and now *this*." He looks over at Damien. "This is a goddamn problem. You know that is against the rules as it is, but since he's your brother, I allowed it to slide. But now, he's putting us in fucking war *again*."

This is what I've always hated about Mafia families.

The higher-ups want you to do every-fucking-thing for them.

I'm fucking sick and tired of it.

I shove my chair to the side and point at him how he just did me. "You want to talk about war?" I raise my voice so loud that it hurts my lungs as I speak. "How many *wars* have I fought for you? I was there when your uncle wanted to kill you, to take your fucking throne. I had the chance to choose his side, but I chose *yours*, killing some of my own friends who had chosen the opposite. Hell, we fucking killed Emilio's dad!" I dash across my desk, growing closer to them, and slam my fist against my chest.

"I went to war because you had fallen in love with a fucking Marchetti and kidnapped her. I think I've gone to war for a lot of reckless shit for you, and I will gladly go to war for my wife." I signal toward him and Damien. "With or without you guys."

"Well, shit," Damien says, whistling as Antonio walks to the bar.

Antonio grabs a glass and fills it with whiskey. "Let's get ready for war then, shall we, gentlemen?" He raises his glass, a deadly smirk on his face. "It's been a while since I've had free rein to kill motherfuckers. I've missed it."

As if Yaroslav could sense trouble, he calls me twenty minutes after Damien and Antonio leave.

"It's about fucking time," I say, answering his call.

"I was in the hospital." His voice sounds raspy and tired. "I instructed Dima to get in touch with you, but he got busy. He said you married the woman, but I've yet to see the money in my bank account. That's a problem, Bellini."

"I have your money and can transfer it to you now."

"No, I want cash, like last time. I don't deal with bank-account bullshit. Too many Feds always lurking around."

"Fine. Cash it is."

"I can't meet today. Tomorrow. One o'clock. Same place we met last time."

"I'll see you tomorrow. Don't be fucking late." I end the call.

39

Genesis

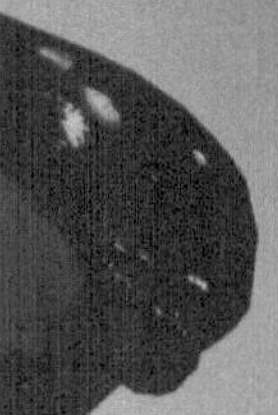

PREGNANT.

I stare at the pregnancy test.

It's my third one.

All of them have said the same.

I rub my stomach, stare into the mirror, and softly smile.

There's a baby in here.

"Hello," I whisper. "I'm going to be your mama."

This morning, the cycle-tracking app on my phone notified me that my period was late. I wanted to wait to take the pregnancy tests until Julian got home, but I was scared.

If I wasn't pregnant, I knew I'd get emotional.

I'd probably cry.

I didn't want him to see that.

I was also excited as hell, and I've never been one for patience.

Julian is meeting with Yaroslav today to pay the balance of my debt.

That chapter with Dima is over.

No longer do I have to look over my shoulder, wondering if a crazy-ass, snake-tatted Russian will take me or kill me.

I grab my phone and sit on the closed toilet seat, speechless and trying to form words in my head. My hand shakes as I text Julian.

> Me: I have the biggest surprise for you when you get home.

My phone beeps with his reply seconds later.

> Julian: What's that?

> Me: You have to wait until you get home.

> Julian: I don't like waiting.

> Me: Too bad. This might be your favorite, and I want to see your face when I tell you.

My response might give away the obvious, but oh well.

Even if he asks if the surprise is that I'm pregnant, I won't tell him until he's in front of me.

Tonight, I'm making dinner, and we have *a lot* to celebrate.

EMILIO DROVE me to Safe Hearts today.

I'm teaching a quick class, and then I'll have him take me to the grocery store and go home. Most of the day, I've been brainstorming how to tell Julian about our good news.

I'm in the restroom, washing my hands, when Sage rushes inside. She slams the door shut behind her, resting her back against it, and she's trembling.

"Genesis," she says, her breathing rapid as she bows her head, "I need your help."

When she lifts her head, I gasp at the bruise under her right eye and rush over to her.

"Who did this to you?" I ask her.

"My stepfather." She winces, as if in pain. "He beat my sister and me up. She's outside but too afraid to come in. Will you please help me convince her to?"

I nod. "Let me go get Emilio."

Unlike Julian, Emilio doesn't sit in class while I teach. He either sits in his car out front or in the lobby. He regularly complains about shelter-sitting, as he likes to call it.

She nods, opening the door, but moves in the opposite direction of where Emilio is.

"Wait," I say, stopping her.

"She's out back, and we don't have much time!" She grabs my hand, using all her power to pull me in the direction of the back door.

A few women and girls stare at us.

One picks up her phone, as if taping the scene.

I've gone out the back door numerous times when taking out the trash or accepting a new delivery. It's where we receive most of our donations as well.

I follow her outside, and she slams the door shut behind us. It's rainy and gross, and I wish we'd grabbed an umbrella.

But I thought of her sister's safety first.

That's what matters most.

"Where's your sister?" I ask Sage, who turns around and looks at me.

A black van swerves in front of me, blocking me from the door. The door opens, and just as I scream for help, someone grabs me. I kick my feet as they slam their hand over my mouth to muffle me. Their arm wraps around my neck, causing me to choke, and I fight as they drag me toward the van.

The man throws me inside, pins me down, and smacks tape over my mouth. I attempt to crawl away from him and jump out of the van, but he slides the door shut and backhands me in the face.

"Stay there, you dumb fucking bitch, before I break your leg so you can't try to run," a man snarls.

I curl forward at his Russian accent, and a tear slips down my cheek. Glancing over, I see Sage balled in a corner, her knees to her chest and crying.

"He said she might be a fighter," the man in the driver's seat says, but I can't see him. "Put her ass to sleep."

"No!" I scream, attempting to crawl away in panic.

The man smacks me again, harder this time, and as I fall back, he grabs me by my hair and shoves a rag against my face.

My eyes grow heavy.

My shoulders slump.

And everything turns black.

40

Julian

I keep rereading Genesis's text on my phone.

> Genesis: Too bad. This might be your favorite, and I want to see your face when I tell you.

Please let it be that she's pregnant.

She hasn't mentioned a period, and we've been trying like crazy.

Today might be the best damn day of my life.

I'll get Yaroslav off my back, and Genesis and I can live our lives without thinking about fucking Russians.

Sure, I'll always have to watch my back for enemies, but Dima is constantly on my mind.

Antonio and Damien are with me.

I slip my phone into my pocket when we pull up to the same warehouse where I met Yaroslav when I paid him the initial deposit for Genesis. The only other vehicle is a black Suburban with a yellow snake bumper sticker.

"Let's go get this shit over with," I say from the back seat.

Antonio drove, and Damien is in the passenger seat.

I snatch the duffel bag with my cash and hop out of the car.

Damien and Antonio do the same. The warehouse door is unlocked, and we let ourselves in. Last time I was here with Yaroslav, he had a guard at the door.

Maybe he knows he can trust me now since we had no problem with payment before.

Or maybe something's up, and this won't go as easy as I hoped.

A man is in the corner, shirtless, punching a boxing bag hanging from the ceiling. The other is spread out in a chair, eating ramen noodles and screaming at the TV.

"All right, where the fuck is Yaroslav, you fucking imbeciles?" Antonio yells, snapping his fingers and motioning for them to come closer.

The man takes another slurp of his noodles before setting down the bowl. The other guy steadies the boxing bag before stalking toward us. I've never seen a motherfucker flex his muscles so much. He looks like a lame Popeye impersonator.

"Who the fuck are you?" I ask. "And where the fuck is Yaroslav?"

Noodle Fuck rubs his hands together, a sly smirk on his face.

I've seen enough *you've been owned* facial expressions at the casino to know a shit show is about to ensue.

"We're here to represent Dima," Popeye asks replies, snorting a few times.

"Where's Yaroslav?"

The two assholes share a look and snicker.

Yes, they fucking snicker, like Antonio's six-year-old daughter does when she steals your last fucking Oreo.

"Yaroslav is no longer boss," Noodles says. "Dima is in charge now." He jerks his head toward the duffel bag. "You can leave the cash with us."

"We're not leaving shit with you," Damien says, snarling his lip. "Call Yaroslav or Dima and tell them to get their asses here *now*."

"Or what?" Popeye mockingly shimmies his shoulders.

I don't have time for this bullshit, so I do what every sane man does. I pull my Glock from my pants and point it at them.

Antonio and Damien do the same.

Noodles fumbles with his pants before pointing his pistol at us.

The other guy dashes over to the boxing bag, as if he left his gun there. For shit and giggles, I fire off in his direction a few times. Antonio laughs as the man hops around, dodging the bullets. I wait until my last fire before hitting him in the ankle.

"What the fuck?" he cries out, falling to the floor and cupping his ankle.

"Dima said to leave the cash," Noodles grumbles, not even bothering to help the man now screaming in agony.

"It's a fucking ankle wound. Relax," Damien says in annoyance. "Dumb fucker is acting like he has an actual injury over there."

Noodles stares at each of us as if we're crazy and isn't sure who to point his gun at. So, he makes a show of going one by one, over and over again. Any of the three of us could easily shoot him in a second.

"Call Dima, tell him I'm not leaving the cash and to get his ass here so we can sign this contract," I demand, playing with my gun's trigger and wondering how much bullshit I'd have to deal with if I just shot this fucker in the face.

Noodles scoffs, jerking his gun from Damien to me. "You think Dima cares about a contract his father arranged?" He throws his head back, laughing like a fucking hyena. "He's killing all his father's contracts. No longer will he play nice with any of you Italian motherfuckers who think you're better than us." He levels and hardens his stare on Antonio. "That changes now. We'll show all you *bosses*." He stops to spit at Antonio's shoes before whipping his cold stare to me and curling his upper lip. "You stole something from Dima, and he wants it back."

"Call Dima and tell him we can make an arrangement," I say, lying.

Antonio lowers his gun to fish his phone from his pocket. "I'm calling Dima myself."

"Good luck," Noodles says. "He won't answer. Let's just say, he has a new wife who'll be entertaining him."

I charge forward, grab the man, and ram my gun against his skull. "Where is Dima?"

Antonio strolls across the warehouse to the guy who's still whining about his wound. He stands tall over him, shooting three shots into his head, and slams his foot into the guy's skull.

"Start talking, or I'll do worse with you," he tells Noodles, aiming his gun at him.

"You won't kill me." Noodles seems too sure of himself. "You don't want to start a war."

I shoot him in the leg. "A war has already been started. Now, we need to figure out if you'll be the next casualty of it."

He cries out in pain, similar to how his sidekick did, but doesn't fall on the ground.

"I won't tell you where they took her," he says. "I do, I die."

"You don't tell me *right now*, you also die," I point out, shooting him in the other leg. I inch forward so I'm in his face. "And it won't be a fast death, like your buddy over there. First, I'll let one of my men torture you for hours, and then I'll gouge one of your eyes out and let a vulture eat it in front of you before laying your organs all around the city and sending your family a map to find each of them." I butt my gun against his cheek. "Don't test me."

His attention floats to his dead friend.

Dima set him up for death here.

He knew these men would die as soon as we realized him nor Yaroslav was coming. I know the second it dawns on this idiot, and he stumbles back a step. I do it with him, not letting my gun fall from his head.

"You help me out, I'll make sure you live," I offer.

"You're lying," Noodles says, sweat now falling down his forehead, and he keeps swallowing.

"I respect your loyalty," Antonio says, straightening his back and lowering his gun from Noodles. He throws out his arms. "As the boss of the Lombardi family, I reward men who help me. You said you hated being treated as if you were beneath us. How about I let you *join us*?"

The man's nostrils flare, and with his shot leg, he grows weak. I hold him up, stopping him from falling.

"You're lying," he sputters.

Antonio jerks his head toward Damien. "You see this man here?"

"Yeah?" Noodles sways from side to side, somewhat losing consciousness.

"Jesus, have none of you been shot before?" I hiss.

Antonio slaps Damien's shoulder. "This man here, he worked for the Marchettis. Now, I went to war with the Marchettis. He told me information I wanted to know, and instead of killing him, I made him my underboss."

Damien nods in agreement, lowering his gun. "Best decision I ever made. Not once has he seen me as a man from the other side. I'm his equal, unlike I was with Marchetti."

Noodles gulps a few more times.

He pays a glance to each of us, as if trying to catch one in a lie.

"What do you say?" Antonio asks with the skill of the best salesman in the world. "Join my family. Come be appreciated."

"O-okay," Noodles stutters out.

Damien grabs his chair, dragging it over to us, and motions for him to sit.

See how fucking nice we are.

We're here to be your friend.

Have a seat, you piece of shit.

I kneel in front of him. "Would you like some water?"

Noodles nods, and Damien goes to the mini fridge next, pulling out a bottle of water. He uncaps it and hands it to Noodles.

He loudly gulps it down.

I kneel to Noodles's eye level. "Now, tell us Dima's plan."

He squints at Antonio. "You promise to have my back?"

Antonio nods. "Scout's fucking honor."

"Dima … he didn't tell me much," Noodles starts. "He doesn't really share much with me. Says I'm dumb, but, uh, I know Yaroslav is dead and Dima is coming for the girl."

"What do you mean, *coming for the girl*?" I grit out, spit flying with each word. My heart hammers in my chest, and I want to dig my fist into this fucker's brain to know all the details.

"I don't know," he rambles. "All he said was to come here, get your money, kill you, and then he was going to get the girl." He raises his voice, and it sounds more pleading. "That's all I know, man!"

I shoot him in the head, annoyed and frustrated.

Damien shoots him next, as if he needed to get his anger out as well.

Antonio stalks toward him to slit his throat. "If you want to be a made man, know your fucking history, you fucking idiot. We don't allow random motherfuckers to join our family."

I hurriedly grab my phone from my pocket and call Genesis's phone.

No answer.

I call it again.

No answer.

My next call is to Emilio.

"What's up?" he answers.

"Where's Genesis?"

"We're at the shelter."

"Do you have eyes on her at the shelter?"

"She left her classroom and went to the restroom."

"Go into the restroom and get her."

"You want me to go into the women's restroom?" He lowers his voice. "In a place like this, I'm not sure that's a good idea. I'm not about to fucking scare these women."

"Ask another woman or Lora to go in there."

"One sec."

I hear conversation in the background, making out Emilio asking someone to check on Genesis.

I grab Noodles's phone from his pocket and follow Antonio and Damien out of the warehouse.

"She's not in the restroom," Emilio says, now panicked. "The woman said she walked out back with another girl."

"Go find her!" I scream into the phone.

"Already on my way!" Emilio says, and I can tell he's running.

The three of us load into Antonio's car, and he speeds away from the warehouse.

"Emilio!" I yell into the phone. "Do you have her?"

"No," he huffs out. "She's gone."

41

Genesis

Today was supposed to be happy.

A celebration of a new milestone in our lives.

But that's ruined.

Regret flows through me.

I should've never followed Sage out of Safe Hearts.

In the back of my mind, I thought the threat of Dima was gone.

As I come into consciousness, I see only darkness. The floor is cold beneath me, and the stench of cigarettes, bad odor, and mold surrounds me.

Something covers my head, but when I attempt to take it off, I realize my arms and feet are restrained.

My breath knocks from my lungs when someone pulls the bag off my head, and my mouth is taped shut. I struggle, trying to tug my way out of the restraints. My wrists and ankles already burn.

The man in my father's office, who Dima burned with the cigar, stands in front of me. Hearing a whimper, I peek over to find Sage tied up in a chair a few feet away from me.

There's no bag over her head, but she has duct tape over her mouth, like mine.

Her gaze pings from the man to me.

Frantic.

Back and forth, over and over again.

Her eyes are wide, but she's not fighting to release herself, like I am.

Is she here because of me?

Or am I here because of her?

The door opens, and Dima walks in, dressed in a black suit and holding a gun.

My blood chills.

I expected him, but still, seeing him here makes everything so much more real.

The light flickers above us, and we're in some dim warehouse building. I don't hear the flow of traffic, just the whoosh of the wind and Dima's footsteps as he comes closer.

His threatening stare is pinned on me, as if Sage weren't even here. He plays with his thick gold ring, sliding it up and down his finger.

"Hello, *nevesta*," he says, putting so much emphasis on the last word.

I jerk my head from side to side, saying, "I'm not your fucking wife," beneath the tape.

He steeples his fingers together and taps them against his mouth before making a *tsk* sound. "Now, I'd prefer to have you tied up in our bedroom, but since you've been a bad girl, here will suffice for now."

I wrestle with my restraints, pleading with my body to get stronger so I can break out of them.

Dima laughs, rolling up his sleeve, showing off a large snake tattoo, and finally takes a glance at Sage. An evil chuckle rolls off his tongue as he takes two long strides toward her.

She hisses when he jerks her head to the side, forcing her to look at me. "You can thank your sister here for reuniting us." He roughly taps Sage's cheek. Dropping her head, he walks in front of me.

I wince, pain riding up my face when he rips off the tape.

"Sister?" I shriek, setting my eyes on Sage.

She's not as shocked as I am.

She knew.

A tear falls down my cheek, and she turns her head away, looking away.

Dima laughs again and rips the tape off Sage's mouth. "Oh, that's not even the biggest secret she's kept from you."

42

Julian

ANTONIO SPEEDS straight to the shelter and swerves into the back alley, where Emilio awaits us.

I jump out of the car and punch Emilio in the face.

"Shit," he hisses, rubbing his jaw. "I deserved that."

I shake out my fist. "You'd better hope we find her."

Emilio nods, his face burning. "I won't sleep until we do."

He knows he fucked up. While we all bitch anytime we have *bodyguard duty*, we know it's still an important job. The person we're watching needs to stay safe. It stings when shit goes wrong as a result of our incompetence.

Emilio and I grew up together. Both our fathers were Lombardi capos, and now, both of them are dead. Enemies murdered mine, but Emilio's father?

We murdered him.

He'd chosen Antonio's uncle's side during the civil war. I'd never seen Emilio so torn when he had to turn his back on his own blood. There was an internal struggle, but Emilio's father was also a piece of shit, not a good one, like mine.

Like me, Emilio has seen a lot of death.

Also like me, he holds most of that shit inside.

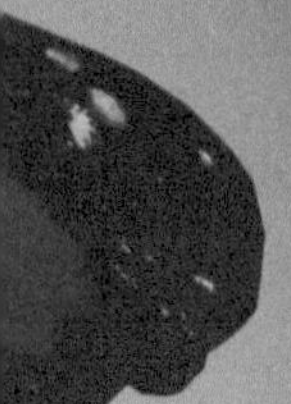

Damien steps out of the car, kicking a takeout container away with his foot. "We'll find her. Don't worry, Julian."

His assurance doesn't help.

I'll fucking worry until Genesis is back in my arms.

Emilio jerks his head toward the back door, and we follow him. He knocks on it, and Ollie answers, sticking his head out and waving us inside. The five of us walk toward Lora's office in a straight line as women and children gape at us.

Ollie slaps me on my back when we reach the doorway. "I pulled up the security footage. We have the make and model of the van and the plate number."

I jerk my chin toward him. "I appreciate it, man."

Lora jumps up from her chair when we enter. Her eyes are red and puffy, and a wadded tissue is in her hand.

"Julian!" She rushes over to hug me. "I'm so sorry! Safe Hearts has always been a safe space. Nothing like this has ever happened before."

I tap her shoulder in comfort. "It's not your fault, Lora. You just stay calm and take care of the shelter. We'll find Genesis."

"Please"—her lower lip trembles—"you have to."

Damien helps her back to her seat as Ollie shoves a laptop in front of my face. Unblinking, I watch the video surveillance of what happened when the fuckers took Genesis. I have Ollie replay it over a dozen times, taking in every single detail.

I note the time stamps. The height of the men. How many there are. What Genesis was wearing.

Every single detail is embedded in my brain.

Emilio and Antonio are at my back, doing the same thing.

"Email that to me," I tell Ollie, and he salutes me.

"I pulled Sage's file," Lora says grimly, opening a drawer and dropping a folder in front of me. "The girl wasn't much of a talker, so our information is limited. I'm hoping there's enough to find Genesis. I suggest we call law enforcement, and they can—"

"No," Antonio says, speaking over her. "No need for that."

Lora warily stares at him. "Okay," she whispers, as if questioning if she's morally okay with overstepping this line.

She has to know what Antonio meant.

I open the folder, and my phone rings before I have the chance to read over it.

Derrick's name flashes on my screen.

I hold the phone up toward Lora. "The police."

Lora's shoulders ease an inch.

There. Maybe that'll make her feel somewhat better.

She doesn't need to know he's on our payroll.

"Talk to me," I say, answering the call as Antonio starts flipping through the pages of Sage's folder.

"Sage Losev," he starts. "Her stepfather, Denis 'Bird Eye' Losev, works for the Morozova family. He was given the nickname because he used to pluck out birds' eyes when he was a kid. Fucking weird and inhumane."

"Motherfucker," I hiss beneath my breath, struggling to control the urge not to throw my phone through the damn wall.

"There's more."

"Go on."

"Rumor is, she's Carlisle Astor's secret child. The Feds have been looking into his transactions, and we found multiple payments to Denis's wife, dating back twenty years ago."

I bare my teeth. "Get me Denis's address."

"Texting it to you now." He ends the call.

A BEAT-UP purple minivan sits in the driveway of the duplex home.

We've been sitting outside, across the street, for five minutes and haven't seen any movement.

Five minutes longer than what I'd like, but I need to be smart in every move I make.

"Hotheaded men always die faster than those who keep cool heads." That's what my father used to say. "Only be a hothead when you're kicking another man's ass. Otherwise, be calculated about every step you make."

On the drive here, Damien called Pippa and told her to find every online trace of Sage—all her social media accounts, anywhere she tagged her locations, or family members.

I stare at the home, already knowing Genesis isn't in there.

All this place will have are clues that will lead me to her.

The front door's screen is ripped, one of the windows has cardboard covering a hole, and there's a yard sign that says *No soliciting, assholes.*

I tuck my Glock into one pocket, grip my pistol, and slip out of Antonio's car. He and Damien do the same. I stalk straight to the door, taking long strides, and kick it open.

How's that for soliciting, assholes?

"Denis?" a raspy, feminine voice calls out from down the hall. "Is that you?"

Damien clicks the front door shut, and none of us says a word as we walk through the living room and into the kitchen.

A woman wearing a stained SpongeBob robe stops, mid-bite of a slice of toast. "Can I help you?"

Her eyes are droopy, but she looks nowhere near fazed that three armed strangers are in her home. It's like this is a regular Saturday for her.

"Where is she?" I demand, aiming my gun at her head.

"Who?" Her gaze slips between us three men, and it dawns on her. "Oh, you're here for *her.*"

I take a step closer. "*Her*?"

"Genesis," she spits, as if the name makes her sick. "Carlisle's golden daughter, the only one he cared about." She stretches her arm across the table to snatch a pack of cigarettes and a lighter.

"Where is she?" I push.

She sticks the cigarette in her mouth, lighting it, and doesn't say a word.

I lower the gun to pluck the cigarette from her mouth, throw it on the floor, and kneel in front of her. "Tell me where she is, or I'll light this house on fire with you inside it."

Ignoring me, she grabs another cigarette. When she goes for her lighter, I throw it off the table.

She blows out a spent breath. "She's with *her husband*, Dima." Her upper lip snarls. "Son of a bitch thought she was better than my sweet Sage. She deserved to be with him, to be the Bratva queen."

I raise my gun, holding it to the woman's head. "What's Dima's address?"

"How am I supposed to know?" She attempts to jerk away, but I don't allow it. "You think Dima just hands out his address to people? No one knows where Dima lives because that's how he wants it."

I click the trigger. "Where's your husband?"

She scoffs. "Working. Fucking a mistress. Snorting coke up his nose. How am I supposed to know? His location is just as much of a mystery as Dima's residence."

"She's useless," Damien comments.

I swipe her phone from the table and push it into my pocket. "Come on," I tell her. "We're going for a ride."

I don't tell her until we're outside that her seat is in the trunk.

For years, I was trained to hunt and kill.

To trace and hack.

I'll find Genesis, and I'll kill every motherfucker in my way.

43

Genesis

Kidnapped.

A secret sister.

Secrets.

It's like I'm in a damn movie plot.

"What other secrets?" I ask Sage, still trying to wrap my head around the bombshell Dima dropped.

Endless questions float through my mind.

I fell right into their trap, and now, I need to dig myself out.

Sage shrinks back in her chair, refusing to look at me.

Dima and his man's attention are glued to us, as if they're ready for a show.

I shiver, freezing, and jerk my hands, as if I suddenly gained the strength to break free.

"Oh, Sage, don't be shy now," Dima taunts.

The man in the corner drops his head back, laughing.

When Sage doesn't say a word, Dima charges toward her. He grabs the back of her chair, jerking it over so she's facing me. When she still doesn't speak, he snatches a fistful of her hair. She hisses in pain when he yanks her head back, forcing her to look at me.

"Tell her everything," Dima goads, holding her in place. "Tell your dear old sister how you set her up."

Tears sting my eyes as Sage keeps her mouth shut.

Dima steps between us to smack her across the face. "You don't start giving my wife answers, I'll rip your fucking tongue out."

I bite back the urge to correct that I'm not—nor will I ever be—his wife, but poking the armed bear isn't the smart way to stay alive.

It's not just *my* life I have to worry about.

It's also my baby's.

I need to keep us both alive.

"I set you up," she bites out toward me.

All the shyness she had at the shelter is gone.

Her real viciousness is coming through.

"That much is obvious," I snap. "*Why* did you do it?"

Sage narrows her eyes at me but turns to peer at Dima over her shoulder when he pulls away from her. She looks at him differently than me.

While I'm staring at him with hatred, her gaze is brimmed with adoration.

"Using the shelter to get to you was Sage, her mother, and stepfather's idea," Dima announces to the room, as if we were on a game show and he was giving us all the rules. "Poor Sage has abandonment issues."

"Why?" I ask Sage again, proud of how strong I'm keeping my voice level. I won't let these assholes see me break down. "Why'd you do this?"

"Because I hate you," she screams, attempting to jerk toward me, but the restraints stop her. "Every day, growing up, I wished you'd die, so I could take your place as our father's favorite daughter. You're nothing but a rich bitch who got the life I wanted."

I wince at her cruel words.

"I didn't even know you existed," I tell her. "That sounds like an issue you should hate my father for. *Not me*."

"You got the mansion, the education, the attention," she says, mocking my voice. "You know what I got? Nothing. The child support our father did pay went straight into my mother and stepfather's pockets. I had no choice. To make ends meet, my family and I worked for the Morozovas. They're the ones who've kept us fed and a roof over our heads." She glances at Dima. "This is my family, and I had no choice."

"Everyone has a choice in what they do. It might not be the easiest, but there's always a choice."

"That's where you're naive, Genesis. We don't have the same choices." She sneers at me. "Unlike you, I don't have a line of men willing to pay a million dollars for me. In this world, there are the used and the users. I've always been the used, and nothing will ever change."

Dima nods in agreement, stopping behind her to play with her hair. "Sage is right there."

She smiles up at him.

"This is what happens when you're the used." He pulls out his gun, shooting her in the back of the head.

I scream bloody murder.

All the control I had over my emotions flies out the window.

I keep screaming and screaming and screaming, praying someone will hear me. Sage's body slumps forward in her chair, and a tear slips down my cheek.

I turn my head, looking away from her, and scream, "Somebody help me!"

I cry out in pain when Dima slaps me across the face twice.

"You're a monster," I snarl at him. "A fucking monster."

He kneels beside me, running his hand along my cheek. His ring is cold against my skin.

"Now, wife, that isn't very nice." He stretches out his leg to kick Sage's chair over. "That bitch disrespected you. Seeing that hurt on your face was killing me. I didn't like it. She was a threat to you, so I needed to get rid of it." Leaning forward, he runs his nose over my hair and deeply inhales. "I will always kill for you, my wife. Now, let's get you home."

44

Julian

I HEAR SAGE'S MOM, Cindy's, body roll in the trunk when Antonio takes a right turn.

No, she's not dead.

I prefer not to kill women.

We only tied her up and stuffed her in the trunk with Antonio's dirty gym clothes and the threat that if she didn't cooperate, she'd never make it out of the trunk.

I've spent the ride scouring her phone.

I read the text thread between her and Carlisle, further proving what a piece of shit he was. Cindy's hatred of Genesis are clear in the texts, like it was Genesis's fault that Carlisle was a shitty dad to Sage. As far as I know, she didn't even know about Sage.

Trust me, if she had, Genesis would have done anything to help her.

It's what she did today, and it got her fucking kidnapped.

My blood boils when I open Cindy and Sage's thread. Sage brags that everything is falling perfectly in plan at the shelter and that she hopes Dima kills Genesis. It was a setup, and they used Genesis's kindness as a weakness.

You can't kill people with kindness.

Kindness kills you.

When I'm finished, I call Denis.

"Look who finally got out of bed," he answers, grunting into the phone.

"She got out of bed and found me in your home," I say into the speaker.

"Who's this?"

"Julian Bellini. I have your wife."

"Hold on one sec." He pauses for a second. "Yeah, let me get a double cheeseburger with extra cheese, a large fry, and a Diet Coke." After finishing his order, he rejoins the conversation, as if this were a casual call. "Now, what were you saying?"

My nostrils flare. "I have your wife, and I'll slit her fucking throat and mail you her body if you don't tell me where mine is."

"You think I give a fuck if you kill her?" Amusement floods his voice, as if they'd just added another burger to his order. "I got a hundred-grand life insurance on her I could sure use. Can you do me a favor and make sure she'll be easily identifiable? It'll make the process go faster."

How the hell can any man in this world not want to kill everyone in it if their wife was in danger?

"Where's Genesis?" I grind out. "Don't think I'll stop with Cindy. I'm coming for you next."

"It's after noon. My guess is, she's already on her way out of the country. Now, let a man enjoy his lunch." He ends the call.

When I attempt to call him back, he ignores the call.

I've never felt so useless.

As someone who usually has the upper hand, I have a headache, being in the opposite position.

I toss Cindy's phone to the side when mine rings.

Cristian Marchetti's name flashes on my screen.

"Marchetti," I answer.

"I heard about Genesis," he says, completely unemotional. "I reached out to a source and learned some information that might be helpful."

"What's that?"

"He claims Dima killed Yaroslav."

"Who's your source?"

"He's agreed to meet with you. Come to my office at the mansion."

ANTONIO ROLLS down his window when we reach the Marchetti mansion gate, and the guard waves him through.

Cindy bangs in the trunk as we slowly make our way up the drive. I've never been to the Marchetti mansion before, but from what I've heard, the ground is nearly sacred to Cristian.

The three of us step out of the car and nearly sprint into the mansion. I want all the answers because the longer Genesis is gone, the harder it'll be to find her.

Benny is waiting for us in the foyer and waves us forward. We follow him straight into an office, where Cristian is rooted behind his desk. A large family mural is behind him. As we move deeper into the room, Benny shuts the door behind him.

Two chairs sit in front of Cristian's desk, and when I notice the bald, wrinkled man in one of them, I charge toward him.

"Whoa," Benny says, stepping in front of me and pressing his hand to my chest.

"This motherfucker—" I thrust my finger in the air.

"Is my informant and here to help you," Cristian states, sounding bored and reclining in his chair. "Boris, tell the man what he wants to know so he can find his wife, and I can get all of you out of my goddamn office."

Boris is Yaroslav's underboss. He was at the meeting when I made the first payment for the Genesis deal.

Benny makes sure I'm cool before stepping away, and I circle the chair to look Boris in the face.

Boris stares at me with sunken eyes. "Dima has your wife." He settles his hands in his lap, straightening his back.

This has to be a fucking setup.

"Why are you telling me this?" I spit.

"The enemy of my enemy is my friend." He adjusts his tie. "I was Yaroslav's underboss for four decades. I swore an oath to him, not to his murderer."

"How can you be so sure Dima killed him?"

"Dima took him home from the hospital, claiming he'd take care of him." His lips twist into a sneer. "Hours later, Dima claims Yaroslav was taking a bath and accidentally drowned. Yaroslav didn't take baths." He slams his hand on the armrest. "No one kills my boss and gets away with it."

"Is your plan to kill Dima?" Antonio asks, stepping around the chair to stand beside me. "Are your men planning to rebel to vindicate Yaroslav's death?"

"Dima has a plan. He's going to kill anyone who had unwavering loyalty to Yaroslav or questions his death. He's already called out a hit on me because I told our men he was the one who had killed our boss," Boris says. "If I'm going to die, I might as well take the fucker down who killed my friend, my boss, and who now sees me as next on their hit list."

"Man, I have a love-hate relationship with rats," Benny comments.

Boris's head snaps in his direction, as if that's the worst insult he's ever been given. "This is my first time saying one negative thing about the Morozova family. My loyalty has outlasted two marriages. This isn't me being a rat. It's me getting revenge, and as an old man, I'll get it better with you men than I will alone."

"How do I know you're not setting us up?" I ask, crossing my arms.

Boris exhales an exhausted sigh. "I could understand your question if I only went to you, but I'm sitting here, in front of the three cruelest Mafia families in the country. Do you think Dima wants a war with you? He wants a healthy relationship with the Marchettis." His gaze flicks to Cristian. "Word is, he plans to reach out to you as the new Bratva boss. He wants to make deals and get you on his good side."

Cristian shakes his head. "As much as I hate it, my son-in-law is a Lombardi. My loyalty is to him and my daughter." He scrubs a hand over his jaw. "If Dima even *thinks* about having a war with the Lombardis, then it's my war as well."

Antonio peers at him over his shoulder. "That might be the nicest shit you've ever said to me, Dad."

"You call me Dad again, and I'll shoot a hole in your head," Cristian comments. "I might not go to war with you, but I don't like you."

Antonio looks at Boris. "We're still working on our relationship."

"It would have helped if you hadn't kidnapped my fucking daughter," Cristian snaps.

"Where did he take Genesis?" I ask Boris, not interested in the Marchetti-Lombardi drama.

"Russia," Boris replies.

"Russia?" I roar.

"What the fuck?" Benny hisses.

"That motherfucker," Antonio mutters.

"Who takes their hostages to goddamn Russia?" Damien asks.

"A man who doesn't see her as a hostage. He sees her as a lifetime prisoner," Boris states.

45

Genesis

"GET RID OF HER FUCKING BODY," Dima tells the guy in the warehouse, pointing at Sage. "This stays between us. Tell Denis and Cindy that Sage ran off after we got Genesis."

The man pushes himself off the wall. "Got it, boss. You want me to bury her, drop her in the Hudson, or what?"

"Bury her." Dima steps behind me, extracting a pocketknife and opening it. "But make sure she's cut into pieces and scattered."

I swallow down the vomit making its way up my throat. My muscles tense when he cuts the ropes restraining my arms before doing the same with the ones on my legs.

Grabbing my elbow, he pulls me to my feet, steadying me, and leads me toward the door. I attempt to yank away from him, but he tightens his hold on me.

A black SUV is parked outside the warehouse, which is surrounded by old buildings with empty parking lots.

The second Dima's grasp on me loosens, I make a run for it. The driver's door opens, and the same burly man from my father's office steps out and grabs my waist.

I cry out, beating my fist against his sweaty back as he tosses me in the SUV's leather back seat. The windows are so darkly tinted that I can't see out.

Dima joins me, slamming the door. His beady eyes are narrowed in my direction as he shakes his head in disapproval.

The doors lock, and Dima snatches my wrist. He holds up my hand, inspecting it, and I attempt to scoot back when he plays with my wedding ring. He overpowers me and slides the ring off.

As soon as he releases me, I lunge forward, attempting to grab it. He snatches me around my neck with his free hand, pushing me back, and rolls down his window. Making a show of inspecting the ring, he turns it between his fingers before tossing it out the window.

"No," I can't help but shriek. "Why would you do that?"

He rolls up the window, looking smug. "Why would you marry another man when you were promised to me?"

I level my shoulders and voice. "Your father changed that promise. He gave me to Julian."

Blame it on Yaroslav.

Deflect, deflect.

He shakes his head. "My father never got the money."

"Julian has it. He'll pay whatever."

He wiggles his thick finger in the air, pulling up his sleeve. "Fuck the money. I'd rather have you."

I inhale three deep breaths.

Think, Genesis. Think.

"Dima," I say, trying my hardest to remain calm as I reach out and stroke his shoulder, "you want me to be your wife?"

"Yes." His eyes are on my hand. "And I always get what I want, *nevesta*." He grabs my hand from his shoulder and kisses the palm. "You are now mine. The best man won."

I bite my lip, nodding.

Not telling him he's so wrong.

For now, I need to stay on his good side.

Like so many people have with me, I'll play nice to his face.

Then, I'll turn just as cruel as everyone else when the time is right.

It's up to me to outsmart and escape this man.

It's time for me to stop being nice and start being smart.

WHEN WE'RE inside a home and what Dima called *our bedroom for now*, he hands me a passport. "Your new name is Anya Morozova while we're traveling."

I open the passport, seeing my picture and new name. "Why do I need a passport?"

"We're going to Russia, *nevesta*."

My heartbeat turns heavy, but I do my best to remain calm. "Russia? Why can't I stay here and be your wife?"

"For now, it's safest if you're there. You'll stay with my family."

"Will you be there?" I ask, forcing disappointment in my voice. I even pout out my lower lip.

He stares down at me, pleased. "I'll fly back and forth. I need to get you out of the marriage here, and then when I return to Russia, we'll marry there."

No way in hell is this motherfucker taking me to Russia.

I don't even know how I'd flee from Russia.

Time is of the essence.

"I'm sorry for marrying him, *muzh*," I say, calling him my husband in Russian and resting my palm on his chest.

He rears back, a satisfied smirk on his evil face.

I drop my hand down, massaging his stomach. "Marrying

Julian hurt you, but I was so confused. He told me you didn't want me, that you signed me over to him for the money."

"Good thing we fixed that then, huh?" He rests his large palm on my face, dragging his thumb over my bottom lip. "Now, you're mine."

I tip my head down, making a show of sniffing myself. "I'm all gross from being tied up in that warehouse. Can I shower before we leave?"

He cocks his head to the side.

"Just really quick, *alone*," I rush out. "Then, we'll leave, get married, and have a great honeymoon."

God, please don't let him try to join me.

A bang on the door interrupts us.

"Boss!" a man calls from the other side of the door. "We need to talk!"

"A quick shower," Dima huffs out. "Our flight leaves in forty-five minutes."

"Thank you." Lifting on my tiptoes, I kiss his cheek and scurry to the adjoining bathroom. As soon as I shut the door, I lock it, turn on the shower, and begin my hunt.

As quiet as I can, I go through the bathroom drawers first.

All I find weapon-wise is a pair of scissors, and I take them with me.

I run into the attached closet, searching through it next, and smile when I find a gun, stuffed behind a stack of socks in a drawer.

Jackpot.

What an idiot, letting me in here, knowing there's a weapon.

I grab the gun, inspecting it.

Now, I'm not experienced with guns, but I've been doing my fair share of research on them lately. I've watched a few videos on proper gun safety and how to use them. I also witnessed Julian kill my father's attorney and Dima kill Sage, watching how they handled the guns while doing it.

Deep down, I wanted to be prepared in case this ever happened.

I check the gun for bullets, finding it loaded, and snatch one of Dima's hoodies. I slip it over my head, check the gun's safety is on, and shove it in the front hoodie pocket. My search continues for any other weapons.

I freeze when there's a knock on the bathroom door.

"Why's this locked, *nevesta*?" Dima asks through it.

I hurriedly strip out of my clothes, tucking the gun and scissors in the back of my pants on the floor, and jump in the shower. "Sorry, can't hear you!" I soak my hair as fast as I can. "Almost finished!"

I turn off the water and jump out of the shower. Shivering, I redress, move the hoodie from my pants to the front hoodie pocket, and crack open the door just as Dima threatens to kick it down.

"Sorry," I say, poking my head through the crack. I tug on the hoodie string around my neck. "I borrowed one of your shirts. I like to wear my hubby's clothes." I fake a smile.

He pushes the door open, causing me to tumble back a few steps, and enters the bathroom. "You ready to go?"

"Do you have a blow-dryer?" I ask, twirling a wet strand around my finger.

He does. I saw it during my search.

"Yeah." He grabs the strand from me and wraps it around his finger, giving it a slight tug. "It's in the bottom-right drawer."

I peek around him, biting my lip, and look at the bottom drawer. "Are you sure you want me to go through your drawers? I didn't because I know how people like their privacy."

He drops my hair, running his tongue over the front of his tooth. "I'll grab it for you, but you need to hurry, *nevesta*. We're short on time."

As soon as he turns around, walking toward the marble

double vanity, I slowly draw the gun from my hoodie pocket. It's risky since there's a mirror, but it's now or never.

As soon as he glances down in the drawer, I raise the gun and shoot.

The gunshot is loud, and I see him attempt to reach for his gun as soon as I pull the trigger, but it's too late. My heart nearly stops as I watch the bullet collide with his head. His head flings forward, hitting the mirror, and he slumps against the counter.

I cover my mouth, shocked that I did it.

How did he make it so easy for me?

I guess there are perks to people believing you're weaker than them.

Dima saw me as the used.

I played that part until it was time to prove him wrong.

My eyes widen as realization hits me.

I killed someone. I'm a murderer.

Now, I need to finish my plan and finish it fast.

I counted at least three other men in the house when we arrived. Unless they're deaf or wearing headphones, they had to hear the gunshot and will probably be up soon to investigate.

Rushing over to Dima, I check his pulse.

The move reminds me so much of when I did the same to my father in his office. I grin when I don't feel anything.

Now, I need to figure out how to get out of here.

I tug Dima's body down to the floor, a smear of blood following him, and search his pockets for his phone.

I tap the screen as soon as I do, finding it locked.

Shit.

Kneeling, I put the phone in front of his face.

It still doesn't unlock.

"Dima! I heard a gunshot!" the same guy who interrupted us before yells through the bedroom door. "Is everything okay?"

Fuck!

I don't reply, hoping no response will be good enough.

"Boss, tell me everything is okay!" He wiggles the doorknob, and I'm thankful Dima locked it earlier. "If you don't, I'm breaking down the door!"

"Dima is in the shower," I shout. "Everything is good!"

"Why'd I hear a gunshot then?"

My head grows dizzy. "It was an accident. He was showing me what'd happen if I tried to run and shot the ceiling."

I try to unlock the phone with facial recognition again.

Cursing when it doesn't work, I crawl across the floor, over his blood, and snatch his gun, just in case.

Two guns are always better than one, especially when dealing with psychopaths.

"Open the door and let me find out myself, cunt," the man says, and it sounds like he's kicking the door.

Turning the shower on again, I strip out of my clothes and change into Dima's robe. I drop the gun and scissors in the robe's pocket and race toward the bedroom door, wiping off any blood on me on the way.

The guy stops his kicking when I crack the door open.

He tries to open it farther, but I block his way into the room.

I rest my hand on my hip, staring him down. "Dima is not happy about you interrupting our shower."

"Dima doesn't shower in the middle of the day."

"We got kind of dirty … you know …"

A sinister smirk forms on his face as his eyes roam down my body. "I don't believe you." He shoves me out of the way.

I stumble back as he forces himself into the room.

I'm so screwed.

As soon as his back is to me, I raise my gun and shoot.

The first shot misses him, hitting the wall.

My pulse races.

My hands start shaking.

I have to be quick.

He turns, grabbing for his gun. I white-knuckle the gun,

touching the trigger, and I shoot again just as he's facing me. He falls back a step as a bullet connects with his face. His body sways to the side, and he's struggling to grip his gun.

Not wanting to risk his men hearing another gunshot, I pull out the scissors and charge toward him. He drops the gun, and I raise my arm, stabbing him in the neck and pushing him down.

He collapses onto the carpet with a heavy thud. Blood gushes from his cheek and neck as I stab him again and again.

I stare down at his dead, bloody body when I'm finished.

I jump to my feet, close and lock the bedroom door, and fall next to Dima's dead man. Blood seeps around his body, his eyes wide open and his thumb still on the gun.

"Tell me you have one," I mutter to myself, searching for his phone.

My adrenaline pumps out of control.

"Yes!" I whisper to myself when I find the flip phone.

I open it, finding everything in Russian.

That's at least one good thing I can appreciate my father for —making sure I knew how to speak the language of the men he sold me to.

I'm nearly out of breath, nearly in a daze, as I realize I don't know Julian's number by heart.

Out of options, I dial 911.

I listen to the ringing, and as soon as the operator answers, I say, "My name is Genesis. Dima Morozova kidnapped me."

"Ma'am, do you know where you are?" he asks.

"No." My mouth is so dry that I'm shocked I can form words. "Can you trace this phone?"

"I'm sorry, but it's not coming up as traceable for me," he says in a cool voice, his words slow, as if he wants to relax me. "Can you describe your surroundings for me, Genesis?"

"I'm in a house."

I jump to my feet, nearly tripping over the man's body, and

rush to the window, looking out it. There's nothing distinguishable. We're on some kind of hidden estate.

"Can you get in contact with NY FBI agent Derrick"—shutting my eyes, I try to remember the last name the prosecutor had said during his speech, and my body shudders when I do. "Green. Agent Derrick Green. Tell him Dima Morozova kidnapped Genesis Bellini and we're at his house. There are other armed men here. Get here fast!"

Julian

I'M SPEEDING to Dima's house—address provided by good ol' Boris. Before this, I'd left Cindy in the trunk at the Marchetti residence, instructing one of his men to drop her off in the middle of nowhere when I gave him the go-ahead. I'm not letting her go until I have Genesis. Leaving her in the middle of nowhere will give her time to think about her bad decisions as she walks home.

My phone rings, and Derrick's name flashes on the screen.

"Genesis called 911," he says when I answer and put the call on speaker. "She's at Dima's house."

I cut a right, following the GPS. "Is she alive?"

"Unless her ghost called, yes, she's alive."

"Fuck off," I grind out. "Is she safe or still in harm's way?" I slam my foot on the gas pedal. "How many men are there?"

"She told the operator she killed Dima and one of his men in self-defense. She's upstairs, so she doesn't know who else is downstairs. She did note that even though it was hard to see outside on the drive there, she thinks there are guards at the gate because they stopped to talk to a group of men."

"She killed Dima?" Antonio whistles, impressed. "Damn, Genesis."

"That'ta girl," Damien comments from the back seat.

"I'm on my way to Dima's residence now," Derrick says.

"I'm four minutes out," I tell him.

"Squad cars are behind me, FYI. If you make it there before I do, don't do anything stupid that they can put you in prison for."

"Tell them to turn around," I instruct. "I got this handled."

"No can do, Julian. There was a 911 call. It's on record, and it's our duty to respond. It's also the Morozovas, a family we've wanted to catch for a while. No way are we losing our chance to rid them from the streets."

"It sounds like they're gone from there now anyway. Dima and Yaroslav are dead."

"Yaroslav is dead?"

"Dima killed him."

Derrick curses under his breath. "Man, I'd never join one of these families."

"We're not all like that," Antonio corrects. "The rats always end up dying at some point. Those who are smart and loyal survive."

"Loyalty is subjective," Derrick comments.

"See you there, Derrick." I end the call and slow my speed as Dima's residence comes into view.

It's private, like Boris said, and spans at least ten acres. The home is made of stone, almost castle-like, and I park on the side of the road when I spot two armed guards at the gate.

"You ready?" I ask the guys, opening the glove compartment and grabbing my Glock.

Damien turns the safety off his AK and unrolls his window.

Antonio holds his gun, ready to fire at any moment.

Cristian and Benny Marchetti are in the SUV behind us. While they usually don't involve themselves in other families' issues, Neomi told Benny she'd file for divorce if he didn't help get Genesis back to safety.

Benny immediately grabbed his gun and jacket, telling us to come on.

Love does some crazy shit to men's brains.

I shift the SUV into drive and floor it toward the gate. As soon as the guards notice us, they raise their guns. Damien sticks his AK through the window, ducking low, as I speed toward them.

Damien's bullets hit both men right between their eyes, and they crumple to the ground. I swerve, running one over, and crash through the gate. A man sprints toward us, a rifle in his hand, and stops in front of us in the driveway. He gets three bullets out before I run him over as if he were nothing but a mere speed bump.

Looking in my rearview mirror, I see Cristian Marchetti following right behind. Benny thrusts his body out the window, shooting two men standing alongside the fence, as Cristian runs over another.

I love bowling with motherfuckers as the pins.

As soon as we reach the house, I shift the car into park, jump out, and run into the house. A man sitting in the foyer, headphones on, jumps up from his chair.

He scrambles for his gun, but I shoot him in the head before he gets the chance to find it.

What kind of dumb motherfucker wears headphones when you have a hostage in the building?

Antonio, Damien, Benny, and Cristian are behind me.

"Genesis!" I scream, darting up the stairs while the others search the house. "Genesis!"

As soon as I make it on the second floor, a door opens, and Genesis darts out of the bedroom.

"Julian!" she sobs, running straight into my arms, shoving

her face into my shoulder. "They killed Sage … I killed them." She digs her fingernails into my shirt. "I'm a murderer."

I cup the back of her head, massaging her wet hair.

While I'm proud of Genesis for killing Dima, I know it'll haunt her.

Most people aren't made for murder.

While I have dreams of murder instead of nightmares, Genesis is the opposite. Her heart is too pure.

Good people aren't made to kill.

The unfortunate thing is, sometimes, they have to.

"No, Genesis," I say, kissing the top of her head. "You're a survivor. You did what you had to do."

"You're also a badass, Genesis," Damien says, standing behind me. "You outsmarted a Bratva boss and killed his ass. Good for you." He squeezes Genesis's shoulder as he passes us. "Where's the body?"

Genesis pulls away a few inches, pointing toward the door she ran through. "In there."

We all look toward the door at the sound of sirens.

"Fuck," Cristian grumbles, massaging his forehead. "Who called the cops?"

"That'd, uh … be me," Genesis mutters.

"You really need to memorize my number, baby." I smack another kiss to her head while massaging her shoulder.

Cristian, Benny, Damien, and Antonio disappear into the bedroom.

"Jesus," I hear.

We walk toward the stairway banister, looking down on the first floor, to find Derrick. A group of officers are behind him.

"I'll assume Dima killed his men at the gate," he comments, checking the pulse of the dead man in the foyer.

"That's right," I reply. "Everyone was dead when we arrived."

He shakes his head, attempting to hide a grin.

"Come on, baby," I say to Genesis. "Let's get you home."

"You take her," Antonio says. "Damien and I will ride back with Marchetti."

Benny exits the room, holding up a pair of Chanel flats. "Do these belong to you, Genesis?"

She nods.

He hands them to her.

"Thank you," she says, holding on to my shoulder and slipping them on.

I can tell she's still in shock. If dead bodies are in there, that means she's been sitting with them.

"I want pictures of the bodies," I tell Benny. "And their phones."

He nods in response.

Genesis holds my hand as we walk down the stairs, and Derrick walks with us outside. Cop cars line the drive, and I hear one call for ambulances through his radio.

"I appreciate you not doing *too much* damage," Derrick tells me before lowering his voice so only I can hear. "We will need to bring her in for questioning."

"Not today you won't," I reply.

He nods. "But we will."

"When she feels up to it."

He nods again. "I'll give you a police escort back so you can get her home faster."

"Appreciate it." I clap him on the back.

He smirks, sliding on his sunglasses. "See, isn't it nice, somewhat obeying the law sometimes?"

"Sorry to break it to you, Derrick, but you sold half your soul to the dark side when you began working with me."

He shrugs. "At least I didn't sell all of it."

I help Genesis into the SUV, buckling her in, and she grabs the sides of my face. Her hands tremble, and she stares up at me with shuttered eyes.

"Julian, I fucking love you," she says, her tone urgent. "The entire time I sat there on the phone with 911, all I could think about was how I needed to tell you that. I had known I had to get rid of Dima because no other man would ever be my love, my husband, but you."

Derrick steps away, giving us our moment, and I see the smile on his face.

I've never felt my heart warm.

Never felt a happiness beam inside me.

I caress her cheek with my knuckle. "Genesis, I think I started falling in love with you years ago, that day in my mother's kitchen. I pretended to glare at you, but the truth is, watching you was all it took for me to ignore the pain as she stitched me up. You're my peace, my chaos, my everything." I press a light kiss to her lips and wipe blood off her cheek. "If something had happened to you, I'd have lost a piece of myself."

She settles her cheek into my palm, and a tear falls down her face. "Let's go home. I want to show you your surprise."

47

Genesis

Julian takes my hand as he makes a U-turn out of Dima's driveway. We pass cop cars and dead men. As we're pulling out onto the street, two EMTs speed toward Dima's house.

We're quiet, and I shut my eyes.

I immediately open them as the memory of me stabbing Dima's man floats into my mind. At that moment, I zoned out, disassociated, and all I thought about was my baby's and my lives.

After killing Dima's guy, I had to either sit there in his blood or clean myself off. I was too scared to get in the shower, in fear that another one of his men could come after me, I had to scoot Dima's body to the side to wet a washcloth in the sink and clean the blood from my body.

I changed out of his robe and back into my clothes, and I waited for the police. My body shook as I slouched in a corner, hiding, in case someone tried to kill me before they arrived.

Julian's hand moves from mine when his phone rings. Grabbing it from the cupholder, he checks the caller ID before answering.

"Hi, Lora," he says. "Yes, she's safe." Peering over at me, he mouths, "*Are you okay to talk?*"

I nod, taking the phone from him.

"Hi, Lora," I say around a gulp.

"Oh, Genesis," she says, her voice hitching with emotion. "I'm so sorry. Going forward, I promise, I'll do better at vetting who stays with us here. This should've never happened to you."

"Lora, this wasn't your fault," I say. "You were only trying to help Sage. We all were."

"I'm glad you're safe, honey. Please keep in touch."

"Of course." After ending the call with her, I glance at Julian. "How'd Lora know Sage wasn't innocent?"

"We watched the camera footage." He clenches his jaw, tightening his fingers around the steering wheel. "Sage met with the men before she lured you out of the restroom. At first, we weren't sure why, but as we started putting the clues together, we figured it out."

"So, you know why?" I ask, my voice wavering.

He gives me a look, waiting for me to answer my own question.

"I know she was my sister," I say with sadness. "Dima made a show of telling me before he shot Sage in the head."

Not one expression passes over his face.

I swear, I can almost see him fighting back a smile.

"Ah," he says. "I was wondering what had happened to her." He makes a right at a Stop sign.

"You wondered, but didn't care?"

"I hoped she'd faced the same fate as Dima."

I frown. "That's not very nice, Julian."

His strong hand takes mine again. "It wasn't nice for her to set you up."

"That doesn't mean she deserved to die."

"She knew what would happen if Dima got to you. Had it not

been for her actions today, you wouldn't be shaking in my car after murdering two men."

I stare down at our joined hands, noticing for the first time that *I am* shaking.

"Had she not set you up, I wouldn't have been trying to come up with a plan to find you in fucking Russia. There was a chance Dima would kill you, but Sage didn't worry about that either. She didn't care whether you lived or died."

My shoulders slump. "I wish she'd just told Dima no."

"She didn't, and that cost her, her life. Don't feel bad for her."

"Easier said than done."

"I do not envy those with large hearts," he says under his breath.

MY MIND IS SET when we get home.

I'll block out everything bad that happened today.

Dima will not ruin this moment for us.

His darkness will not spoil our happiness.

I escaped him, *killed* him, and now, he's no longer a threat.

Maybe Julian and I can get our happily ever after.

The air-conditioning is cold when we enter our home.

"Let's get you cleaned up," Julian says. "You need to rest. We'll order takeout and eat in bed."

"Are you staying with me tonight?" I whisper as he scoops me up into his arms.

"They'd have to kill me before I left your side." He carries me upstairs, straight to the bathroom, and lowers me to my feet.

I kick off my flats as he turns on the water, and he returns to help me undress. After checking the water temperature, he kisses my forehead and helps me into the shower.

I sigh, tension gradually releasing from my muscles as the hot water splashes my body. Moments later, a naked Julian joins me. I scoot back, giving him room.

Tipping my head back, I allow water to run over my face and down my hair. As my head lowers, I pretend not to see the traces of blood running alongside the water down the drain.

I cleaned the blood off my body in Dima's bathroom, but there was still some caked in my hair and beneath my nails. Julian soaps a washcloth and gently starts washing my body. I relax against his touch and the heat of the water.

Unlike me, Julian doesn't seem exhausted at all.

This is just another day for him.

A single tear slips down my cheek.

I'm not sure *what* the tear is for.

What happened with Dima, that Julian saved me, or that I'm finally getting what we've talked about?

I gulp, mad at myself for getting emotional.

Everyone around me is ruthless. Maybe that's how I need to be too.

"Julian," I say, shutting my eyes.

He stops mid-grab of the shampoo and sets it down.

Stepping closer, he runs the pad of his thumb along my cheek. "Genesis, everyone reacts to these situations differently. While some prefer to talk about it, others don't. We can talk about it right now, tonight, or any other time." He drops his head to kiss my cheek. "However, you'd prefer to get it out—tears, letting your anger out on me, whatever—I'm here for you."

Another tear falls down my cheek from the other eye.

I brush my fingers along his chest, my voice sounding hoarse as I say, "I was so scared, Julian."

He drags me into his chest, holding me tight and resting his chin on my head.

"I killed a man," I say against his skin. "I killed *two* men."

He shakes his head. "Genesis, you fought for your life. That's it."

"I didn't just fight for my life." I inch back, grab his hand to interlace our fingers, and smooth it down my stomach. "I fought for *our baby's* and my lives."

He pauses, his gaze moving from my stomach to my eyes. "Are you serious?"

I shyly smile at him. "I am."

A wide grin spreads across his face.

I've *never* seen him smile so big.

His lips brush against mine before he before drops to his knees and softly kisses my stomach. "We're having a baby, Genesis." Staring up at me, he blinks water from his eyes and then nuzzles his rugged cheek against my skin.

Reaching down, I run my hand through his hair. "We're having a baby."

A lightness forms in my chest, and excitement pours through me.

Today has been an emotional roller coaster.

It went from the high of seeing the positive signs on the pregnancy tests, to the horror of being kidnapped by Dima, to this intimate moment now.

This is what I fought for.

For this.

For us.

For our life together.

I WAKE up to an empty bed.

Reaching across it, I look around for Julian, but there's no sign of him.

The bathroom light isn't on, so I scoot out of bed, taking the sheet with me, and walk across the bedroom. A sliver of light shines from beneath the door. I ease the door open and tiptoe toward the banister. Peeking down, I see Julian sitting at the island, FaceTiming on his phone.

"I'm going to be a dad," he says into the phone, Damien's face on the screen.

"Are you serious?" Damien asks before I hear Pippa shout, "Oh my freaking God! You'd better not be lying!"

"Look at that big-ass smile on his face," Damien points out. "He's not kidding. After what happened today, other than when he found out Genesis was okay, that's the only thing that could make him happy."

"Awww, a happy Julian is a cute Julian," Pippa comments cheerfully.

I crack a smile, imagining Julian narrowing his eyes at her too-happy tone.

"Look, honey, he's growing a heart." She claps. "I'm so happy for you two! Alessia is going to be so excited that she's getting a cousin! Another Bellini baby! I need to call Genesis."

"Not tonight," Julian hurriedly says, as if he saw her reaching for her phone.

She sighs. "I know. Damien told me I had to wait until tomorrow." Another sigh. "Poor thing, but also what a fucking badass. She killed a fucking Mafia boss."

"Bratva," Julian and Damien correct at the same time.

"Semantics," Pippa shouts at them.

"All right, I have to go," Julian tells them. "I just couldn't wait to tell you, bro. I feel like I'm on top of the world."

"You are," Damien says. "I'm happy for you and Genesis, brother. I was worried about you for a while. It might've been hell for the both of you, but I'm happy Genesis was brought into your life. She's who you needed to save you."

I slam a hand over my mouth as tears prick at my eyes.

Jesus. Is this what pregnancy does to you?

I've never been much of a crier, but these tear ducts are a-flowing.

Julian tells them goodbye, and I dash back to the bedroom, jumping back into bed. I situate myself to how I was lying before, pretending to sleep as I hear Julian's footsteps come up the stairs.

"I know you're awake, eavesdropper," he says with a chuckle. "You could've come down and joined the conversation."

I sit up in bed. "I was trying to only be halfway rude."

He's shirtless, but since he put his sweats back on, he takes them off before climbing back into bed, wearing only his boxer briefs.

He reaches across the bed, dragging me closer, and I turn on my side to face him. I settle myself as he loops his arm around my shoulders, and I relax my head against his warm chest.

I trace one of his tattoos with my finger. "Two people who felt like they had no one will now have everything they've ever wanted," I whisper.

He takes my hand, moving it from his chest, and trails kisses along my palm. "Destiny was just waiting for us."

I let out a breath when he bends forward, spans his hands along the flares of my waist, and pulls me onto his lap so I'm straddling him.

"Thank you for saving yourself and our baby." He opens his hand, smoothing it over my bare stomach. "You were so brave, and you did it for us." Grabbing the back of my head, he drags my face toward his. "I'm ready for our future, Genesis. A real wedding, our baby—*babies* if you'll let me be lucky enough to keep trying. Fuck a contract. I just want you."

"A big Bellini family," I whisper.

He nods, swiping his nose against mine. "A big Bellini family."

"Just like your mother wanted." I press a soft kiss to his lips, but he deepens it.

"I love you, Genesis," he says when we finally take a break for air. "You are now the reason I'll make sure I stay breathing. I never thought I'd be lucky enough for love. I always thought men like me didn't deserve it, but even if I don't, you're giving it to me anyway."

48

Julian

Four Months Later

I ADJUST MY BOW TIE, staring at my reflection in the mirror.

For a man who doesn't look any different, I *am*.

Damien steps behind me, doing the same. "I appreciate you inviting me to this one." He slaps my shoulder. "Glad you didn't leave me out."

I flip him off. "You'd have objected if you'd been invited to the first wedding."

When his bow tie is straight, he backtracks a few steps to sit on a chair. "Nah, if I'd done that, you'd have probably shot me." He scoots toward the edge, resting his elbows on his thighs. "Though I'd have just made you annul it later."

"You wouldn't have made me do shit." I spin on my heel to face him.

"True. You were so obsessed with Genesis that I could've offered you a billion dollars and control of the world in exchange for not marrying her, and you'd have still told me to fuck myself."

"Damn straight." I snatch my tux jacket and pull it over my

shoulders. "And still shot you because the offer would've pissed me off."

The door opens, interrupting our conversation, and Antonio steps inside the Groom Room.

Antonio shuts the door, turning to look at us, stone-faced. "Not to sound like a drag on your wedding day, but we have a problem."

"When don't we have a problem?" Damien says, already sounding stressed, all the amusement from our conversation gone.

I stare at Antonio grimly, waiting for whatever bad news is coming my way.

Whatever it is, it'd better not affect my wedding today.

Genesis already had one subpar ceremony. I won't allow that to happen again.

"Pissed-off Russians are blowing up my phone," Antonio states before stopping. "Not physically, metaphorically."

It's wild that we have to clarify that.

But men in our world have an affinity for blowing shit up.

We've murdered every Russian who was aware of Dima's plan to kidnap Genesis, including Denis. That motherfucker got a personal three-hour torture session from me before I gutted him, hung him up by chains in a warehouse, and left him there for two more days before dropping him in the ocean.

"Tell the Russians to kiss our Italian asses." Damien kicks his feet up onto the table. "Dima murdered Yaroslav, *their boss*. They should be happy the disloyal fuck, his son or not, is gone."

Antonio kicks Damien's feet off the table and sits beside him. "Dima's cousin is coming from Russia to take control of the family here. None of them are pissed at us, but they want a contract."

"We don't owe them shit," I sneer. "Did you tell them Dima took my wife? If anything, they owe us a fucking favor. A huge fucking one. Tell them I want a shipment of their fucking eyeballs for my wedding gift."

"What kind of contract do they want?" Damien asks.

"Marriage."

Damien lets out a breath through clenched teeth.

"He wants one of our men to wed his daughter," Antonio adds.

All attention slips to me.

"The fuck are you looking at me for?" I ask. "We're at my wedding, so don't get any ideas."

"Calm down. We're not planning to make you a polygamist," Damien says. "We're brainstorming. Start doing the same."

"We only have …" I pause to think of options.

"Emilio or Leo," Antonio says. "I vote Emilio." Leo is Antonio's cousin.

I shake my head. "Emilio will say no. He doesn't want a wife."

Antonio strokes his jaw. "He won't have a choice."

"I think a wife would be good for Emilio," Damien inputs, as if we were parents discussing sending him to boarding school for bad grades, not forcing him to marry a stranger.

I point at each of them. "Fine, it's Emilio. But don't you inform him of this decision until *after* my wedding." I straighten my lapels.

"Having sane Russians on board with us will help," Antonio continues. "The Irish are still pissed at us. Even though Riona is in charge, I have a feeling the higher ups in Ireland aren't happy about a woman being in charge."

Riona is currently the boss of the Irish mob, based out of Boston. She's the first woman to carry the position after murdering her father. I like Riona, father murderer or not. She's coolheaded for the most part, and she broke the marriage contract with Damien so he could marry Pippa.

"Fuck the Irish," I say.

Antonio stands, buttoning his blazer. "We'll discuss this later. Genesis will probably kick your ass if she walks down the aisle and you're nowhere to be seen."

THIS MORNING, I went to my father's gravestone and told him he was right.

Every parent loves hearing that.

He'd told me and Damien that, someday, we'd find a woman we loved as much as he loved my mother. He swore, one day, a woman would bring us to our knees and she'd become the reason we stayed alive.

Sometimes, in the back of my mind, I wonder if he ever saw Genesis as that woman for me. If he already knew.

I'd sworn to him, there was no heart for me to give to a woman. Genesis proved that wrong. She pushed her manicured hand into my chest, planting roots and helping my heart to grow large enough to fit room for herself there.

For our growing family.

The music starts, and everyone in the pews turns quiet. The cathedral is full of guests. All attention turns to Genesis as she struts down the aisle with Uncle Mick by her side.

We take regular date nights to the pizzeria. At first, and even though they didn't voice it, I could tell they were concerned about my affiliation with the Lombardi family, as they had been with my father. But after so many years after losing my mother, they said they regretted ending their relationship with her. Time is too short, and it was one of their biggest regrets. I'm also extremely careful with them. Other than today, we only see them during date nights at the pizzeria.

My lips twitch into a smile as my eyes are glued to her. She's headed straight to me, her baby bump on display in her white dress.

Her eyes aren't on anyone but me.

I mouth, "*So fucking stunning,*" to her, and she blows me a kiss.

She's made me the luckiest man alive.

As she grows closer, I hear a slight squeal from Darcy.

Even though this is her second time as the maid of honor, she took the duty very seriously. Amara is our flower girl, and she made a show of stopping to show her ballerina moves each time she dropped a flower.

Genesis's bridesmaids—Pippa, Gigi, Neomi, and her sisters —are behind Darcy. Her choosing them as bridesmaids became a problem.

Cristian and Benny wouldn't allow another man—*one of my groomsmen*—to walk them down the aisle. That resulted in them becoming part of my wedding party.

Who'd have thought my groomsmen would consist of Lombardis and Marchettis?

It's fucking comical.

The closer Genesis gets to me, the more she takes my breath away.

When they reach me, Uncle Mick hugs her, then me, before taking his seat between Aunt Belinda and Betty. Betty gives me a thumbs-up, and I shake my head.

My smile meets Genesis's as she stands before me. I grab her hand in mine, pulling her closer until we're only inches apart. I inhale her sweet scent.

Father Jerome steps before us to start the ceremony. He almost bowed out when he saw Antonio during the wedding rehearsal two nights ago. In order to attend the wedding, Antonio had to take a trip to the confessional and then recite a shit ton of Hail Marys.

Happiness seeps into my cruel bones, into my hardened

heart, as I repeat my vows to Genesis.

"You may kiss the bride," Father Jerome finally says.

I wrap my arms around her waist and kiss her hard and deep.

Like it's been killing me, standing here, waiting to have my lips against hers again. Like I'm not a man who kisses her nearly a hundred times a day.

A simple contract led us to this.

No, *my family* led me to this.

Deep down, I know they accepted Genesis into their lives because they knew she'd be good for me. They saw the good in her heart and how trustworthy she is. I'll never take her for granted.

WE DON'T FLY out for our honeymoon until tomorrow morning, but we're starting it tonight at a suite at the Park Hyatt hotel.

It's after midnight when we finally arrive at the hotel. Pippa and Antonio threw us a long but extremely generous reception dinner. For so long, I'd thought I didn't have family, but I'm learning you don't have to share blood to be family.

It's been a busy few months. I made Genesis wait a few weeks before allowing her to return to Safe Hearts. She was pissed, but she had no idea I had an ulterior motive.

Safe Hearts Mission now has its own butterfly house. With the building structure and codes, we had to settle for that rather than a butterfly garden. The children love it, and sometimes, Genesis teaches her classes in there. As someone who's never been a butterfly person, I'm not going to lie—it's cool.

To make up for the lack of a garden, I had that installed at our house, near the patio. Every morning, she sits out there and reads, works on teaching plans, or schedules social media posts for Safe Hearts.

I want to give Genesis everything she's ever wanted in life for giving me something I thought I'd never have—happiness.

I'm shirtless in bed, my back propped up against the headboard, as Genesis crawls up the bed to straddle me. She told me to get comfortable as she changed into the sexiest white lingerie I've ever seen in my life.

Genesis smooths her thumb against the bandage on my chest. "What's this? Tell me you didn't get shot before our wedding this morning?"

I chuckle over the fact that that's her first thought. Shaking my head, I carefully peel back the bandage to reveal my new tattoo.

"You said this was where you wanted your name," I say when the full tattoo is uncovered.

Her breathing hitches as she stares at her name in cursive writing with a crown covering half the *G*.

"When we decide on a name, our baby's name will be right beside yours." I run my hand over her stomach, giving it three gentle taps.

It's what I do every night—a reminder to our baby that Daddy is here and he loves her.

Yes, her.

We're having a girl.

Dropping her head, she plants a kiss on my lips. "I love you."

"Love you too, baby." I run my tongue along the seam of her lips while lowering my hand down her stomach, dipping it below her panties to cup her pussy.

I groan as soon as I feel the wetness.

My wife is always ready for me.

"We need to get these off," I moan. "How bad do you care if I rip them off?"

"I bought three pairs of them because I knew there was a chance you would."

I rip the panties in one swift movement and play with her clit.

"Ride my cock, baby," I instruct her, helping her lift herself.

My hands stay on her hips as she grabs my hard cock, stroking it once. I hiss through my teeth as I lower her onto it.

She's always so wet and warm.

So tight.

No other pussy will ever be better.

I raise one of my hands to her back, unclasping her bra and tossing it to the side. She throws her head back as I lift both hands, cupping her swollen breasts.

"Yes," she moans, gyrating her hips as I play with her nipple, running my thumb over it.

I lick my lips, taking one in my mouth.

A few seconds later, I relax, allowing her to find her rhythm and take control.

"God, I love your big cock," she moans, setting her palms on my chest and swaying her hips.

"Fuck yeah, baby."

I settle my hands back on her hips, lifting her on and off my cock, and she starts wildly riding me.

Her eyes shutter as she takes in the pleasure while I press my hips forward, meeting her thrust for thrust.

As she rides me, her breasts jiggle in my face. My mouth waters as I raise my chin to press my face between them and suck on a nipple.

"God, I love you," she says.

I lean forward for a better angle as she bounces on my dick. She's fucking me so hard that my back keeps ramming into the headboard.

I can always tell when she's close because she goes fucking hard.

My baby works for her orgasm.

Her legs tremble as she throws her head back, moaning my name and telling me how much she loves me.

That's another sign I know she's close.

She throws out, "*I love you*" and "*I love your cock.*"

"Yes, baby," I grunt out. "Come on your husband's cock. Give it to me. Use this dick for all your needs."

She fucks me harder.

The headboard hits the wall.

Not even ten seconds later, I feel her pussy constrict around my cock, and she moans out my name, along with another appreciative comment about my big dick.

I'm so close myself.

Gripping Genesis's hips, I flip her onto her stomach, her ass in the air. I slap it a few times, and my dick is soaked with her cum as I thrust inside her.

She plants her elbows on the bed as I raise her hips higher, fucking her as hard as she fucked me, grunting how much I love her with each stroke.

I fuck her as hard as I love her.

As I get close, my cock growing bigger and ready to bust in her sweet pussy, I roll her onto her back. I push my body between her legs, entering her missionary, and she wraps her legs around my waist.

I slowly make love to my wife.

Five Months Later

Women are fucking warriors.

Genesis was in labor for twelve hours.

Twelve. Fucking. Hours.

I've been around strong, murderous men all my life, but never seen someone as strong as her.

"Have Mom and Dad decided on a name yet?" the nurse asks as I sit beside Genesis on the hospital bed, running my thumb over our baby girl's hair.

She's beautiful.

I've never seen or held anything more precious.

Staring down at her, I smile.

I had no idea I could fall in love with someone so fast. The moment she came into this world, crying at the top of her lungs, I knew she'd be my entire world.

Genesis's and my entire world because I can see the love radiating off Genesis.

She'll be a great mom.

Speaking of mothers.

We haven't heard from hers since she called her about Prosecutor Cliff Sikes mentioning her. They put a warrant out for her mother's arrest, but as far as we knew, she's still out of the country. My guess is she'll never come back, and Genesis has stopped reaching out to her.

Genesis glances up at me with tired eyes. "What about Melissa?" There's no missing the nervousness in her voice, like she isn't sure if the idea will excite or sadden me.

"Melissa," I say, repeating the word slowly. I'm quiet for a moment before softening my voice. "What do you think, baby girl? Do you want to be named after your aunt?"

Our baby coos.

I grin.

"I think that's a yes," Genesis says around a light laugh as a tear slips down her cheek.

I tip my head forward to kiss her forehead before staring up at the ceiling. "Look, Ma. You have another granddaughter."

I sniffle, holding myself back from getting emotional.

I won't lie and say I managed that same strength when I held her for the first time. It was like my heart was fully filled with warmth in a way it never had been.

While Genesis had helped heal it, my baby girl was the finishing piece for it.

"Melissa is a beautiful name." The nurse smiles, taking in the moment. "Please let me know if you need anything."

Genesis's cheeks are flushed as her eyes well with tears.

"Baby," I whisper, cupping her face with my hand, "we did it."

"We did it," she says, releasing a full-on sob.

"Thank you for giving me something to live for," I say, stroking her skin. "For so long, I thought my life had done nothing but crumble to ruins. But here you came into my life, building me up inch by inch until I reached happiness."

She grabs my free hand in hers and squeezes it as I snuggle closer to them.

Genesis created my light.

My happiness.

My new beginning.

ALSO BY CHARITY FERRELL

LUCKY KING SERIES

Sinful Sacrifice

Sinful Hearts

MARCHETTI MAFIA SERIES

Gorgeous Monster

Gorgeous Prince

Gorgeous Villain

BLUE BEECH SERIES

Just A Fling

Just One Night

Just Exes

Just Neighbors

Just Roommates

Just Friends

TWISTED FOX SERIES

Stirred

Shaken

Straight Up

Chaser

Last Round

ONLY YOU SERIES: A BLUE BEECH SECOND GENERATION

Only Rivals

Only Fate

STANDALONES

Bad For You

Beneath Our Faults

Beneath Our Loss

Pretty and Reckless

Thorns and Roses

Wild Thoughts

RISKY DUET

Risky

Worth The Risk

ABOUT THE AUTHOR

Charity Ferrell is a USA Today and Wall Street Journal best-selling author of the Twisted Fox and Blue Beech series. She resides in Indianapolis, Indiana. She loves writing about broken people finding love while adding humor and heartbreak along with it. Angst is her happy place.

When she's not writing, she's making a Starbucks run, shopping online, or spending time with her family.

www.ingramcontent.com/pod-product-compliance
Lightning Source LLC
Chambersburg PA
CBHW061629190726
48289CB00006B/1533